# Hominins - Past and Present

Storyline Books

835 West 21st Street,
North Vancouver V7P2C3,
British Columbia,
Canada

https://storylinebooks.com

Copyright © 2020 by Maurice Schmidt
First Edition — 2020. Title: Hominins - Past & Present
     All rights reserved.
     Innovation, Science and Economic Development Canada
     Canadian Intellectual Property Office (CIPO)
     Certificate of Registration for Copyright
     Application Reference Number 1174720 October 09, 2020
     Authorization code: 8656961

Disclaimer

ISBN

978-1-7770574-2-8 (Paperback)
978-1-7770574-3-5 (eBook)
978-1-7770574-4-2 (Hardcover)

BISAC Codes: Book Industry Standards & Communications

Fiction / Science Fiction / General
Fiction / Nature & Environment
Fiction / Romance / Historical / Ancient World

Distributed to the Kindle Direct Publishing and IngramSpark.

# BOOK COVER

The dynamics of our planet reach far and wide. From the core of iron at its center to the magnetosphere surrounding us, our day-to-day life is subject to forces that are measured in thousands, even millions, of years. As the continents drift on a sea of magma, the cargo of life they carry adapts to find niches on the flotsam, evolving to meet the demands of existence. A mold for success brings similarities that manifest themselves today as they did in primitive times. Remove the disguise of the present, and underneath lies the imprint of past errors.

The intersection between species challenges them to cohabit a slice of time in harmony. Why is it that the interface that marked the encounter between Homo Neanderthalensis and Homo sapiens left one group extinct and the other there to dominate, not only its contenders but all of life's tree?

This is a fictional account of when these two hominin species crossed paths with nature's prevalent forces, setting the scene. Has civilization learned from these past events? Maybe, maybe not, but be reminded, the natural world will have the last word.

# SYNOPSIS

Across the globe, modern humans struggle with racial and ethnic strife despite belonging to the same species, Homo sapiens. Imagine a world with multiple species in the Homo genus, as was the case 30 to 40 thousand years ago. How would we characterize their interaction? It seems reasonable to expect heightened discord, with one group ostracizing the other, merely because they look different? For evidence, we need not look far. Stemming from our considered superiority, the state of the entire ecosystem stands as an indictment to our mistreatment of it. Our impact is pervasive. Even those of our kind are often singled out for egregious injustice. Why can we not share this planet as equals with all of nature's elements, despite our differences? It was not long ago that we were just another creature in a realm rich in diversity, a true Eden for all its participants, as equals. That was before we established our dominance.

After hundreds of thousands of years as a successful species, our precursor Homo Neanderthalensis was undoubtedly under stress as a species. This was due to a series of ice ages that altered the flora and fauna they depended on. However, it is reasonable to assume that they would have regenerated after the last of the ice ages, as they had previously done if given a fighting chance.

At this juncture, coincidence would have our species migrate out of Africa and spread across Europe, where we encountered them for the first time. When we now examine Europeans, we find that 3% of their DNA is Neanderthal. Scientists have also ascertained that females of modern humans would not have been able to carry to term offspring from male Neanderthals, while female Neanderthals could produce viable progenies from modern human males. It is via this route that we can account for the traces of Neanderthal DNA in Europeans. I put it to you, what is the narrative behind these facts? Undoubtedly, our propensity for violence against our type, compounded by misogynistic tendencies, stands in stark relief. Are these contributors to the decline of the Neanderthal? Add to this our poor record with differences in ethnicity, caste, class, gender, and social standings, and you have certainty that modern humans would not condone a contender at the top of the food chain.

Earth's magnetosphere is currently, and was at that time, in an excursion phase with the potential for a polar magnetic reversal. This weakens the protective shield allowing solar radiation to penetrate the atmosphere. The result is an increased risk of cancer, the severity of which correlates with the extent of the disruption. Add to this the eruption of the supervolcano at Naples, also around that time, producing a volcanic winter lasting several years, and you have the confluence of circumstances that threatened the Neanderthals with extinction. As their numbers declined, lack of genetic diversity trapped them in a vicious cycle, dooming them as a species.

This book is a fictional account of the first encounter between these two species.

# TRIGGER

Genetic studies have unveiled commonalities between species, lent greater certainty to the evolutionary tree of life, and mapped the progressive dispersal of life forms across the globe. Combined with geological studies, which provide an understanding of plate tectonics and continental drift, the effects on the distribution of species can be explained with a great degree of accuracy.

Above us, the ever-present solar orb streams a lethal cocktail of radiation to threaten life of its tenuous hold. On the other hand, the magnetosphere, driven by the dynamo at the planet's core, moderates the effects of the sun, allowing energy so vital to us, to penetrate and sustain life on the earth. Fluctuations in these dynamics manifest in climate changes which alternate between extremes of temperature. Additionally and sporadically, the magma within vents pent-up forces disrupting the fragile ecosystem with catastrophic eruptions. Life either clings to its niche, adapts, or succumbs. Sometimes, new players enter and disrupt the status quo or occupy opportunities that open up.

Circumstance sets the scene for the two species', Homo Neanderthalensis and Homo sapiens, to meet as chronicled by this book. Meanwhile, we, here in the 21$^{st}$ century, look on and struggle with our dysfunctional relationships and the forces of nature bide their time, ready to intervene.

# WHY I WROTE THIS BOOK

The overriding reason is that I had something to say. I wished to delineate contemporary challenges in the context of ancient times. I also wanted to remind us of our place in the ecosystem since we are inextricably intertwined with it, despite our dominant position in the hierarchy of life. Setting the scene in primitive times affords the opportunity to imagine a world in its original state, pristine and without the stamp of our authority over it.

The license of fiction allows exaggeration to make these points, and to this end, I wanted to express my perspective, granting that it is just one amongst many. I have no intention to impose mine on anyone, but instead, offer the enjoyment that the imagery invokes.

Finally, the creative process of developing the plot and expressing thoughts in words is a sheer joy. Seeing the finished product in the tangible form of a book and its persistence into the future is, admittedly, another reason for writing the book.

Do enjoy the reading of it.

# WHY YOU SHOULD READ THIS BOOK

Firstly to just enjoy the unfolding plot while at the same time immersing yourself in an era of primitive man. Imagine life before civilization, where the rudiments of life require a dint of effort well beyond today's organized supply chains and emphasis on material wealth.

These are people who do not have the benefit of norms of behavior handed down over generations. In their tightly knit groups, their conduct is governed by a narrow community without broader input.

# INTRODUCTION

The novel juxtaposes Stone Age life and life today. Parallels are there to be seen, but it is the repetition of history, then and now, that circumstance imposes on the storyline. The motivations of the leading players and how they evolve as characters add a dimension to the drama, enticing you to remain engaged.

Although the setting of the narrative covers two vastly different time periods, it remains grounded in normal human responses to circumstances. I hope that it conjures up images that are parallel to your daily routine. I challenge you to map out alternative paths in the storyline in your mind and enjoy living their fiction and see where they lead you.

Thanks to Peter, my brother, for proofreading the book.

I dedicate this book to Karyn.

# Table of Contents

# 1    Creatures

The tide of life waxes and wanes as the planet tilts its face to the warmth of the sun in its progression around the ecliptic. First this way, then that, the brushstrokes of the seasons paint a kaleidoscope of colors across the landscape, and in concert, the kingdom of creatures follows its ordinance.

Underfoot, the dynamo ceaselessly turns around its core of iron, guarding its cargo of creatures on the mantle against the lethal flux of the solar wind with a magnetic tide that flows along its longitude.

According to their kind, creatures of the forest and seas, with hopes and desires, live without discord or vengeance, in harmony within an ocean of water, wind, rain, and sunshine, content in their designated branch in the tree of life.

However, some with invasive tendencies seek dominance over others, usurping the natural order, bending it to their perverse will. With no regard for consequences, not realizing the loss of the Eden they were born to, they plunder and despoil their inheritance. They seek to differentiate themselves from other creatures of the realm with cunning and avarice, only to leave a trail of destruction. Poorer in their consequences, they wallow in a toxic legacy of a planet stripped of the complement of its earlier diversity. Their neighbors stand apart, subjugated until their commonality is unfathomable. Even as fellow creatures in a world so obviously meant for sharing on an equal footing, they deny themselves the richness by this omission and are poorer for it.

## 2    Valley

Hyrax stands at his sentry, scanning the valley and sky for threats. High on a boulder, he surveys his extended family of alpine marmots foraging for insects and vegetation on the meadow below. As the largest of the group, he asserts his dominance with a strong flap of his tail and aggressively charging at his male companions who scurry out of reach. As is custom, he signals to an underling to take over the watch so he can mark out the perimeter of his territory to discourage foreigners from potential encroachment. Returning to the observatory, with chest filled and head thrust forward, he proclaims authority over his subjects and jurisdiction, vocalizing his leadership with emphatic whistles.

Midway through his soliloquy, a shadow, partly veiled by the glaring sun, catches his attention. Abruptly he ends his refrain and whistles a sequence of high-pitched warnings. Elle, an adolescent female, follows his gaze apprehensively. With only seconds to react, the terror overhead grows larger, descending at a frightening speed. It approaches with the sun at its rear, obscuring its flight. Frantic to escape its claws, all semblance of control is lost for a brief moment; escape the only prerogative, the group scatters. As the sweep of its wings leaves a rush of wind, it passes over. Thankfully, its target stands beyond, frozen with fear at the bank of the stream. A furry field mouse hopelessly parries its foe in vain, as the eagle tears into the soft fur with a vice-like grip to dispatch the life from the creature in one swoop. Nonchalantly, it rises from the water's edge, over the embankment and canopy of trees while the group of marmots belatedly scatter under boulders, logs, and brushes and into tunnels with practiced speed.

The raptor makes for a ledge against the cliff, and they listen as the young nestling eagerly anticipates the feeding. The gruesome tearing of flesh from its body is unmistakable as it is sated. A stillness holds sway as the mammals struggle to grasp the import of the unsettling event, the precariousness of life, and the value of each moment of life. The loss to the neighbors is heartfelt, just as birth alters the dynamic, so too death leaves a vacuum not filled in the same mold. The furry mouse will leave a void. Along with other creatures in the valley, all share a subliminal dialog, an unstructured communique of warning signals and messages of weather changes and food sources. The alteration will yield a different result, but life finds a way to persist.

In the straw-colored grass, tunnels lead through the dense growth from the rock face at the water's edge. With three stripes on her back instead of the usual four, Trine, the companion to the slain mouse, stares out at the scene of the attack. Desperate to understand the loss, she cautiously moves forward. In the aftermath of deathly silence that followed, the shriek of alarm as the shadow passed overhead remained imprinted on her consciousness. Struggling for an alternate explanation, she looks about then sadly turns to make her way back through the passage in the grass to a nest under the branches of a tree. No older than a week, a litter lies in the soft down, oblivious to the loss. They suckle until satisfied as she listlessly considers her grief. Yes, life must go on. She will have to shoulder the burden of upbringing alone, a fate she has previously endured. She casts about for a distraction from her thoughts only to see a group of finches congregating in swaying grasses under the shelter of a nearby tree. Their subdued demeanor is a testament to the fear they feel should one of them befall the same assault. Trine sees Zinnia, the roller, who is first to shake off the effects. She somberly resumes her search for food as her offspring follow suit; a signal to others in her blue-feathered group and indirectly to the field mouse that the danger has passed, life must go on. For emphasis, she pauses for her mate, Cyan, to nestles up to her for comfort to dispel the scene from his mind. Trine takes heart from the guidance that Zinnia offers, and gradually, normality returns as the inhabitants resume their activities. Emphasis

In the ravine, twisted ivy leading up from the mossy ground cover into the dark reaches of the heavy foliage of a tree, a woodpecker climbs up the trunk, making its way to peer out from an opening. Aoki joins Ruka in quiet contemplation of the happenings, their shy habit, and consequently, infrequent ventures into the open provide immunity to attack by raptors. Care is a necessary precaution, one that led to their shyness, given the startling beauty of their red crests that is liable to attract unwelcome interest. Plainly visible on a ledge of the far cliff, the eagle stands at its post, omnipotent, in command of all below. The woodpeckers return to the gloom of the forest to make their way to the cones protruding in bunches on the far periphery of the tree. There they satisfy their hunger on the seeds before sheltering in their hollow for the night.

At the foot of the cliff, Hyrax takes up his post on a boulder exposed to the last rays of the sun. Ever watchful of the eagle, he cautions the pups of the group as they playfully practice wrestling with their siblings in the broken rock-strewn landscape. In their juvenile reliance on the adults for protection, they scurry around the fallen boulders, unconcerned at the fallen mammal's misfortune or the danger overhead. Making the most of the failing light, the activities dispel the intruding coldness as the sun sinks in the west.

Eyther looks down from the ledge while Ayrial attends to the fledging as the last vestiges of winter's snow still line the surrounds of the nest of twigs. The view extends across the alpine meadow to the stream and the facing heights on the far side, glowing red as evening sets. Above the cliffs, reaching up to the peaks, snow steadfastly holds fast despite the warmth of summer. Below, the river winds its way across smooth rock pools down cascading falls, gurgling in its passage to disappear around a bend, obscured by branches reaching up from the dark of the green conifer trees. Clouds skid across the sky to a bank in the north as a cold breeze picks up in anticipation of an unseasonal cold front. In a matter of days, the young one will be ready to part the nest and venture out into the beckoning world just in time for the encroaching cold of winter.

As darkness settles across the valley, gusts of wind herald an oncoming storm. The commune, with Hyrax as the leader and his mate Shyrax, make for the shallow reaches of overhanging rock-faces where deep tunnels lead to the communal sleeping area. There they huddle against the frigidity in a world where fear, contentment, and weather extremes share a common certainty. Elle spends a fitful night struggling for warmth as a blast of early winter wind steals into every corner.

## 2.1   Preparations

Zinnia stirs from a restless sleep as the first light of dawn breaks. The canopy of pine needles of the tree they had sought refuge in provided some shelter from the storm but the buffeting wind and biting cold made for frequent wakeful moments as the branches swayed in the gusts. Shaking off the remaining droplets, the fledglings stir and, with subdued cries, voice their need for food. Cyan transitions from sleep to alertness in moments, as is his habit. He leads the group from the shelter of the tree to the grasses below, which hang under the snow's weight. The storm has discouraged insects from emerging, leaving only seeds in the swards of reeds alongside the stream for the birds to feast on. With their hunger partially sated, they slake their thirst in the running water and begin scratching for grubs in exposed areas where the storm has not left its white blanket.

Zinnia bustles between her offspring, encouraging them to feed while food is still available. She senses that the season is fading quicker than normally. Their long migration will require them to be at peak strength for the arduous flight. She has been quietly struggling with a troubling change to the direction she should navigate when they set out. Her sight, which enables her to visualize the magnetic field, has been disturbed. Instead of just one, two paths appear in the sky, and she cannot understand what this means. The drop in temperature alarms her because it means they need to leave earlier than usual.

## 2.2　Stirrings

In the sleeping chamber, deep within the burrow, Elle stirs from a fitful sleep. An inexplicable tremor vibrates through the chamber. Barely discernible, it is enough to interrupt her rest only to find that all is quiet. Waiting for a recurrence, alert in the cold blackness, she waits. The minutes pass, waiting, waiting...nothing. Sleep eventually overtakes her but as time passes, the trembling restarts, merging with her dreams until the reality of it startles her to wakefulness. Listening, puzzling, what is it? Nothing, all is still. The heavy breathing from the rest of the family of marmots indicates that they are oblivious to the disturbance. By morning, Elle wakes, tired and irritable, uncertain whether it was just a dream. She shakes off the lingering uncertainty by reassuring herself that the den, burrowed with the hardened nails of their paws, all of ten feet down through soil and stones, could not possibly harbor a secret. Dawn finally breaks, and in rising, she shakes off the cold of the night, and daylight begins to dispel her concerns.

The daily routine of life soon establishes itself as Shyrax, the group's dominant female, foists her will on the females in the group. She taunts their playfulness with overbearing supervision, harshly separates them from the young males' interests, and confiscates delicacies found in the meadow for herself. Her counterpart, Hyrax, lords it over his male subjects with severe reprimands, muscles his way into their games, overpowering them as he imposes his size on them. Between Hyrax and Shyrax, they maintain a lifelong monogamous relationship and rigid control over their progeny. Foreign marmots are aggressively discouraged with a scented perimeter to mark the territory. This is Hyrax's preoccupation, flapping his tail on the ground for emphasis as he proceeds. In daring to cross the boundary, a ferocious attack will soon expel an intruder as Hyrax asserts the defense of his dominion.

The family has grown to number twenty, with Elle being one of the later additions. The established order offers security, but restrictively provides little room for individuality or self-expression. Abortions usually result from pregnancies to any of the females other than Shyrax, who targets these unfortunate females with malignant attention, imposing on them until the stress terminates the gestation.

On this day, Elle receives the brunt of Shyrax's attention as she struggles to dismiss the remnants of the night's interruptions. Absentmindedly, she strays into the fringe of the forest bordering the meadow to escape her attention. The forest's quiet gloom holds a certain foreboding, emphasized by the strictures placed on them against entry into this domain. Out of sight of the protective gaze of Hyrax or his appointed sentry, dangers are more pronounced. Cougars, Foxes, and Lynxes present a heightened risk, especially to juveniles. Deathly quiet greets Elle as she strays deeper into the shadowy world. The sigh of the wind in the coniferous trees dampens all sounds, and the matted floor silences even the rustle of leaves underfoot. Immersed in this realm so near to her usual limited range, her mood lifts, replaced by the excitement of the unknown and hidden dangers as natural protective instincts bring to focus a rush of alertness. Enthralled, she glances about and cautiously steps forward, taking care to avoid unnecessary movements that may attract attention. The terrain drops off to a glade as the trees make way to a sparkling stream at the foot of a series of rapids leading from the craggy cliffs. She hesitates at the fringe of the opening and listens for unseen dangers. All is quiet. The tranquility washes over her emphasizing the freedom without Shyrax's constant attention. She is not immune to the need for caution and the importance of the protective umbrella that Hyrax has ensured over the years. Should she want to establish her own independence, the opportunity for reproduction would necessitate venturing out into the unknown in search of a partner with whom to start her own family? She knows her male siblings likewise find themselves in the same predicament. The freedom of her excursion has brought to the fore those considerations.

On better judgment, she sets aside the temptation to press on and turns back, resolving to return whenever the demands of the commune are too much. This will be her secret get-away to escape from the claustrophobic constraints when needed. Stealthily she makes her way back to the meadow and silently merges with her siblings, unnoticed by Shyrax.

Invigorated by the foray beyond the confines of home range, she joins in the playful exuberance of her siblings until the light fades to evening, and they return to the sleeping burrow. Tiredness overtakes the group, and soon, immersed in sleep, stillness descends on them. Lying with her ear to the ground, the trembling sensation from the previous night, once again, becomes apparent, only to stop for a while before resuming. Suddenly a more substantial jolt echoes through the chamber, waking some of the family. In the blackness, Elle senses their perplexity but without explanation. Unsure of its source, they soon fall asleep. All is quiet, and no further trembling occurs for the rest of the night. Each night Elle expectantly waits for a resumption of the vibration, but there is none, and the concern fades into the recesses of her mind.

## 2.3   Glade

Elle's habit of rising early, well before the other marmots, has certain advantages. She can enjoy the freedom of the meadow to herself without being harassed by Shyrax. She eagerly peers out of the burrow at the verdant green pasture and ventures out. The recurring vibrations during the night still haunt her, but the unease lifts when supplanted by a greater danger, that of the constant presence of the eagles on the cliffs. Without Hyrax's oversight and systems of warning whistles, she must take care. At least this is a more tangible apprehension than the vague, irregular trembling that seemed to come from nowhere at night. She makes haste for the safety of the forbidden forest, hidden from the constant gaze of the eagles. Trembling with excitement, she cautiously moves forward through the trees to a sparkling stream and rapids descending from craggy heights she had found during her previous venture into the unknown. The glade brings back the peacefulness she so enjoyed in the last visit. Edging forward into the open, she reaches the water's edge glances about. All is still.

Once sure of being unobserved, she nibbles at the succulent watercress growing in a dense mat in the shallow edge of the river and wades closer to the rushing water. Invigorated by the frigid water on her thick fur, she forgets her need for apprehension, splashing about in youthful pleasure. The moments pass in the sheer joy of the moment. Then remembering the need for caution, she looks about. Nothing? Holding still, stilling her excitement, she waits. Suddenly, sensing an observer, she darts for the cover of the forest growth and stops to look back. Still nothing? After a while, there is a movement in the bushes on the far bank. Retreating deeper into the undergrowth, she waits, tensed, and ready for flight. Could it merely be the wind in the leaves? Unsure of her instincts, she remains concealed and watches. At length, there is a repeat, something stirs in the brush. To her surprise, a marmot emerges into the open and brazenly makes its way down to the stream. Entranced, Elle takes in the scene. It is a stranger, young, like herself but a male. Could he be part of a group? She allows time to pass and from her concealment observes as he too tastes the watercress, looks about, and for a few moments, playfully splashes in the shallows.

Confident of their insular seclusion, she ventures closer. He immediately stops his activities and stares across the water at her approach. Separated by the gushing water, they look at each for long moments as she feels her heart racing. At these closer quarters, she can see that he is quite large and robust despite his apparent youthfulness. He, taken by her grace and shiny mottle colored fur, stands transfixed. Frozen in position, they lock eyes with each other. Is this the long-awaited opportunity to start her own colony? As these thoughts begin to intrude on her consciousness, a sudden shrill cry from above interrupts the spell. With practiced speed, Elle, recognizing the ever-present threat of the eagle, darts for the cover of the forest with him doing likewise on his side of the ravine. The danger circles overhead. Safe in knowing that they were not seen, Elle calms herself since the eagle would not announce its presence before an attack. The other marmot is lost in the foliage of the other bank. They emerge sufficiently to reveal their concealment but dare not venture out. For a long while, the eagle continues circling, until the two recognize the futility of waiting and disconsolately retreat to their respective colonies.

\* \* \*

Ayrial lazily circles in the morning thermals rising off the face off the cliffs in the warmth of the sun's rays. A shrill cry to Eyther, his partner, informs her that he will look further along the ridge to locate prey for their fledgling. The two marmots darting for cover on the banks of the stream catch his eye. Observing from a distance, he waits for his chance. The call, unfortunately, alerted them to his presence. In the undergrowth, they are safe from attack, but maybe, just maybe, they will relax their guard, offering a chance to swoop down for the kill. At length, they move away, and he turns elsewhere to look for food.

\* \* \*

The woodpecker pair, Aoki and Ruka, silently observe life on the meadow from the safety of the forest's edge. They see Elle, somewhat subdued, emerging from the shadows to join her fellow juveniles at play under the watchful eyes of Hyrax and Shyrax.

10

There are Zinnia and Cyan. Like them, woodpeckers must soon move to warmer climes, although their journey is not as far. They patiently wait for the cue from the rollers to begin their expedition, but inexplicably they seem to be waiting longer than usual. What can be the reason? The anxiety of the delay is beginning to take its toll as they worry that the timing may affect their food supply at the destination.

Meanwhile, Trine, the field mouse, has had a busy morning. As the sole provider for her litter, she must keep up her strength to ensure a healthy milk supply for her offspring to suckle. She periodically returns to her nest in the grass to satisfy their hunger and provide warmth. They are still too young to stray from the nest for seeds, so her task is to divide her time between feeding herself and providing them with comfort. The group of rollers led by Zinnia and Cyan provides a distraction for Trine as they busy themselves with their fattening to endure their migration.

The days are progressively getting colder and the nights longer. The birds and mice share a common intent: to prepare themselves and their offspring for the long winter. The marmots also have their annual cycle to prepare for; their hibernation deep within their burrow will be a safeguard against the extremes of winter.

*  *  *

Back in the burrow in the dark of night, Elle fitfully tosses and turns as her emotions alternate between excitements at having met the stranger at the glade only to be replaced by alarm at the recurring vibrations. There is also the urging to prepare for the imminent hibernation.

The next day, a dull morning greets them with Hyrax proclaiming the last day of fall and only two days to the start of hibernation. This signals a frantic rush to line the burrow with fresh grasses and stock up with tubers, bulbs, and edible roots. The juveniles use the opportunity to play their games while the adults are distracted with hectic activity. Elle feels torn between helping the adults, joining in the spirited fun of the younger ones, or sneaking off to meet with her stranger. The day ends in unfulfilled frustration and only one day left to risk setting off on a clandestine venture of independence and self-reliance.

11

# 3    Forestland 39,000 Year Ago

Moraine rises to a blustery day with a fresh sprinkling of snow on the trees and across land still frozen in patches from last winter. It is a clear day, the sky a pale blue, and the sun offering little warmth. She exits the communal sleeping quarters, a hut made of reusable branches strapped together with strips of bark. Mud applied to the gaps keeps out the wind but not the penetrating cold. Pine needles woven into mats line the roof to shed rain, keeping the interior dry. If they need to strike camp, to follow the roving herds, they can disassemble the structures at a moment's notice.

In the absence of men, the camp is quiet as the women take the opportunity to linger longer before attending to their duties. Moraine, one to enjoy the solitude of the forests, decides to walk up an incline at the back of the camp and over the top to the adjoining valley. Generally, her habit is to proceed down to the rapidly flowing river at the foot of the camp rather than this seldom-frequented route. The group rarely stays in one place for more than a season in their nomadic lifestyle, limiting exploration of the locale in more detail. As she crests the rise, the trees give way to tundra and show undulating scrub-clad hills steadily rising to distant peaks gleaming the white of perpetual ice. Hesitant to venture too far alone, she pauses to consider the extent to which she should proceed and collect her bearings for a return path. The excitement of the solitude and gusts of wind that sigh in the branches of the trees reaching up from the valley leads her further. Descending a slope, she nears a sheer drop with a view of a tributary glistening between thickets of trees below. Looking over her shoulder, she shrugs to dispel lingering concerns for going too far. Deciding to skirt along the edge of the cliff, she hopes to descend if she can find a stretch that is not too steep. Walking parallel to the river with a contour of the land, she presumes that at a point further on, the tributary will merge with the main river, and the cliff will dissipate. Where the two streams merge, she can optionally walk up the tributary or follow the main river back to camp. With this plan in place, she carries on confidently. The view off the edge of the cliff presents an enticing landscape over the tops of the trees. Closer at hand, the glint of sunlight off the cascading stream and stands of reeds where the terrain flattens out to one side of the rivulet, add to the spectacle. Gatherings of robins and rollers congregate in the branches above her, signaling their readiness for the annual

13

migration to warmer climes. She delights in the mix of birdsong as they enthusiastically preen themselves in preparation for the journey, apparently using the precipice as a launch platform. Stepping onto a protruding slab of stone with an uninterrupted view, she pauses for a moment. The serenity of the place calms the remnants of the clamor that camp life imposes. A life spent in close quarters has its disadvantages. The men constantly jostle for attention, and the women fret over the division of duties. The sages espouse wisdom built on mishaps and errors in their past, to right the wrongs of their own ways. The younger ones like herself have to endure the brunt of these competing forces. Here in the quiet of the world, she can collect her thoughts and build an inner fortitude to face the return of the men from their hunting expedition. Scouts located the tracks of a herd of reindeer. The numbers warrant a sizable party to steer and trap them up a blind valley for selective culling. The intent is usually to harvest the older deer. In the excitement of the moment, excesses often result in more than the required number of dead animals. She will have to endure tales of boastful bravery as they elaborate on their escapade. After days of labor, smoking the meat under fires, a full larder will ensure a supply of food for the winter. Moraine heaves a sigh to shrug off these thoughts when a movement between the trees at the water's edge at the foot of the cliff catches her attention. Looking closer, she expects a bear or cougar to emerge from the ticket, but the obscuring trees frustrate her attempts to see clearly. The outline was that of a crouching man in a fur coat, but that is not possible; the nearest clan is many days' march to the north or east. Moving a few steps along does not improve her vantage, and the mystery persists, but she cannot shake the prospect of it being a person. Redoubling her effort to find a way down, she strides on, but at the confluence of the two rivers, the cliff remains undiminished. It has merely closed in on the tributary forming a narrow gorge where the two rivers meet. The roar of the water drowns out all other sounds in the turbulence of the merger. Further down the river's main course, the cliff gives way to a slope.

Realizing that her choice was incorrect, she recognizes that she should have walked in the other direction. The sun has risen to a noon elevation for autumn and, concerned that her clan will be alarmed at her absence, she reluctantly heads down to the main river to the camp. Exploration of the tributary and its mystery will have to wait for another day.

As she steps into the encampment, she shudders at the approach of Gramater. The wizened old woman makes it her business to rule over the younger women with severity and holds inexplicable malice reserved for Moraine. As midwife and medicine woman for the clan, she dispenses life and death as she sees fit. All tremble under her unchallenged matriarchal dominance.

She emits a rasping sound to clear her throat before gesticulating with her leathery index finger, "Where have you been while we work our hands to the bone?" Before Moraine can reply, "When the men return, they will need wood for the smoking. I want a pile right here." She gestures to the storage covering, "Enough to last for a few days. Take an ax and get busy."

Thankful at the curtailed questioning and a fresh opportunity to escape the confines of the camp, she hastens to get some rope and an ax and quickly sets out. After multiple trips to gather branches and logs from the cold and dark forest, the sheltered storage area is filled. She then turns to help with food preparation for the evening meal.

As darkness descends, she settles into the warmth of her spot in the sleeping area. Her mind returns to the scene from the cliff. Tossing and turning with an unsettling disquiet that she cannot fathom, the more she thinks about it, the more certainty there is that it was not an animal, but a person.

## 3.1   Foreigners

The following day is warmer. A quick breakfast and on the pretext of having more wood to collect, she walks down the path with an ax in hand. At the river, she proceeds upwards towards the tributary with its mystery, a person, or an animal. The confluence is trickier to negotiate than expected. The rushing waters join in a turbulent torrent, which bars passage to any but the most determined. Undaunted, she navigates the swirling waters by wading chest-deep in the freezing river. Proceeding around a bend in the course and hugging the edge of overhanging rocks where the flow is calmer, she struggles but maintains a footing to emerge on a beach of rounded pebbles, wet and shivering. The foot of the tributary lies before her with the cliff on her left, offset from the water's edge by a shallow embankment. Walking is more straightforward as she makes headway up the valley. The warmth of the sun and the activity soon dry the soft fur of her skirt and leggings as she proceeds at a pace.

Not far off in the distance, she sees the protruding rock at the top of the cliff, the observatory from where she saw the movements obscured by the trees on the previous day. Slowing her stride, cautiously blending with the vegetation to camouflage her approach, she moves forward, stopping periodically to scan for movement. Suddenly, with a jolt, she stops dead. Just ahead and to her right, at the water's edge, the murmur of a voice is audible above the gurgling river. Freezing to the spot, she tries to find the source but to no avail. Backing away, she retreats to a safer distance following the curve of the river. From a concealing brush, she peers up-river. There, a man and child sit on a large smooth rock that is partly interrupting the flow of water. He appears to be speaking to the boy who, from her vantage, looks to be about ten years old. The man, a robust figure with a shock of straw-colored hair, looks down at the child speaking in a low voice. At the distance between them, the conversation is not audible, but the intimacy of the exchange is evident. The boy bends over in a coughing spell, and the man comforts him with his arm over his shoulder. Tortured concern crosses the man's face until the child recovers. He then gestures at the far bank and the ridge of the valley, seemingly indicating a route over the top and points to the robins as they follow the direction of his gestures. The boy shows some excitement at the man's suggestion but soon lapses into a pained look and begins coughing again. The warmth of the sun's rays spotlighting their position brings some relief for the juvenile, and a cheerful smile quickly appears on his face. Oblivious to Moraine's presence, she watches, spellbound by the fluctuating mood of the two, as the condition changes from despondency to relief to cheerfulness. Torn between stepping out to partake in their tender affection for each other, to offer assistance, but in fear of startling them or provoking aggression, she desists. Moraine's slender form would be no match for the strongly built and conditioned frame of the man.

As the sun sinks to the horizon, a shadow falls across the stream. The man takes the boy by the hand and helps him off the boulder. They proceed up towards the cliff. Not to lose sight of them, she follows at a safe distance. At the foot of the cliff, trees obscure the entrance to a cave, which would not easily be located without foreknowledge of its presence. Moraine hears muffled sounds from within the depth of the grotto of at least two other voices acknowledging their return. She lingers a while but noting the sun's position in the sky, decides to return to the camp.

Running to make up for the lost time, she ponders the circumstances of the group. The man is thick set, not much taller than herself, who as a young adult is smaller than her siblings and other females of her age. His broad forehead leads to bushy eyebrows, an elegant nose, and a balanced jaw with a scattering of facial hairs in the same color as the rest of his hair. Compared to the boys in her clan, the youth has a gangly frame, probably heralding a growth spurt to come as he matures. The impression gained at the distance that separated them suggests that a failure to arrest his ailment might retard his growth. The poignancy of the relationship between them was the most striking feature of her observation. A closeness that is lacking in the interplay between people in her clan who obsess over duties and conformance to each's role in the unspoken hierarchy within the group. A preordained mold set by the elders for each person dominates the relationships and behaviors of every person. Moraine always feels constrained by the expectations set for her, longing for the freedom of self-expression.

A sense of helplessness pervades her thoughts in thinking of the apparent effect on the youth's condition. She feels an urge to contribute to a solution. Fording the confluence of the two rivers is easier in the downward rush of water, but care is necessary; a single slip will almost certainly be fatal. She is soon on a path leading to the settlement. After gathering a few branches and collecting the ax from where she abandoned it earlier, she strolls into the camp, on the pretext of returning from a wood chore. With relief, she manages to enter unobserved and blends into a group preparing food for the evening meal.

In the cold of night, she relives the events until an idea to bring relief to the child dawns on her. Rising before dawn, while everyone else is still soundly asleep, she stealthily makes her way to the work shelter. There she rummages through the stock of medicinal herbs stored in a curious mix of earthenware containers. Avoiding some with dangerous-looking X's marked on them, she locates what she is looking for next to a disused bed used for the woman's midwife duties. Gramater, renowned for her ability to remedy various ailments, stores her potions here under strict instructions that the hut is out of bounds to everyone except a select group whom she is mentoring in the art of healing childbirth. Testing the ingredients, the paste of ivy and menthol herbs smells right, and the taste confirms that it clears the sinuses. Dispensing parts of the contents into a smaller chiseled stone vessel with a lid, she quickly exits and hides it under a brush behind the shed and feigns sleep back in the sleeping quarters.

Eager to revisit the scene of the previous day, she manages to elude the attention of the mater, and before the sun reaches halfway to noon, she finds herself back at her observatory. There is no sign of the two, so she unobtrusively places the urn with a sprig of flowers on the rock and returns to her post to watch. It is again warmer than the day of the storm, and she can see the sun rays creeping ever closer to the rock as it rises towards noon. As expected, the two saunter down the hill from the cave and approach the stream. Initially, they stand at the river's edge, pointing at a group of fish making their way up the flow, flashing their shiny flanks as they leap over some rapids. The boy is first to see the urn. He points to the object and draws his companion's attention to it. The man's reaction is immediate. With a practiced motion, he grabs the boy to his chest, and even under the watchful eyes of Moraine, he magically disappears, camouflaged by the surrounding vegetation. Time stretches as Moraine anticipates the man's return but nothing. He remains out of sight. With her heart pounding in her chest, it dawns on her that he will probably scout the area before venturing back to the rock. Realizing that he may locate her at her post, she decides to retreat further downstream. Moving quietly away, she gathers herself behind a secluded boulder in some marshy reeds. Deeming it unsafe to venture closer to see whether the man collects the proffered medicine, Moraine reluctantly decides to return on another day and heads for the camp.

## 3.2   Return

At the camp, frenetic activities are underway. A runner has returned from the hunting expedition to signal to the women that the men are bringing a significant number of carcasses for processing.   They are due to arrive around noon on the following day. The number of fires needs to be increased, and the larder expanded to accommodate the meat with additional ice blocks to preserve the food. True to form, Gramater takes command of the preparations, issuing orders as she wanders about checking on progress, scolding at the incompetence of first this person then the next.

She instructs, "Dig the fire-pit deeper! More, deeper. Yes, now expand it outwards."

Hobbling over to another group, "You! Why so slow – get a move on, we don't have all day", she says, gesticulating with her walking stick to another group to supplement the team. Dissenting voices are rare as each person tries to evade her focus.

Moraine finds the niche that removes her from supervision by collecting snow from the forest for compacting into blocks. Packed on a sleigh, she drags the chunks to the larder, where she builds a cubicle for the meat.

By nightfall, the preparations are complete, and Gramater does a final round of checking. Singling out Moraine's ice blockhouse for scrutiny, she questions, "The blocks need to be larger, and you need a foundation layer, so the meat does not get exposed to the dirt. Stupid!" Jabbing the ice cubes with her stick, she proclaims, "More compacting is needed. It is too soft. First thing tomorrow, see to it that you fix these problems. How do you think you will find a man to put up with such sloppy work?"

Moraine silently endures the criticisms knowing better than to antagonize her.

Day breaks to a gentle drizzle with temperatures tending colder as the day progresses. By noon, a steady downpour brings rain and sleet with gusts of wind, undoing all the preparations of the previous day. The waterlogged fire pits are useless, and the firewood is too wet to support burning. To add to the problems, the returning party arrives late, drenched, and down-spirited, expecting a welcoming party only to find the villagers holed up in their huts, reluctant to face the elements. The reindeer carcasses have to be jammed into Moraine's ice storage chambers to wait for the weather to clear. By nightfall, with the area reduced to muddy slush from the trampling of so many boots, a foul mood pervades the residents. Accusations over minor offenses and arguments flare up periodically until finally dwindling as the cold bites and exhaustion brings sleep.

Moraine finds relief from the tension by dwelling on her expedition to the neighbors. The dichotomy of life in the settlement compared to the gentle interaction between the boy and the man stands in stark relief. As her mind ponders the characteristics of the two, she recalls events from her earlier years when her group met another nomadic group, and an exchange of news, methods, and travels took place. Included in that group were two adults, a male, a female, and a child. They had a similar build to the man and the boy she saw at the tributary. Alarmingly, wooden shackles secured them to a stake in plain sight at the edge of the settlement. The backs of their clothing showed rips with the obvious explanation being that they endured some form of beating. Their demeanor was downcast as they meekly endured taunts at the hands of an ill-tempered overseer who required them to perform various menial labor. Most surprisingly, Moraine's group condoned the behavior as if it was normal. The child was only about four years old and had an uncanny resemblance to the overseer. By the callous treatment metered out, it was clear that the status of the threesome was that of subhuman slaves. Even the wolf-like dogs that wandered around the compound received better treatment.

Sitting bolt upright on the straw mattress, Moraine suddenly realizes that because they look different, her acquaintances from the valley are in danger of similar treatment by her group if found. The imperative is that they must remain hidden or better still, move to safety elsewhere.

In the morning, the wind and clouds continue to dispense misery on the residents as temperatures remain at the freezing level. All activity is curtailed, and angry outbursts flare up at the slightest provocation.

Tusk, one of the young men of the hunting party, uses the confines of the hut and a captive audience to boast of his exploits. He regales them with stories of his bravery and punctuates his monolog with a diatribe on the shortcomings of the reception party. With domineering self-importance, he brushes aside anyone interrupting his monopoly. Reaching for his club, menacingly heavy with an intricately carved bone handle and shaft with a stone stub at the end, he points to the marks representing each deer that died at his hands, thirty, and a record. For each notch, he has a story of his exploits and a boastful claim. He glances at Moraine for affirmation of his greatness, a gesture that Gramater notices with interest. She has long considered Moraine for a match to this man of substance. He projects an authoritarian manner, a means to check Moraine's independence and rebellious streak.

At a break when Tusk has to stop to eat, Moraine takes the opportunity to exit the claustrophobic interior. The bracing wind and rain is a welcome relief. Gramater watches from a side entrance to see Moraine stop, glance about, and proceed to Gramater's work shelter. She emerges, looks for anyone observing her movements, decides that all is clear, and disappears into the forest, heading down the slope to the river.

Gramater gestures Tusk to a corner. At her urging, he steps aside, and she whispers, "Moraine is up to something. Follow her; there down that path. I want to know what she is doing. Now go!"

Tusk, the grandson of Gramater's deceased sister and only surviving blood relative, is the occasional recipient of meager privileges the matriarch condescends to hand out.

Aroused at the license to give reign to his inner urgings, Tusk sets out at a trot. With some difficulty, he manages to close the gap on Moraine as she fleet-footed makes her way along the edge of the river. As the bank separating the river from the cliffs narrows, he is forced to slow down so as not to be seen.

Talking to himself, he says, "She must realize she is heading down a cul-de-sac, surely. What can she want there of all places? Curious."

With rising anticipation, murmuring to himself, "Hmm. It's a good place to corner her and have my way with her. The old geyser's message was clear."

As he rounds a bend in the course of the ever-narrowing escarpment, the cliff encroaches to within feet of the rushing water. From his vantage, he sees her stop, test the water with her foot, and shiver as if intending to wade into the turbulence.

"She is trapped; nowhere to go but back."

Expecting her to retreat, he conceals himself in some bushes alongside the path and watches, muttering, "I'll ambush her as she passes."

To his surprise, she steps into the rushing water. Hugging the edge of a bolder, she disappears around the corner, holding some article over her head as if to prevent it from getting wet.

"Darn! This is madness!"

Striding to the end of the cul-de-sac, he hesitantly enters the rushing water to follow. The current is surprisingly strong. At waist deep, he stops, uncertain that he can ford the rushing water. Testing it with a few more steps, he sees her further along the beach and retreats in fear of the current as the depth increases. A second attempt yields the same result, and this time he catches a glimpse of her disappearing at a brisk walk into the thicket lining the tributary.

Disconcerted, he curses his cowardice and retraces his steps to the camp, hoping to evade the attention of the old woman. He will have to tell Gramater that she eluded him further up the tributary. Cold and wet, he enters the encampment from the rear. As he proceeds to join the clansmen, a tap on his shoulder stops him in his tracks.

The old woman prods him with her walking stick, "Where is she?"

"I lost her further up the river. She was carrying something."

Annoyed at the response, "Yes, yes, I am aware of that. I want to know what she was doing."

Tusk timidly ventures, "We can ask her when she gets back."

"Stupid dolt! Are you interested in taking her as your woman? Think man! You need to know what her secrets are. Tomorrow I want you to follow her again."

"The waters are very dangerous. She crosses where only a small person can cross. I can take a party further up the tributary where the cliffs give way and come down the river from the top to wait for her where I lost her."

"No, no. Just you. No party. I will tell you when she leaves, so be ready."

## 3.3  Gramater

Tusk leaves her presence. Alone, Gramater's hidden anger spills over. Taking up her walking stick, she repeatedly beats the covering of her sleeping area. Red-faced and panting from the exertion, she tries to calm her thoughts, muttering, "Curse her, I will get her … just be patient. Poisoning her mother at the birth of the brat was satisfying but not enough. Killed the wrong damn person. Meant to rubbish the brat, Moraine. Instead, the mother goes and dies. Anyhow that is long past. My vengeance must, it will be satisfied! Every day the brat is more rebellious. She needs to be taught a lesson. Brought under control."

Agonizing afresh over her three stillborn children to Eagor and his subsequent abandonment for another woman, she curses that day. Left barren and unable to conceive, the thought of his infidelity still rankles Gramater. The daughter from that union, herself, fell pregnant, and in performing the midwife duties, Gramater's attempt to abort the prospective child by poisoning the mother failed. The child, Moraine, survived, but the mother did not. The father, suspicious of the mother's death, brought Moraine up under constant protective supervision until his death while on a hunting expedition. By then, Moraine was old enough to fend for herself. She proved to be a resourceful, independent person who stood her ground when challenged. A rebellious trait that further exasperated Gramater, being accustomed to subservience by all her minions.

With vengeful glee, she saw an opportunity. "Grooming Tusk to lead the clan when I am gone will kill two birds with one stone. Bring Moraine to heel and, in doing so, promote Tusk in the eyes of the clan and secure a continuance of the Gramater bloodline."

## 3.4   Potion

Moraine takes to running to dispel the cold and quickly covers the distance to the clandestine vantage point with a view of the rock at the water's edge. The rock is deserted, and the jar, left there yesterday, gone. After a long wait, she decides to approach the cave at the foot of the cliff. Stealthily making her way through the undergrowth, she draws near and listens; nothing, all is quiet. What can this mean? After a while, she despondently descends to the river, leaves the second potion on the rock, and heads back to camp. En-route, she senses someone following but all attempts at seeing the person allude her.

At the camp, the mater curiously says nothing as she enters the encampment, despite seeing her approach. Tusk, too, behaves abnormally, taking to leering at her across the communal space.

Brilliant sunshine greets the following day, but a cold wind spoils an otherwise pleasant day. The loss of two days is made up in a frenzy of activity to secure the meat from spoiling, smoking, and drying it to a hardened condition for storage. They gorge themselves in the excess and a rare display of joviality spent dancing and drinking to the successful hunt and in the knowledge of a secure larder for the lean period ahead. The beverages, laced with fermented berries, add an artificial exuberance to the festivities. Tusk increasingly abandons his limited self-control, regaling the audience with elaborations on his earlier boasts.

In a lull, he corners Moraine, knowingly winking at her, hinting at her absence the day before, "Say Moraine, how was the swim, a little cold?"

Moraine, who has fretted all day at not being able to disappear up the valley because of the workload, manages to disguise her alarm, "Oh, that, yes, it was cold."

"That is an odd place to go for a swim. What were you doing there?"

Without a plausible explanation, she decides to brush him off, "Excuse me, they are waiting for me at the smoke pits. I have work to do" and squirms past him.

It is clear that he followed her but probably not beyond the confluence of the two rivers. Her secret is still safe but obviously in danger. What to do? She must warn the man, but they may not speak the same language. The rest of the day is fraught with anxiety. Can she locate the man? How to stress urgency? Will Tusk follow her again? These questions vex without answers. By nightfall, she concludes that one of two possibilities may eventuate. If Tusk follows, she will have to abandon the excursion. On the other hand, if Tusk does not follow, she will have to impress on the man and his group to leave forthwith.

Waking before sunrise Moraine silently makes her way to the work shelter.

"Oh no, it is the last of the potion. Gramater will be fuming when she discovers that it is missing. I just hope this cures the boy; I have nothing more to offer them."

On impulse, she decides to take some of the other supplies; salves for wounds, lotions for cold sores, and balms to relieve insect bites.

"What is this? Marked with an X, must be something special. I had better leave it."

With her needs in a pouch, she returns to the communal sleeping quarters to wait for sunrise. A chorus of snoring, a legacy of over-indulging on the previous day, continues unabatedly. Recalling the frigid waters, she quietly adds additional fur clothing to her leather bag. Undecided, she ponders, should she sneak out while everyone is asleep, or wait for them to wake to better follow Tusk's movements. Deciding on the latter, she pretends to sleep and watches his movements. Finally, he stirs, then dresses, and exits to relieve himself. Moraine makes her move, takes up her pouch, slips out a backway, walks down to the river, and circles back through the undergrowth to watch Tusks. He completes his ablution, and as he enters the shelter, Gramater calls him aside, speaking in undertones, gesturing in the direction she walked. He then points in the opposite direction, indicating the hill at the back of the camp and promptly sets out in that direction with his club in hand. Confused, Moraine follows at a distance to see him walk up the escarpment and veer right along the ridge following the route above the cliffs overlooking

27

the tributary. His intent is now clear. He means to descend to the river further upstream and follow down the valley's course from that angle. She guesses that he fears braving the current at the confluence of the two rivers, as he did on the day he followed her.

He and Gramater are in cahoots, and the old woman is fully aware of the missing potions, muttering to herself, "The woman has eyes in the back of her head."

The danger to the man and the people in the cave is extreme; her duty is now clear, she must warn them.

## 3.5    Tusk

Tusk walks at a brisk pace through the wooded area, skirting the top of the cliffs, using his club as a lever to step over obstacles. Now and then, he peers over the edge looking for Moraine. At length, feeling he has outpaced her, he decides to stop on a ledge overlooking the riverine below. He has a clear view of the likely path she will follow. At length, she emerges in the distance from a cluster of trees and slows to a cautious pace, edging forward while looking ahead as if expecting something there. Curious at her behavior, Tusk leans forward to see past some intervening shrubs. Moraine stops in her progress and appears to fumble in her leather rucksack. She removes, what at the distance looks like several stoneware containers, carefully places them next to her, and glances about to make sure she has not been seen. Sure, in her seclusion, she leaves her rucksack under a bush and proceeds along the water's edge away to a protruding rock, places the containers on the rock, and returns to her backpack to wait.

Tusk can barely make out her presence through the obscuring growth and has to edge nearer to the overhang to improve his view. Still not clear enough, he decides to lie on his belly and creeps closer to the edge. Uncomfortable in the downward sloping position, he moves to a sitting position and waits. The tension mounts as the moments pass with Moraine expectantly observing the articles she left on the rock, and he, keenly waiting for an event to unfold. The minutes pass, and as the time stretches, the apprehension dissipates. Just as he begins to relax, startled he sees a man approaching her from the rear. With unusual yellow straw-colored hair, the man darts from one intervening brush to another to maintain his concealment. Still unaware of the approaching man, she remains focussed on the rock until a rustle interrupts her attention, and she turns to see the man just meters away from her. Stuck by the unfolding drama, Tusk leans forward, and in doing so, his club rolls off the edge of the cliff, clattering as hits first one protruding ledge and another further down. The pair turn in unison to locate the disturbance and catch a glimpse of Tusk as he tries to conceal his presence by lying on his back. Moraine freezes in position, and the stranger immediately dissolves in the bush as if by magic.

\* \* \*

Moraine, in moments, gathers her thoughts. With her intent dashed, the prospect of staging her presence after the man discovers the medicines lies in tatters. Worst of all, her deception must now be apparent to Tusk. On impulse, she decides to cast her lot with that of the strangers, this much she owes them; her doings have heightened their danger. Taking up her rucksack, she sprints across the clearing to the rock with the pouch of remedies, grabs them, and under cover of trees to obscure Tusk's view of her movements, heads up the embankment to the caves. As she covers the remaining distance, the stranger steps out of the brush and bars her way. Stopping dead, in a sign of surrender, she stretches out her hand holding out the medications and waits for his reaction.

\* \* \*

Having lost sight of his quarry when she disappeared behind the rocky protrusions of the cliff face, Tusk angrily takes his frustration out on a tree, ripping a branch from the stem. After a while, with no further activity below, cursing, he heads for camp. Walking on, it dawns on him that the events offer opportunities. Moraine will be more vulnerable to him and realizing, "Yes; the stranger, he looks familiar ... Of course, just like the savages that other clans held captive. That is it; they held them as slaves."

A plan takes form in his mind, urging him to hurry; he needs to return with a few men.

Unsurprisingly Gramater sees him enter the encampment and pulls him aside. Catching his breath, he blurts out his story.

Patting him on his shoulder, she says, "You did well, son. Let me think. You say you only saw one man, right."

"Yes, just the one."

"Well, it is quite possible that there are more. You need to take two armed men and approach from the bottom and another two to close off the top end. Trap them where they are. Do you think they can cross the river?"

"No, no, the stream is flowing too fast. They would be washed away."

"Okay. That's the plan. Now listen. I want you to capture them alive, if possible."

"And Moraine?"

"Moraine needs to be disciplined, and I think you are just the person to do that. She needs to be taught a lesson," emphasizing the point by stabbing her gnarled finger into his chest.

As Tusk dashes off to find recruits, Gramater mutters to herself, "You idiot. So predictable, nothing motivates stupid men more than the thought of owning a woman." Shouting after him, "Do not fail!"

Within minutes, he has his task force ready and commands, "You and you, that way up the river to the tributary. Stick to the edge of the cliff and wade through the water to the landing further up the tributary. The water reaches chest height, no problem – as I did," he lies.

Pointing to a surly, muscular man with a stocky frame and a small, skinny person next to him, "Scat, you lead. Runt, you do what Scat tells you to do. No arguments, and both of you, make sure you follow my instructions."

"You two, Wart and Rasp, come with me. Now, all of you remember, corner them; I want them alive. Rasp, you get ropes; we will have to tie them up. Leave Moraine to me, okay! Let's go!"

Remembering, he shouts after the departing group, "If you see them give three short whistles and repeat that until you get an answering whistle. We will do the same. When we are ready to close in on them, I will give three long whistles. Go now!"

# 4    Stranger

The stranger stands his ground, barring entrance to the cave. An impasse, what to do? Seeing Tusk's club lying in the undergrowth, Moraine slowly moves to it, extracts it from its lodging, and points to the top of the cliff where they saw Tusk standing. Using the club, she indicates a hitting action against her head and points to the cliff, then to the man. The man seems to understand but remains unmoved. Fumbling through her bag, she removes the pouch of medicines and points to the cave where she presumes the boy remains hidden. Placing the pouch and the club on the ground, she indicates to him to take them. He seems to understand, takes up the articles, and suggests to her to follow. As Moraine's eyes adjust to the gloom, she sees the remnants of a fire glowing in a corner. The boy stands to one side. Two women of a similar frame and coloring to the man stand opposite in an alert posture with sticks in hand, ready to defend themselves if necessary. Moraine takes in the scene, and they silently wait for a reaction from her. Against a wall of the grotto, she sees a fresco of a hunt, showing men with long spears following deer and other creatures with tusks. The art is a delicate mix of yellow ochre and red with long charcoal lines and a curious symbol of two pairs of diagonally intersecting parallel lines engraved into the stone.

 On the ground lie slate shards with similar symbols scratched on them. Picking one up and turning it over, she sees an intersecting pair of sprigs of flowers with leaves at the base, painted on it. Struck by the intricacy of the drawings and moved by the portrayal, she hesitates, then sensing an opportunity, slowly steps closer to the pictures on the rock faces. All eyes follow her, and the tension of the encounter dissolves with each step.

Spellbound, she takes in the drawings. Then turns to point to her chest, says, "Moraine!" Repeating her name a few times.

The taller of the two women replies, "Quill," and points to the other woman and says, "Fern."

The boy, looking brighter than previously, warily moves forward to her, takes her hand, turns to the man, and says words that have no meaning to Moraine. The man smiles in return, and the spell is broken. They move closer and exchange words that hold no threat. Relieved at having crossed the initial hurdle, the danger outside remains to be articulated. Moraine gently prises Tusk's club from the man's hand and points upwards, then with a slicing action across her throat, indicates the danger. Repeating the gestures three times, provokes a discussion between the three adults. Judging by their expressions, they seem to understand. Moraine takes the initiative to impress on them the need to run from the cave. After a few repetitions, the man grasps the significance of the peril they face and instructs the others to gather their things. Indicating to the boy, like the other day, they are to travel over the ridge on the far side of the river. The boy's face immediately lightens up, and he rushes to the far end of the cave to collect his meager possessions from where he must have slept and gathered up the slate shards and assorted hollow bone implements. Rolling up the sleeping mat and while the others do likewise, he waits at the entrance for the adults to follow with Moraine standing next to him. On an impulse, he returns to the cave where Moraine left Tusk's club. Taking it, he hands it to Slate, who tests its weight and examines its carvings then deposits it to his backpack.

Rejoining Moraine, she indicates to him, "Me Moraine. You?"

The boy replies, "Broach."

Pointing to the boy, then the man, she says, "Broach. What is his name?"

"Slate." Gesturing to the taller of the two women, then the other, he says, "Quill, Fern."

Repeating Moraine says, nodding, "Slate, Broach, Quill, Fern, Moraine."

Within minutes, the group is ready to leave. Proceeding along the edge of the cliff, a short distance, Slate stops at a mound of stones. Bending down, he observes a moment of silence, paying homage to a person buried there. The two women and the child do likewise and, in a downcast demeanor, move on. Taking a painted shard from a pouch, Broach buries it below some of the surface stones as a tear rolls off his cheek, then he too moves on in silence. Moraine can but wonder at what tragedy lies there.

33

## 4.1  Ambush

Tusk and his group make quick progress along the ridge then take a short cut to strike diagonally along the top to avoid the broad curve of the river below. Soon they emerge from a thicket again at the top of the precipice. Frustrated at finding the cliff now higher than anticipated, he decides to continue further along as the river winds away to his right. He has a clear view down the valley in a while, but the perspective upstream shows a thickening of the forest growth, offering concealment to anyone on foot along the river's edge. Further up, the river plunges from his elevation down into the gorge is a spectacular waterfall, a height of at least fifty persons. Assessing the situation, he concludes that it is a natural cup-de-sac, which will trap the fugitives.

Indicating to his fellows, he says, "Okay, this is where we stop and watch. Scat and Runt, moving up from the bottom, will corner them at the foot of the waterfall. It should soon be over. Pity we didn't take the bottom route. We will be missing the fun."

His accomplice, Rasp, suggests, "Why don't we roll some rocks into position. We can scare them as they pass."

"Okay, but don't forget; we need them alive. Stay out of sight until I give the signal."

With that, they prepare some boulders ready for dislodging to plummet over the edge at the right time and conceal themselves behind vegetation to wait. Tusk finds a comfortable position to watch the imminent drama. At length, Moraine, a child, two women, and a man appear in the distance. The man leads the way, glancing about for danger, scanning the cliff face for movements, and pointing out possible danger points. As they approach the denser vegetation directly below Tusk, Wart and his companion, Scat, appears further downstream. They obviously cannot see the fugitives from their vantage, as they cautiously move forward. Tusk whistles three short whistles in quick succession. The men in the rear stop to listen as he repeats the signal twice more. They immediately answer with three short whistles of their own and take a more defensive stand, guardedly moving forward, but the fugitives have moved into the dense woodland, still out of sight. At Tusk's command, his group on the ridge release a few boulders, which tumble and ricochet off intervening protrusions to crash in the woods below. He follows up with three long whistles to signal to the group below to go on the attack.

\* \* \*

The whistles, disguised as bird calls, do not fool Slate. He urges his group to a trot, expecting some form of attack. Although the boulders fell harmlessly to their rear, it means the enemy on the cliff has seen their progress; they should expect a repeat of the attack ahead or the foe hopes to turn them back. The answering whistles from downstream means an attack from the rear is the immediate danger. The vegetation progressively gets denser as they proceed until it is quite a struggle to make headway.

Turning to his followers, in a low guttural voice that Moraine cannot understand, with gestures, he clarifies that they must not break branches and twigs so that they do not give away the path they are following through the undergrowth. In this manner, they move on with more caution, bearing right towards the sound of the river. Following the course of the river, as it bends to the right, the slope to the foot of the cliff widens. The ridge that lines the valley rises to broken crags, separated by steep gullies, tending in the same direction as the stream. Up ahead, through the obscuring leaves and branches, Moraine makes out the glint of water, falling down one of the gullies in an impressive waterfall. As they approach the foot of the falls, the noise rises to a deafening roar, and mist swirls in a cloud that dampens the foliage to dripping wet. Moss lines the forest floor and boulders at the edge of the river. Moraine fears that they have reached a dead-end, but Slate confidently walks forwards, clearly familiar with the surroundings. He stops at the edge of a circular cauldron of roiling water into which the water gushes from the height of the cliff.

The noise drowns out any attempt at speaking, so Slate gestures that the group must wait, and he disappears back along the path that they came on. The minutes pass as Moraine wonders how they will evade the pursuers. Eventually, he reappears and indicates that two people are in pursuit but have deviated from the route leading to the foot of the falls. He urges speed and takes to walking in the shallows along the edge of the pool of water. Submerged rocks make for difficult progress as he leads them ever closer to the cascading water. Proceeding deeper, the frigid water reaches to chest level as he braces himself, holding the boy to his chest, he strides into the falling water, disappearing into the shower of water. Moraine is last to enter, unsure what to expect. Holding the rucksack above her head, she negotiates the slippery stones underfoot and enters the drumming maelstrom and moments later, emerges in a grotto obscured from the outside by a curtain of water. The overhanging rock provides shelter from the falling water, but the mist soaks the inner rock faces and beach. Soaked but temporarily safe from the pursuers, Slate leads along the side of the sheet of water to the far end of the river and out into an open space. A steep wooded incline, lined by a continuation of the cliff of the far bank, peters out at the height of the slope. Skirting the cliff face, the view to the opposite bank through the partially obscuring foliage shows Tusk in the distance with three other men standing at the edge of the cliff where he rolled the boulders into the ravine. They appear to be trying to locate the fugitives and the two at the foot of the cliff. Slate wastes no time in distancing his party from the scene and leads up the incline and over the ridge where a new vista opens up. Snow-clad mountains with intervening valleys stretch across the horizon with a section of lower elevation in the middle. It is towards this gap in the mountain range that he points but orders a stop and opportunity to rest, eat from the hastily gathered provisions from earlier in the day, and dry out in the sunshine.

* * *

Tusk abandons the need for stealth when after a while, there remains no sign of the fugitives. He resorts to shouting down at the pair at the foot of the cliff, "Idiots! Have you let them double back?"

Scat shouts back, "No. They must be here somewhere. Will keep searching," then mumbling in a lower voice, "irritating fool."

"Try nearer the cliff. There may be a cave, Maybe boulders behind which to hide. We will stay at this end where we have a clear view through the vegetation in case they are going back the way they came. The area at the base of the cliff is not visible from here. Scat, station Runt to guard that area."

"Runt, ignore him, come with me."

Runt replies, "There must be a crossing up ahead."

With sunset approaching, the two in the riverine finally locate the passage behind the waterfall. Scat, the leader, wet from negotiating the water, emerges on the far bank, walks to an open stretch away from the roaring water, and signals to Tusk on the distant cliff pointing to the waterfall as the route taken by fugitives.

Exasperated, Tusk vents his anger on his underling, Rasp, who ventured that Moraine had outsmarted them, "Dolt! You think this is funny. We'll track them, day and night, but I'll get them and, you Rasp, you'll be carrying the provisions. Runt is supposedly so good at tracking, he'll have a job. Back to camp now. Be ready in the morning."

## 4.2    Chase

Slate leads the way halfway up the rise from the hidden path under the waterfall and turns to follow the contour of the hill with the main river far below and to the right. Lying ahead is a gap in the distant mountains, which seems to indicate the source of the river. He notes that the migrating birds are headed in that direction giving him confidence in his choice of path. With a determined stride, he steps on. Fern and Quill follow with Moraine and Broach bringing up the rear. They trudge along in silence, each in their thoughts. As the sun nears the horizon, Slate calls a halt. From this vantage, he has a clear view of the route they have followed. He finds a comfortable position from where he can maintain that view to watch for any followers. Moraine, some feet away with Broach at her side, watches his movements. Periodically, his gaze shifts to a thicket a small distance from their position. There is a movement within. He waits. After a while, a pheasant emerges, hesitates, and then scratches about for seeds on the ground. Gesturing us to be still, Slate backs away in a crouching position with this spear in hand. He skirts around a bush and circles behind the ticket. The pheasant ceases feeding and returns to the dark of the thicket. A single squawk of alarm is all Moraine hears as the life of the fowl ends. Carrying the lifeless pheasant, Slate returns to the group with a signal to follow. Noiselessly the group obeys, and he leads to an obscuring rocky outcrop where he strikes a flint stone to produce a spark and ignite some tinder-dry leaves and twigs under a spit for roasting the bird, having removed the feathers.

Once sated and having stored a remaining portion in a leather pouch, the group settles down for the evening. In the twilight, there is a sense of cohesiveness that settles over the group. For the first time, they turn to each other, and Broach is the first to talk. He stayed near Moraine's side for much of the time. There is an unspoken companionship between the two, as the youngest in the group. A staccato of attempts at conversation fails as the others join in with gesticulations and exaggerated facial expressions to emphasize their meaning. The comedy of it eventually becomes apparent as the boy begins to giggle, and the others try to hold back their laughter. Even Slate's usual serious demeanor gives way to a broad smile revealing healthy white teeth. Unable to contain themselves, they break out into prolonged laughter, dissipating the remnants of a tension-filled day.

By the dim coals of the fire and after renewed attempts, Broach and Moraine achieve a semblance of dialogue with the others joining in. Moraine realizes that she will have to adapt to their language rather than expect all four of them to learn hers. Gradually she learns that they have been on the move for many months before settling in at the cave they vacated. It offered a degree of security, given its location and access difficulties. On inquiry, Moraine establishes that the person buried there is Broach's mother, Slate's partner. She died of some form of skin ailment compounded by respiratory problems. Pain at the loss is evident as the sadness produces a more subdued end to the exchange. Moraine demonstrates her condolences by hugging the boy gently and extending her hands to the adults to share in their grief.

To shrug off the somberness, Fern explains that she is Slate's sister, and Quill is her cousin making her point by drawing a semblance of a family tree in the sand. Talk turns to lighter subjects as the glowing embers gradually darken and extinguish. Wariness signals a time for sleep.

* * *

Wet and cold to the bone, Tusk vents his fear and frustrations out on Rasp as he struggles to brave the rushing water at the confluence of the two rivers. Humiliated at relying on Rasp to hold his hand to steady him as he struggles against the force of water, transparently shows his usual bravado as insecurities, for the others to see. Once safely on the beach, to reassert his leadership, he administers a punch on Rasp's midriff, on the pretext of him being too slow while in the stream.

The scorn heaped on him by Gramater for allowing the fugitives to escape is a festering sore on his ego. He inexplicably feels compelled to secure her approval, but his attempts to do her bidding only further exasperate him as they come across as fawning ingratiation. To salvage a modicum of self-esteem, he boastfully promised to find the escapees. Now, with a delay of a day, he knows the emptiness of the promise given the head start that they have, but he has no alternative but to continue with the charade. Moving on in a dark and brooding mood, they again have to brave the waters to traverse the passage behind the waterfall. His foul mood persists until they crest the rise on the far side and the distant mountains come into view. Determining that the Moraine and her group will be heading for the gap in the range, he elects to strike out in that direction. Midway through the following day, they, by chance, happen on the rocky outcrop where Slate prepared the meal.

Wart, who has been lagging to avoid Tusk's attention, calls out, "Hey, here! Have a look. I think they spent the night here."

Irritated Tusks comes over and reluctantly admits, "Hmm, flattened grass. This looks like an attempt to hide the coals of a fire. You may be right for a change, Wart." Turning to the group, "I think we are on the right track. I need you to double up. Walk faster now! Rasp bring my things – get a move on!"

* * *

Spectacular mountains flank the side of the valley as Slate leads his group through the pass. Occasionally they descend to the edge of the waters to skirt buttresses that form a barrier that diverts the flow. At other times, they ascend to contours overlooking the river as it carves its way through the mountain range. From these elevated positions, Slate stops to scan downstream for evidence of followers. Anxious to distance them from the pursuers, he nevertheless has to interrupt their progress to hunt for food. Moraine has proven helpful, exhibiting uncanny accuracy with the spear, but they only have one between them having left the spares at the cave. He solves this by fashioning a point to a reed for darting fish, as they make their way upstream to their spawning grounds. With each of the parties equipped with a means to fish, they do not lack for a supply of food. Tusk's club proves to be of little value with the stone stub at the end, which serves more as a tool to administer blows at close quarters.

Moraine looks forward to the evening discussions as she becomes more fluent in their language. Fern proves to be the opposite of her brother, carefree and jovial, while Slate is quiet, intense, and curious, always looking for a deeper meaning to questions and the world around him. Quill is earnest, worries a lot, and has an abiding concern for everyone's wellbeing. She takes over Moraine's supply of potions and helps Broach whenever he is feeling unwell. Broach vacillates between youthful playfulness and exuberance and downcast listlessness whenever his ailments overwhelm him. He, like his deceased mother, shows signs of a skin ailment and respiratory problems. In one of his thoughtful moments, to Moraine's surprise, he takes one of the bone implements from his pouch and begins blowing in the one end. It generates deep humming tones creating an unstructured moving rhythm in low tones rising and falling depending on which holes he depresses. There is a certain wistfulness that inescapably relates to memories of his mother infecting Slate, Quill, and Fern. They silently listen as the sounds wash over them. The bond between them is almost tangible.

Each morning Slate meticulously hides any evidence of their overnight activities. He discards the remnants of the fire into the river, combs the area for any signs of having slept there, and scatters leaves over the place.

On the third day, after a strenuous incline, they reach the headwaters. To the left, a waterfall spills from the heights of a craggy pinnacle, and a saddle of land divides north from the south with a shallow alpine meadow straddling the divide. On the right, a mountain towers up into the only cloud in the bright and otherwise cloudless day. The view ahead shows a series of undulating hills diminishing to a plateau in the hazy distance suggesting a warmer region. Northwards the view traces the passage they walked. They followed up the incline, with ice patches lining the shadowy flanks. The path winds its natural way along the only passable route from the far distance. A variety of birds wing their way overhead in a steady stream in their intent to reach the beckoning warmth of the lands across the plains.

Here, the air, refreshingly cold after the exertion to reach this elevation, affords an opportunity to rest. The majesty of the landscape with looming mountains, emerald green pastures, splashes of color lent by a scattering of alpine flora and water sparkling over rocky rapids, lends an enchantment as it miniaturized the group against the breathless tapestry. Concerns over being followed seep from their minds as they soak in the embrace of nature.

With the rudiments of their language, Moraine poses a question, "Slate, you think – they follow?"

Shrugging, Slate says, "We walked well. Maybe they guess our route, the path, this gap in the mountains."

Fern, expressing the exhilaration of the pass, animatedly gesturing with her arms outstretched, says, "Slate, enjoy the moment. We are safe. Tomorrow we can worry again."

Quill, cautions, "You can't be sure, Fern. They may still be following. As Slate says, there is only one route they could follow, and it is the same one we took."

Slate brings some relief, pointing, "From here down onto the plateau there, say in two more days, we could be safe. Once there, there are many routes, so they won't know which way to go. We must hide our trail to confuse them. We'll rest here until midday, eat, then onwards!"

Moraine turns to Broach, who is somewhat subdued, says, "Broach, the sun. Very bright today. You must cover yourself. Quill, do you have some lotion in that pouch? Maybe, he needs some?"

Quill dutifully applies some to the marks on his face as Broach coughs gently, and Slate looks on with concern. As they silently eat the leftover food from the previous day, Slate moves to a promontory to scan for the best way forward.

In doing a final check for followers, with some irritation, he makes out the group rounding a bend in the river at the very extreme of his visible range. The faint outline of five people is apparent.

"Fern, Quill, Moraine, come look." Pointing, "Can you see them? Look!"

Joining him on the rise, Moraine is quick to locate the procession, "Yes! I can see five people."

Slate says, "I think they are about a half a day away. We need to hurry."

Within minutes, they are on their way, having disguised all evidence of their presence on the slope. Slate urges them to tread carefully to avoid disturbing the vegetation as they walk. He takes an unlikely route into the valley, first skirting along the edge of the mountain on their right, then descending an adjoining valley. Striking out along the contour of the fall of the land, walking is easy, as they rapidly progress in a gradual descent. He comfortably manages Broach on his broad back as they distance themselves from the enemy. By nightfall, satisfied that the chance of the pursuers finding them is minimal, they stop for the night next to a cliff with an overhanging rock-face that offers protection from dew and the elements.

* * *

As they crest the rise, the dilemma is immediately apparent to Tusk. Moraine's group could take any number of paths down the other side of the escarpment.

Exasperated, he vents his frustration, "Left, right, straight on, we should have got here ahead of them."

Shoving Rasp out of his way, "You're always lagging, and we have to wait for you. Useless individual."

Rasp stammers, "All these things I have to carry. I, I can't keep up. Y … you should just go ahead and, and I will catch up."

"Too late now. They are long gone. What a waste."

Scat, who has been looking down the slope, interrupts, challenging Tusk with his burly presence, "Don't blame Rasp, we were slow off the mark, to begin with. We should have got going right away rather than waiting until the next day."

Runt takes the opportunity in a lull, turning he points, "Look. There are three routes they could have taken. If we had more men, we could try all three. Eventually, they will reach the plains over there. When we are closer, we may be able to see which way they went."

"Well, we don't have more men, stupid!"

Scat, irritated, hot and frustrated, imposes, "This gets to me. You lead us on a wild goose chase, and here we are listening to your rantings. For

44

what? Just to satisfy you and the old hag. Just shut up! I'm going back." He begins collecting his things.

Runt ignores the mounting tension between Scat and Tusk, "Wait! Just wait. What we need to do is send more men. We can wait for them. I am a good runner. I can go back and get support, and Gramater can break camp. We have enough provisions from the hunt, so there is no reason for them to stay where they are."

Tusk, torn between retaliating to Scat's implied dominance by Gramater, his inner need to prove his manhood and the looming failure of the chase, wrestles with what to do. His mind twists and turns in agony until he finally succumbs to his need for vengeance against Moraine and his desire to lord it over her and sides with Runt. With an air of bravado and to blunt Scat's attack, he condescendingly says, "Runt, you always think you are so smart. You think your suggestion wasn't obvious. Get your things and go. Go now! What are you waiting for? I need you back here in five days with five more men. Move dammit!"

Scat just shakes his head in annoyance and sits down.

Runt is soon on his way with parting instructions to give Gramater directions so she can follow later with the rest of the clan.

Relieved to be on his own, Runt distances himself from the other four as quickly as possible. Small though he is, his intellect eclipses most of his clan's, but he knows that this risks alienating him if he displays it too obviously. For now, he is thankful to be out of Tusk's obnoxious presence.

The angle of the descent is ideal for covering the ground quickly. He relishes the cool breeze in his hair and the freedom to pace himself without having to adjust for the presence of the other travelers. Within two days, he is back at the camp.

# 5   Undercurrents

Endlessly churning, flexing under the pressure of gravity and heat of nuclear decay, the belly of the earth belches its excesses to relieve the strain. Fever tremors herald the ejecta that emanates from within, producing flotsam on a sea of magma, continents that float like scum, the slag of the furnace below, they are the waste product of an eternal dynamo. On this jetsam, the cargo of life holds desperately to niches in the floating mass, footholds that first provide harbor but are mercilessly winnowed to leave some to morph to a new disguise. The fittest labor on relentlessly, seeking to dominate the weak and infirm, but always at the mercy of what lies underfoot.

Electromagnetic radiation streams from the solar orb overhead, bathing the planet with the lethal effects of its wind, threatening to strip the atmosphere of its protective shield to sterilize the fort of tenuous life. Except for the magnetic dynamo within, deflecting the incoming stream, the inhabitants would stand naked, defenseless before its onslaught.

As Earth relentlessly circles the sun, millennia after millennia, the tilt of its axis wobbles by degrees, and its orbit wavers from a circle to an ellipse and back again. Circumstance sometimes joins the forces of orbital mechanics and the internal working of the world to wreak havoc on its passengers, while life struggles to maintain its foothold. The climate sways between frigid and sweltering; the magnetic barrier oscillates between defense and surrender to the incoming rays. Orchestrated by the collision of continents and the subductions that follow, swollen blisters disgorge their contents in eruptions that blanket the surrounds with ash and rivers of rock. Aerosols of sulfur dioxide in the stratosphere obscure the sunlight inducing volcanic winters, precipitating acid rain, and exacerbating the struggles of nature. This cast of circumstances conspired to impose its will on the world 39,000 years ago, setting the scene for a change in characters in the drama of our ancestors' final act. The clash of the transition to our kind is writ large in the scattering of remains hidden by the passage of millennia, standing inescapably in the DNA we inherit. Freed from constraints, we the survivors spread to inhabit every niche of this wide world, steadfastly eliminating all that challenged for dominance. Rest not, for the conspiring circumstances have no concern for the meager sovereignty we hold; they circle their prey and strike at will when their time is ripe.

"Jane! I think I found the reason for their route", Michel shouts with relief, "It was there staring at me all along. I can connect the dots. It is plain to see".

Somewhat irritated at being interrupted, dropping her analysis, she moves over to the screen to look, "You will have to explain. What have you found?"

Michel excitedly draws a southward arc across the map, with an exaggerated fork as it intersects the mountains of northern Spain, "The magnetic field runs down here from Scandinavia, and as it approaches the mountains, here at the Pyrenees, the gradual divergence into two paths is clearer. It forks instead of heading straight for the magnetic South Pole. Precisely, where the divergence is more apparent, the birds scatter away from their usual path. Your geotagging data from last year shows a slight deviation but not as much as occurred this year. It has been exaggerated. The interesting thing about this is that associates working from the States who routinely monitor the magnetosphere from space using their miniature CubeSat satellite, make no mention of the year over year variation. Even now, with the exaggeration, I have heard no mention of it. If you like, I can logon to their system to check."

Calming down, Jane looks closer, "Yes, I see the deviation. It may explain the drop in numbers that we now see as they return to Europe. I guess that they simply get lost during the return trip. The question is, why the sudden change?"

"On the southward trip, they may get funneled through the mountain pass in the Pyrenees, whereas on the northward journey, they would follow the magnetic field only to be confronted by a mountain."

"Yes, that would be confusing. They may take a while to find their way to the mountain pass."

She returns to the opposite side of the table. A large map, made up of multiple pages stuck together, spreads across the table between them.

Scattered across the floor are sheets that did not make it into the map on the table.

Michel ventures, "Everyone has been so focussed on the climate conditions that I think they have lost sight of a potential polar reversal; the magnetic South Pole has been in an excursion phase for many years."

Jane returns, "Last year Zinnia and Cyan arrived two weeks later than usual. We are already into the third week and still no sign of them. There has to be an explanation?"

Michel suggests, "Maybe they are like the canary in the coalmine. Is it possible that they are ultra-sensitive to changes in the magnetic field?"

"You are the expert on geomagnetism, can that cause a change? Is it a subterranean problem that is out of sight?"

Michel explains, "Like earthquakes, it is difficult to predict when they will occur."

Thinking it over, he considers, "Say, come to think of it, you may have something there! Tectonic subduction has been associated with changes in magnetic fields in the past. If something is happening underfoot, literally, it may have to do with the tectonic plates. The African Plate is pushing northwards under the Eurasian Plate, creating the Alps. There is a supervolcano west of Naples with a caldera, known as the Phlegraean Fields, which has about twenty-four volcanic edifices in the area. There was a major eruption 39,000 years ago and two significant but smaller eruptions subsequently. An anthropologist hypothesizes that the big one may have contributed to the demise of Neanderthals just at a time when modern humans arrived in Europe. World temperatures dropped, causing a volcanic winter that lasted many years."

"That's fascinating. How do you come to know about this?"

"Like most things, there are interdependencies. The subduction associated with the eruption started the magnetic excursion that followed. That is what drew my attention. The magnetic north and south poles did not fully flip at the time but came close to it; the magnetic South Pole split into two, and the force-field surrounding the earth weakened, allowing an increase in the harmful effects of energetic particles from the sun reaching the surface."

Jane asks, "How were the Neanderthals affected?"

"Combined with the periodic ice ages of the time and the volcanic winter that followed the eruption, much of Europe was reduced from forest to steppe tundra. This resulted in a decrease in the numbers of animals like deer and elk that depend on the vegetation. Being meat eaters, the Neanderthals suffered the consequences. Add to that the cold and the radiation from the sun, and you have the circumstances for hardships on an already fragile species having to compete with newly arrived modern humans."

"How cruel circumstance can be? One feels for them. It is quite a sad story ... Are you suggesting that our Robins are being affected by the current magnetic excursion?"

"For that, I have to defer to you. The magnetic excursion we are experiencing now has been ongoing for a couple of decades. You tell me, have the birds been affected?"

Jane replies, "Possibly. It may explain the delays in the migration, but that is not the issue. Why the prolonged delay this year? That is the question. It brings us back to my first question; is there something going on underfoot, literally as I said?"

"Okay, you make a good point. To answer that, I would have to speak to someone who has his or her finger on the pulse of the latest tectonic movements but first, let me see what the latest is from CubeSat." Logging onto the system and zooming into the Pyrenees area shows nothing extraordinary. "Just as I thought, nothing from CubeSat. I think your birds can pick up subtle changes well before all our sophisticated electronics."

Jane hastens, "Well, with that confirmed, don't let me hold you up; do you know someone who can help?"

Pondering, Michel says, "Hmm. There is someone by the name of Enrico. I forget his last name, but he works at the university in Naples. He is involved in this debate about the Neanderthals. He and an anthropologist by the name of Käthe Loeschke have collaborated on this. I must confess, Käthe told me about the Neanderthals. She works at the institute of anthropology at Leipzig. I met her at a conference on geomagnetic effects on technology a few years back."

Jane urges, "If you are going to help me with this geotagging project, we need answers rather quickly. When can you contact them?"

"I can try to track her down at the institute. There must be contact numbers online. Same with Enrico. Tomorrow, okay?"

## 6.1   Team

"Hello, is that Enrico Rossi? This is Michel Brenner."

"How can I help you?

"I have followed some of your writing on plate tectonics. Do you know Käthe Loeschke?"

"Yes, yes. I do."

"I am in the Pyrenees at the moment, working with a friend on bird migrations. Specifically, birds that navigate using magnetic fields, which is my specialty. Can you answer a couple of questions about plate tectonics? Jane, my friend, is with me. Can I conference her in?

"Yes, hello, Jane, how can I help you?"

Michel explains, "We were just wondering whether there has been any unusual tectonic activity in your area recently?"

Enrico replies, "This is a very active site, as you are probably well aware. If you are looking for specific changes, it is difficult to be certain given the noise of competing disturbances. It is both frustrating and concerning because the population here is at risk, and they turn to us to predict the next episode. We try to model early-warning signals, but there are so many variables that we remain uncertain. So to answer your question, there is activity. It is highly variable, but at the same time, that is par for the course."

Jane responds, "We are tracking the migration of birds along the corridor from Germany through to Africa, via the Pyrenees, and find that the migrations are faltering. It is as if something is confusing their flight paths or delaying the migrations. We are not certain."

"Interesting. I can't help you, more than what I have told you but would like to stay in touch to see how matters develop; if you don't mind."

Michel concludes, "Yes, that would be great. We will be talking to Käthe about the evidence of effects on Neanderthals. It is just possible that she will know something about other creatures."

Enrico says, "Okay, I am in fairly regular touch with her. Good luck!"

Ending the call, Michel turns to Jane, "Well, that didn't rule anything out but also didn't shed any more light on the problem."

Jane responds, "Yes. Maybe Käthe can add more. Can you call her now?"

"Sure..."

After a couple of tries to locate her, Käthe's voice, a strong German accent, confirms the connection, "Käthe Loeschke hier."

"Hallo Käthe. Forgive the English, it is Michel Brenner here. Do you remember me from the conference in May?"

"Oh yes, yes, I do remember. You are the expert on geomagnetism, right?"

"Yes, sort of. I have Jane Woodruff, a friend of mine, with me. Jane is studying the migration paths of birds that use the earth's magnetic field for navigation. She wanted to talk to you to see whether you have any spill-over knowledge on the historical effects on creatures other than the Neanderthals."

"Hallo Jane, did you have anything in particular in mind?"

"Hi, Käthe. We may be grasping at straws. Just on the off chance, we thought it worth speaking to you. We are finding it difficult to explain the behavior of birds that depend on the magnetic field. We know that there is an excursion event underway in the south right now. We also know that the excursion event 39,000 years ago happened to coincide with the demise of the Neanderthals. What is your evidence on this?"

Käthe explains, "Radiation from the sun can affect the DNA of individuals. We know this from studies done on modern humans. It is reasonable to assume that the effect on Neanderthals would be similar. The difficulty is that we don't have a whole lot of material in the form of their remains to work with, but indications are that genetic damage did occur at the time of the excursions. They would have suffered from an increase in melanoma, usually in the form of skin cancer. Telltale signs are apparent in the bone marrow."

Pausing for a moment, she continues, "We are currently trying to correlate the migration of deer with that of the Neanderthals who depended on them for food. The advancing cold from the ice ages would have led them in a southerly direction from Germany into France and Spain."

Jane questions, "Is there a relationship to birds?"

"Yes, since you are interested in birds, all I can say is that, to some extent, migrating birds and animal herds follow similar migration routes in the Arctic Circle today. You could say that the birds steer the deer where to go; they are more sensitive to environmental changes than grazing animals. They lead the way. The bones of ancient migrating herds are in more abundance than Neanderthal remains, giving us more to base our conclusions. Using this logic, we are trying to determine the passage of our forebears."

Michel interjects, "I presume you mean that the birds and herds would set off on their migrations at about the same time based on seasonal changes. Once they are en-route, I guess that the magnetic field changes would only affect the birds, not the deer. The deer will follow their usual route, whereas the birds may deviate based on magnetic changes. Do you agree?"

"Yes, that sounds logical."

Jane concludes, "We are back to square one. We still don't know why the birds are late."

Käthe answers, "We are trying to understand what caused the demise of Neanderthals, and the consequences of the magnetic excursion are one of the possible reasons. If you can definitively prove, based on events occurring now, that birds change their migrating habits based on polar excursions, we would be interested in correlating this with evidence of animal migrations to see whether there is a relationship."

Jane asks, "Do you have any suggestions on how we could do this?"

Käthe replies, "In the fall, we will be going on a four-week field trip along the likely migration path that animals followed in their southward journey. Would you be interested in joining us? There will be a lot of walking. As a parallel study, you could look for evidence to support your logic."

Michel says to Jane, "That would be interesting. I could take magnetic field readings, and you could follow the geotagging." Addressing Käthe, he asks, "When will you be setting out?"

Käthe replies, "We are quite flexible. I can send you details of what we have in mind. We were thinking in the fall, but if you prefer other dates, please get back to me; we are open to changes. You would have to self-fund your part of the work."

Jane says, "Okay, that sounds exciting. Let's see, it is March now. I presume you are looking at around October. We will consider it and let you know. Thanks."

They exchange contact information and end the call.

Jane says to Michel, "Quite aside from the contribution it would make to my study, doing it as a field trip, wow that would be fantastic. I wonder whether the university would pay for it ... Are you interested in coming along."

Teasing, he says, "What would you do without me? Of course. It would be great."

"I suggest that we try for a late fall period, just when the birds start their southward migrations."

## 6.2    Field Trip

Michel adjusts his backpack for comfort and helps Jane with hers while Käthe impatiently waits for them. The tablet with an offline version of the route's map is last to be packed, sliding into a back pocket for quick access; finally, the march can begin.

Otto, Käthe's colleague, returns to the vehicle and, using voice controls, enters the coordinates for the village of Foix on the French side of the Pyrenees, applies the autonomous connection parameters, and as the CAV moves away, shouts from the window, "See you at Foix this evening; six PM."

Setting out over a short incline, Michel says to Käthe, "It is hard to believe that these forests replaced the steppe tundra prevalent 30 or 40,000 years ago. The climate must have been quite different."

"Yes, as you probably know, some of these old-growth trees can live about a thousand years, more in some cases. That means about thirty-nine generations since that time. When you think of it like that, a lot can change in that time; ice ages gave way to the climate we now have."

"So, what is your strategy for the route we are following?"

"We previously did two field trips. The first was from Leipzig, the original site of the Neanderthals, to Strasbourg in France. The second was from Strasbourg to Pamiers, here in France at the foot of the Pyrenees. That second leg included Dordogne, where Neanderthal remains are in abundance. We headed directly from Leipzig, over the escarpment to Dordogne in France and now over the Pyrenees and on to Gibraltar. Joining the dots for each location where their bones are found, will provide a path of their retreat to where they finally went extinct."

"I calculated the distance from Pamiers, where we are at the moment, to Gibraltar via Zaragoza and Cuenca in Spain as 1,600 kilometers. Quite a distance! As I said, it should take about four weeks, including sections where we will travel by car. I hope you are up to the walk?"

Jane interrupts, "Michel, you should take a magnetic reading now; to mark the starting point."

"Yes. I did that at the drop-off. South is solidly opposite to North, fully normal. I will take a reading every hour."

Trudging on, they crest a rise and follow a course parallel to the river on their right. To their backs, undulation hills stretch into the distance towards central France. Ahead, the Pyrenees rise to great heights. Käthe's path heads for a gap in the range. As the density of the forest increases, the patches of open meadows are a welcome relief. Birds congregate in the trees lining the edge of the forested area, excitedly signaling to each other as they flit between the grasses and the protection of the trees. The soft sigh of the autumn breeze immerses the hikers in the calm of nature, dispelling the stresses of the planning process. Uplifted at having rid themselves of the confines of city life, the three walk on in silence, each focusing on their individual purposes.

Käthe imagines a time when herds found pasture here and steadily made their way along her chosen course. Driven by the cold embrace of long winters, they intuitively followed a path to the beckoning warmth in the south.

Jane interrupts her thoughts, "Say Käthe, what drew you to study the Neanderthals? It is a fascinating subject, and you get to make these field trips."

"I have always been interested in anthropology. Even as a child. It seemed inevitable that I should end up doing it at university."

"You seem so intensely focussed on the subject. I feel the same about birds. It is hard to explain why I find them so absorbing."

"Yes, I know what you mean. What sealed it for me was when I had my DNA determined. We have a laboratory at the university that tries to extract the DNA from the bones we find. They use sophisticated techniques, not like the commonly available kits you can buy to determine your ancestry. I took part in a study to compare our genome to that of the Neanderthals. It turned out that I have a relatively strong correlation to Neanderthal DNA."

"That's interesting. How do you feel about that? I know some people incorrectly think they were not so intelligent."

"Yes, that idea has been debunked. Is that the word? Most Europeans have around 3% Neanderthal DNA. Not a lot, but mine is slightly higher. I am quite proud of it. It inspired me to learn more."

Laughing, Jane asks, "Are you looking for your great, great, great grandfather?"

"Well, you just never know. We were fortunate to have Svante Pääbo visit our university. He was the first person to map the entire genome of the Neanderthals from bones found in Serbia. A fascinating man, very determined and inspiring. You should read his book on the subject, 'Neanderthal Man.'"

By late afternoon, a tributary leading into the main river blocks their progress. Standing on a protruding rock, they gaze down at the offending stream below. An impasse, which way should they proceed, upriver or down? As Käthe and Michel debate which way to go, Jane watches as the Robins congregate on the edge of the cliff, ready for their migration. They excitedly preen and chatter in expectation; clearly, the pass in the distant mountain range is their route. Returning her attention to the other two, she voices her opinion, pointing, "Look, the birds are heading more or less in the direction of the pass. The best way to get there is to follow the cliff down to the main river and then cross the stream and up the other side. That has to be the shortest route."

Käthe concurs, "Yes. Think like the herds. They would follow the lead of the birds. If we go left, it could take a while before the cliff gives way sufficiently for us to cross the stream."

That said, they make their way towards the main river. As they progress, the elevation down to the stream and the confluence of the two rivers fail to give way to an easy passage down, as hoped but having committed to the chosen direction, they continue. Finally, the cliff peters out, providing a steep descent to the main river from where they walk up to the confluence. The tributary is stronger than expected. Hugging the edge of a

58

rock-face, they successfully negotiate onto a landing at the foot of the tributary.

Käthe observes, "The tributary provides quite a nice protected area between the river and the cliff for the Neanderthals but not so for the herds. It will probably delay us a little, but I think we should explore up-river a bit and see what we find. Besides, we can't cross here anyway. The stream may be broader and shallow enough for a crossing, further along."

As they progress, the chatter of birds lining the trees at the top of the cliff mixes with the splash of the river, providing a dreamlike experience in the greenery of the vegetation. Sure enough, at length, the stream broadens to offer a route across using large boulders as stepping stones. The final stretch requires them to throw their kit onto the far bank and wade waist deep to get there. Drying themselves on a raised platform of rocks overlooking the stream, they take the opportunity for refreshments while admiring the striations on the cliff face on the opposite side.

Jane points to a rock-fall further along, "See there, it looks like a landslide, the cliff must have collapsed some years ago. Vegetation has taken root and is quite well established in the rocks."

Michel says, "Yes. Had we have persevered a little longer when we were up there, we may have been able to get down."

Jane responds, "Yes, just maybe. It looks a little unstable. Hey, that looks like a cave, just a little way from the edge of the rock-fall."

Käthe rejoins, "Wow! Yes, come, let's have a closer look."

Re-crossing the river, they scramble up the embankment to stand at the entrance to the cave. It extends a few meters into the gloom. Excited, they step forward with Käthe leading the way. The floor is dry and littered with blown leaves and twigs.

With a gasp, she stops and exclaims, "My god, rock paintings! Here along the side. Exquisite!"

Michel and Jane rush over and stand amazed.

Before them is a fresco of a hunt, showing hunters with long spears following deer and creatures with tusks. The art is a delicate mix of yellow ochre and red with long lines in charcoal. The condition of the art is remarkably good except for those nearer the entrance to the cave, where the sunlight has faded them.

Käthe is beyond herself with excitement, "Wunderbar, Ich kann es kaum glauben! This is a once-in-a-lifetime experience. I must contact the office to send a team. We need to secure the area and do a formal examination."

Jane, enthralled, examines the pictures as they extend further into the cave, calls, "Käthe, look at this, some sort of symbol. Two pairs of diagonally intersecting parallel lines. It looks like a modern hashtag sign."

Käthe approaches fascinated, "I have never seen anything like it. Mind you, there are photographs of similar markings at the Gorham cave at Gibraltar except that those are not painted. I wonder what it means. It looks like it is the same age as the rest of the drawings. It can't be graffiti."

Stepping out of the cave, she calls Otto and breathlessly explains what they found. "Otto, you need to contact the office. Arrange for a team to come here without delay. We will wait for them. They need to bring along the usual tools and implements for excavation. Who knows what else lies underneath the soil?"

Providing the geographic coordinates and a description of how to get to the location, she ends the call and returns to Jane and Michel, "We will have to shelve our plans to continue the field trip for the moment. Once the team arrives, we can reconsider. Is that okay with you?

Jane, "Yes, this is way too important. I can spend some time observing the birds. Their migration is about to start. Michel, what will you do?"

"Oh, don't worry about me. I enjoy just being here, out in the open. I will set up a tent and take it from there. How long before the team arrives?"

Käthe estimates, "I expect they will be here on the day after tomorrow. I guess that they will take a flight from Leipzig to Foix. These self-driving electric cars are a boon. With the geo-coordinates, they can pick up a car there and guide themselves to the closest point where they can hike the rest of the way. Yes, two days should do it."

\* \* \*

While Käthe photographs the images, takes careful measurements of the floor area, and meticulously explores the immediate surroundings, Jane concentrates on the birds congregating at the cliffs' top. Successive flocks launch themselves in the direction of the mountain pass with lulls between each group. A crescendo of bird calls rises as they form a group and begin their journey, followed by a quiet spell as the next assembly prepares to depart.

Michel wanders further along the face of the cliff to the edge of the landslide. The tumble of rocks extends down to the river creating a small dam where the fast-flowing water carves out a detour around the rock-fall. Jumping from rock to rock, he crosses to the far side of the impasse and proceeds along the course of the river. Following a bend in the valley, he hears the sound of a waterfall, and with every step, a mist of water vapor increasingly soaks the vegetation to dripping wetness. A sheer drop from the top of the cliff greets him, providing a spectacular waterfall down to a pool at its foot. A curtain of pounding water drums out all sound as he breathlessly marvels at the scene. Rich green vegetation crowds in from the banks as the clear water forms a wide pool and then rushes on down the valley. All thought is dispelled by the sound of water and the picture before him. Enthralled, he takes in the scene until the need to return to the group is necessary.

Arriving back at the cave, he describes the cul-de-sac at the end of the ravine and the barrier presented by the waterfall. Käthe is first to observe, "That means that this enclave is secure, the only way for anyone to reach the cave is to follow the route we took. It would mean that the inhabitants of this cave must have felt quite secure here."

Michel returns, "Yes, as long as they keep an eye on the confluence of the two rivers where we had to wade through the torrent. As long as the flow of the water remains strong, it would cut off access, but if it gets too strong, they would be trapped here."

Käthe adds, "Actually, that means that people could live here for protracted periods in safety and may mean that we will find many artifacts below the soil."

Jane joins in, "Yes, but it may also mean that only a few people managed to find the valley in the first instance."

Käthe says, "Okay, you have a point. We will know once the excavations begin."

Jane digresses, "Michel, could you take me to the waterfall? I would like to see whether there are different bird types in the mist, as you describe it."

"Sure. But we will have to do it tomorrow. It is already too late now."

The next day Jane and Michel find themselves gazing at the gushing water as it ceaselessly pours over the lip of the cliff and cascades against protruding rocks on its way down.

Jane issues a challenge, "Come, I dare you, let's swim. It will be cold but invigorating."

"Okay! Beat you in."

Braving the cold, they strike out for the falls and enter the drumming water. Passing through, they find a hidden beach under the overhanging cliff face.

"Wow! Michel. Look, this presents a passage to the far side. Anyone knowing this area intimately would discover it."

"Yes. Amazing. I wonder whether the people from the cave knew about it."

The rest of the day is spent exploring the mist soaked embankment on the far bank and walking up the side a distance to watch the birds in their migration. Immersed in her subject, Michel has to urge a return to camp as the light begins to fade.

Late the next day, the team of four volunteer university students arrives. Käthe is quick to take command of the situation. After showing the new arrivals the paintings and the layout of the cave, she marks out a numbered grid for excavation and provides detailed instruction to the team lead, a postgraduate archaeology student by the name of Ulrich, on how to proceed. They set up their tents along the edge of the river and as darkness descends, sitting around a fire, excitedly speculate on what will be found.

In a matter of a day or two, with minor adjustments to the work plan as progress is made, the team is fully engaged and able to proceed on their own, enabling Jane, Michel, and Käthe to resume their field trip using the path that Michel and Jane found leading under the waterfall.

The temperatures are distinctly cooler as they follow the birds' fall migrations and proceed with the incline along a ridge overlooking the course of the river to the distant gap in the mountain range.

A day and a half later, having reached the divide between north and south, they proceeded along the westerly contour on the pass's south side. Within another day, as they strike camp for the evening, Michel takes his usual measurements of the magnetic waves. Calling Jane, he says, "Look, you can see how the magnetic field diverges, just as we noted in spring."

Jane, looking over his shoulder, says, "Yes, and the birds are in full migration now, which is three weeks later than normal. They must have decided on a direction. Some are heading in a southeasterly direction and others in a south-westerly direction. See the mountains over there in the distance across the plains? They are heading there."

Käthe enjoins, "Guided by the birds, that is where we should be heading. Madrid is more or less in that direction. Of course, in the days of the Neanderthals, there were no towns. I don't expect we will find much in the way of artifacts there. Urban sprawl and human activity will have taken care of that."

Michel says, "Are you saying that there is nothing more for us to do here?"

"No, no, we should spend some time here in the foothills of the Pyrenees, see what we can find, and then skip over Madrid and continue on the other side. Remember, Gibraltar is our destination."

# 7    Descent

Slate, Broach, Quill, Fern, and Moraine make their way along the contour of the land and gradually descend to the lower reaches of the mountains flanking buttresses that extend out from the main escarpment. Slate, keeping an eye on the far off range of mountains in the south, watches as the migrating birds head in that general direction, resolving to follow their lead as soon as he can shake off any likelihood the pursuers will guess their route if they intend to follow. Proceeding at a more leisurely pace, enabling Broach to keep up, allows them to admire the landscape. Moraine enjoys the silent dialog they share, evident by the exhilaration on each of their faces. They take in the peacefulness of the surroundings as eagles soar in leisurely circles in the rising thermals coming off cliffs. Periodic stops provide Slate with the opportunity to scout for venison to provide a steady supply of food for consuming at the nightly rest-overs.

The days pass, and the events at the cave begin to fade. By late afternoon on the fifth day, they reach a stream noisily cascading down rapids leading from a cliff to an alpine meadow below. On the edge of the rivulet, a large boulder, presumably dislodged from the mountain sometime in the past, offers shelter from the wind and protection from overnight dew as it looms over them sitting in its shadow. Downstream the view is of the encroaching forest on each side with pasture on the banks and a larger river at the foot of the slope. The water bubbles over the rock-strewn passage with pools forming where they obstruct the flow where the watercress grows in matted clumps.

Dull clouds and a chill in the air greets them on the following day. The progression of the seasons heralds the coming winter. Even in this unfamiliar territory, Slate, knowing the importance of the progress they have made, mutters in his usual serious manner. "Winter comes soon. We crossed the mountains before the snow falls start." Pointing to the distant mountain range, he says, "In a few days we must set out for those mountains."

Interpreting Slate's plan as a signal that they have successfully shaken off the pursuers, Fern joyfully dances in a circle holding Broach by the hand, "Play us a song, we are out of danger. No enemy to worry about."

To which Broach plays a staccato jig on his bone instrument. The mood is light as they discard any remaining concerns with the pursuers.

By evening, comfortably ensconced in their new home, with the day having been spent exploring the immediate surroundings and adding to their provisions, the evening passes in their now-familiar routine of sharing thoughts and wondering at what lies across the plains and the distant mountains. In the twilight, Quill tends to Broach's sores using the ointments provided by Moraine. Thankful for the obscuring bolder, they are soon fast asleep.

* * *

The next day is a little brighter with the view across the meadow shimmering with dew and the sunlight glistening off the snow-capped mountains that seem to beckon them to come. They all know to take the opportunity to rest ahead of the journey across the plains. As they relax in the shade of the boulder, birds and various animals venture across the meadow. One attracts their attention. A marmot cautiously looks out from the forest edge for threats, finding none, it moves forward to the water's edge. Still nervous at being out in the open, it hesitantly tests the water, then abandoning all restraint, it playfully darts in and out of the water delighting in the cool water. Mesmerized by the scene, Slate and his group watch the creature's enjoyment with Broach captivated by the novel spectacle. A movement in the brush of the opposite bank draws their attention. Another marmot emerges. It, too, is cautious but soon overcome by curiosity; it boldly moves forward. They appear not to know each other. The first marmot is initially unaware of the other until it reaches the edge of the stream. Surprised and alarmed at not having taken sufficient care, it immediately darts for the safety of the forest where it stops and looks back. After a while, it decides that the intruding marmot does not present a danger and slowly moves to return to the river where the other waits. As the distance between them narrows, there is a clear physical attraction evident as male and female. Perchance, Moraine, and Slate's eyes lock in a similar attitude, but a cry from an eagle overhead breaks the spell and the creatures dash for cover in the forest. Gradually they emerge to peer out and track the circling bird of prey as it leisurely flies overhead, unaware of its impact on events on the ground. Long moments pass as the bird continues to turn in its gyrations. Eventually, the marmots tire of waiting and disappear from sight. The glade returns to its previous calm.

An emotional bond between Slate and Moraine persists as they each dwell on their separate thoughts. An unfamiliar exhilaration suffuses Moraine, while Slate feels uncomfortable guilt that tears at his longing for his departed partner. As the day draws to a close and they gather to share the food prepared over a small fire, Slate announces that they should prepare for departing in the morning. Broach, who has not been suffering from his usual ailments, excitedly begins gathering his meager possessions, packs his painted slate stones, and quietly plays a cheerful melody on his musical instrument before settling down for sleep. Fern joins in to hum an accompaniment while Quill dutifully organizes the medications and food they will be taking along.

* * *

Tusk paces back and forth impatiently as they watch the procession of people in the distance, making their way up the incline to the summit of the pass. At midday, the first group finally crested the final stage and exhaustedly seat themselves in a circle to await the stragglers. Bringing up the rear is Gramater, who is sitting in a sling carried between two muscular men. Tusk can hear her voice, which carries over the separating distance, "My back hurts! ... Don't jerk like that. Can't you just walk evenly? ... What on earth I agreed to this for I don't know. We were quite comfortable where we were."

Finally, her porters reach the top, and she is let down. Walking a tight circle stretching her tired body, she quickly takes command of the situation, barking out instructions on setting up the camp. Tusk, who has been trying to avoid her, soon becomes the target of her attention, "Where are they? What have you done to find them?"

Tusk replies, "We ... we don't know where they have gone. We have been waiting for you before starting a search."

"You mean you have been sitting around here on your lazy backsides? You could have fanned out and looked for them."

"Yes, but we would have had to return here every evening and start all over on the next day."

"Obviously, stupid. You will have to do that anyway. Tell me more. What were they doing, and why is Moraine following them? I hope we haven't come all this way on a wild goose chase."

"They were holed up in a cave. There were two women, one a child and a man. They look like ... do you remember the clan we passed last year? Remember? They had some of them shackled as slaves. These were like them. They are not like us."

"What are you saying? Those backward people? They are only good for one thing, and that is as slaves, and you let them escape."

Stammering, Tusk admits, "Yes ... yes. They had a secret route out of the valley; otherwise, we would have got them."

"I can't believe how incompetent you are. Just unbelievable. And ... and what was Moraine doing with them?"

"She seemed to prefer them. They didn't force her to follow. She could have turned back if she wanted to."

"Okay, this is worse than I thought. First, you let some good slaves escape, and now we have Moraine in their clutches."

Angrily stabbing Tusk's chest with her crooked forefinger, "I will not have this. Nobody, and I mean, nobody leaves our clan without my permission and especially not to join some low caste animals that these people are." Screaming, "Do you hear me?"

"Yes ... Gramater. We will find them and bring Moraine back."

"Okay. Now get yourselves into groups and start the search. Today, start today. Right now."

Tusk turns to Runt, "You come with me. Scat, you take Rasp and go in that direction," pointing.

"Rasp, Wart, you two go down that way. Look for any sign of them and report back here by nightfall. Now go!"

Setting off in a westerly direction with Tusk, Runt is first to point out a hint of the group's passage when they find what looks like partial footprints in some moist sand along the edge of a stream. Further investigation reveals nothing to confirm the path they have taken. By nightfall and all the teams back at camp, the only evidence they have remains the partial footprint that Runt found. On the next day, with Runt's finding the only promise of a course to follow, the groups set out again to extend their search beyond the last point they had reached. Two days later, the direction suggested by Runt's find confirms that as being the likely route when they stumble on the remnants of a fire and the remains of a pheasant, a single bone near a deposit of ash.

Back at the camp, Tusk reports to Gramater, "All we have to go on is the partial footprint from two days ago and the ash and bone of a pheasant today. This must be their direction. We need to focus our efforts that way," pointing. "We can send runners that way and extend the search further, but my guess is that they are skirting along the escarpment and gradually downwards. At some point, I think, they will head out over the plain, southwards."

"Okay, if your scouts find them, leave one to watch them and send for reinforcements. If they move on, then leave a trail of broken branches pointing in the direction to take."

"Okay. It is too late now, so we'll set out at dawn."

Five days since the arrival of Gramater pass, as they extend their search. Scat and Runt, working as a pair on this occasion, are first to locate the group in flight. Looking down from a cliff, they see the group near a large boulder partially diverting the flow of a stream. From the obscurity of a brush, they scan the area for a path down and an approach to attack.

Runt, pointing to a cleft in the craggy cliff, says, "Scat, there! Just a way further along. We should be able to get down without much trouble."

69

Scat answers, "Yes. Hmm, yes, ideal. I'll wait here and watch, you go back and bring the others. Let's see, it should take you about a day and a half to get back here. That means tomorrow night. If they start to move, I will leave a trail of sticks pointing the direction. Now run!"

Runt, enjoying what he does best, begins a steady pace back to the summit of the pass. By nightfall, he reaches the camp and reports to Gramater since Tusk is nowhere to be seen. The delight in the old woman's face is evident even through the wrinkles that often disguise her intentions.

Runt sums up the situation, "A group of us can cover the distance by nightfall tomorrow if we hurry. The whole clan will need longer, maybe an extra day or more."

"Okay, as soon as the others return from scouting, we can decide on a group. Good work, Runt. I look forward to putting Moraine right."

In the last light of the day, Tusk and Rasp arrive back from their search, tired and disconsolate without success, but Tusk soon revives at the news from Runt. At Gramater's insistence, she and Tusk finalize the group for recovering Moraine and capturing the foreigners. In addition to Scat, who is still at his observation post and Runt, who knows the way there, Rasp, Wart, and two more, Grate and Grunt, are added. The plan is to set out at first light with Tusk in charge who, with renewed bravado, claims the center of attention, boasting of the need to bring Moraine under his control and prospect of a group of slaves to carry out his bidding.

As estimated by Runt, they arrive at Scat's lookout point as the sun is setting and with just enough time for him to point out the fugitives to Tusk. If they look carefully in the distance, they can make them out preparing a fire for their evening meal.

The plan is to start before dawn. Tusk is to guard the path down to prevent them from escaping back up the cliff. The rest will descend, and Scat and Runt circle down to the bottom while two will flank them on the left and two on the right, effectively circling the group. Each group must take up positions where Tusk can see them in the early light of the day. When everyone is ready, he is to signal the attack with two arms raised. All is set as darkness envelopes them.

# 8    Campi Flegrei

The crust surrounding the mantle strains as pressures build underfoot. The dynamo within churns ceaselessly, spawning seismic waves that weaken the magma chamber above raising pressures that mount in opposition to the force of gravity. Tensions stressed by the contending forces compete for superiority. Gases build, straining the chamber further while the magneto radiating into space falters under the fluctuating flows. The balance maintained for eons seeks a new equilibrium, shifting, shifting to a temporary truce. The semblance of balance holds sporadically in an equilibrium between opposites, staving off a catastrophic conflagration. Tectonic plates jostle for space as they apply the force of their momentum to areas of least resistance. Obstacles in their path undermine their progression, forcing them upward or downward or buckle under the obstructions, concertinaing at the interface to their onslaught. Ranges of mountains grow at the fault lines, and boiling magma edges ever closer to the surface forming blisters ready to be lanced by a break in the temporary truce between the powers that hold sway.

Magnetic forces stream from the subterranean turmoil out into the magnetosphere surrounding the globe, altering the protective shield. Interacting with the incoming solar radiation, they excite electrons to emit photons in flashes of red-green light as they change state, leaving dancing displays in the sky near the poles and elsewhere as subliminal echoes of the undercurrent.

Ultrasensitive to the electromagnetic pathways, some creatures with time evolve the capacity to see these patterns and build a reliance on the aurora as a compass for navigation in their annual migrations. Then as the changes intensify, they puzzle over the divergence from the norm. Oblivious to the linkage of events underfoot and unable to foretell the consequences, they stand rooted by the force of habit. Memory offers no reliance for tens of thousands of years passing between occurrences, leaving nothing as a guide, no contingency plan, the only path open is to react as events unfold.

For those that care to ascertain, the dilemma faced by the creatures of that time presents a warning; take heed and prepare, for, without a plan, fate will exact the maximum in the execution of its dastardly intent. Just as they succumbed to the confluence of these circumstances which cast a shadow over their time, a winter of discontent under a dark sky laden with acids followed, stunting all growth and decimating the herds that depended on the pastures to graze on. Even those higher up in the chain of food fell afoul of the consequences. The penetrating rays from the solar orb compounded their plight, weakening their immunity and laying them bare to disease and pestilence.

Our archaic ancestors, marginalized by waves of ice, a species already on its knees, were stuck down, leaving an impudent rising breed to inherit the legacy. By dint of cunning, these new ones brought the old ones to subservience, subsuming them, dominating them out of existence and, in doing so, left an indisputable fingerprint of their malign nature in our life-blood as evidence; DNA preserved for all to see. To this day, a question mark still hangs over us as we emphasize our differences and negate our biases, traits that we fail to shake off.

Nature cares not. It will revisit the past and deliver punishment in full measure to those that fail to heed the signs. Creatures that can read the writing in the sky tell that the crust underfoot is ripe for a repetition. That the edifice of civilization is like clay, its permanence an illusion, its safeguards like flimsy wisps in the winds of change. The bits and bytes of our communication will be stripped naked before the onslaught, and industry will surely grind to a halt under garbled messages as the solar radiation shreds it of all meaning. Once muted, the semblance of control will crumble. The certainty of the atomic clock will fracture, fission, and the dependence on time cast civilization lose. Discord will reign. The truth of True North will speak with a forked tongue. Ships of the air and sea will lose their bearings. Transport will not transport as all will grind to a halt without a schedule. This is a token of the devastation that the signs foretell.

A great leveling will unmask the sophistication, laying bare the essentials that throb under the civil veneer, reducing it to dog eats dog, shattering the sanctity of interdependence, and giving rise to a ruthless cohort with a singular quest of self-preservation and dominance.

# 9   Shuddering

In the predawn, all is still dark. Trine stirs in the downy warmth of the grass nest, prompting her offspring to nestle closer to suckle. She shakes loose and peaks out at the meadow. In the first-light, she sees Zinnia, the roller on the branches of a nearby tree, transition from sleep to wakefulness, stepping away from her partner, Cyan, fluffing out her feathers and quietly waiting for the darkness to lift. Elle, the juvenile marmot, is the first of her kind to emerge, her snout just visible at the entrance to their burrow.

Time seems suspended at that moment, absent of movement, caught between two states, life in its ordained routine, or the ushering in of a new dispensation. The moment stretches, held like a petrified forest cast in a permanent mold. The suspense mounts as the field mouse, the marmot, and the roller intuitively know that life is about to change, change irrevocably.

The trembling Elle so feared begins, rises, rises to a great tremor, and then like a crack of a lightning bolt, and the whole earth shudders uncontrollably in the aftermath. The mountains heave as if to release a vast reservoir of pent-up anger, dispelling eons of frustrations, they shift and with it, cast loose gravities grip, unleashing landslides that rumble down their faces destroying all obstacles in their way. Down, down, they tear casting aside trees like insignificant twigs, tumbling into ravines, setting off boulders that rip and bounce across the meadows and fields below. Then a momentarily, a pause, deathly quiet by comparison to the preceding cacophony, the lull is only temporary before the quake resumes its terror. Three times it vents its anger before it abates. Expunged of its inner turmoil, it sinks into seemingly profound remorse for its actions with long murmurings before finally holding still.

The landscape so dear to the three creatures lies shattered. By dint of fortune, they barely escape the vengeance of the mountains.

Elle's burrow collapsed, and with it, it buried her siblings and parents. Marmots across the mountain range suffered this same fate as they lay in the depth of their warrens. With their habit of parental dominance and closed community lives now compounded by the scattered remnants that survived, any chance of their paths crossing diminishes, bringing them to the brink of extinction.

The shock of the event reverberates within Elle, disorientating all sense of control. Her mind thrashes about for understanding, some means to fathom flight from fight, seeking the best recourse. Only when quiet settles does calm return. As the dust settles, she begins a desperate search of the rubble for her kin. The fruitlessness, minute by minute, becomes apparent with a dawning sense of foreboding that a solitary lot is her prospect. Hyrax and Shyrax are no more. As the weariness of her search seeps into her being, the adrenaline that sustained her is replaced by the realization that she is injured. Her thigh and left hind leg bare large gashes, leaving a numb sensation in her paw. An excruciating pain permeates the wound. Limping to an area of the meadow where the grass survived the landslide, calming herself to think, she instinctively huddles behind a boulder to avoid the omnipotent glare of an eagle as her pain intensifies. Little does she realize that Eyther and Arial suffer loss too?

The ledge where they so diligently tended their fledgling is gone. At the first rumblings, they eluded the falling rocks, instinctively rising on their wings to escape the carnage, but with dismay, they watched as the ledge disintegrated under an avalanche of stones, boulders, and dust, obliterating any semblance of the nest they so carefully built. Circling the theater of the event, they drew nearer in the hope that their young may have survived, but soon realize that this is in vain. Just one week separated junior from flight and certain escape, but this is not to be. With winter approaching, the prospect of starting anew is dashed, a lonely winter lies ahead for them without an offspring.

Circling higher, they scan the extent of the altered landscape. Some craggy cliffs are reduced in size with a tumble of rubble at their foot. Dust still hangs in the air, the scarred rock-faces just visible through the curtain that obscures the extent of the damage. Rising ever higher, the range extends into the distance, the view to the west and east a blur where a misty haze marks areas of damage. Rotating to a south-easterly perspective, they see a vast column rising to great heights. The billowing cloud streams upward from the ground over the horizon, lingers in the still air before being caught by the winds at a higher elevation, and carried away eastwards. Eyther, glancing at Arial, sees the incomprehensibility of the sight echoed in her eyes. Without a ledge to return to, they continue their slow gyrations on high as if it will turn back time to restart the day on a familiar footing. Ultimately, acceptance of the new fate seeps into a realization of the irrevocability of the here and now and the need to process its aftermath. To distance themselves from the theatre of the pain they carry, they fly to peaks further along the ridge they called home and settle there, silently processing their grief.

Trine, too, is confused. The landslide stopped just short of her nest, but loose rocks ricocheting as they tumbled from above, smashed trees and gouged huge trenches in the meadow. In dismay, just as she thought they may have escaped the damage, one such boulder crushed her nest right next to her and continued until stopping with a spray of water in the stream. The passing force of it flung her aside to land in a skein of debris. Groggy and disoriented, she rose to frantically search for her family in the depression left by the boulder but without success. No amount of scratching in the crumpled grass revealed even a remnant of her little ones. By noon of the day, acceptance began forcing itself on her. Downcast for the second time in her short life, she sheltered in a torn brush to nurse the blow received at being tossed aside so violently and faced the loss of her offspring, seeking solace that time brings to those that wait. Looking about from her concealment, the shattered remnants of the once indestructible cliffs loomed high in their altered state, and even higher above, Eyther and Arial circled. Even at this distance, Trine felt their loss, evident in the slow revolutions of the circles they drew in the sky. Closer at hand, Zinnia, Cyan, and their fledging having emerged unscathed by the events, drew near to each other, nervously anticipating a resumption of the apocalypse, but none came. Their impending migration, now thrown into further disarray, left them at a loss as to what to do next. The patterns in the sky that usually guided their path south seemed more confusing than before, two paths leading south, previously just vague outlines, now stop in evident relief. In the hope of a return to normalcy, they decide to delay their departure and begin foraging in the tumbled landscape for food.

As nightfall approaches, the meadow community hides in temporary shelters as the wind rises, hinting at the approaching winter. A restless night ensues for each of them in their unaccustomed places of rest. A sense of foreboding, portending an uncertain future, holds each in a spell of fear.

# 10   Attack

Imagining the attack and capture of the fleeing five churns endlessly in the mind of Tusk as he lies in the dark waiting for dawn. He visualizes the surprise on Moraine's face, relishing the moment he will be able to claim his prize. Images of his men in a circle around the cowering group glow brightly in his mind. He will step forward and whip the man, the pain of each blow transferred to Moraine until she understands that he, Tusk is master and deserving of her subservience. The chase has been worth every moment as the climax approaches.

As the sky brightens, Tusk stands ready at his elevated position between two towering cliffs looking at the theatre below. He can make out Scat's silhouette in the half-light who appears to be searching for a good view of the others. Tusk can see one of the fugitives stirring from sleep to start the day, oblivious of the looming danger. Finally, Scat locates the rest of his team and signals the attack by raising his two arms.

For a few moments, all action is suspended, everyone freezes in place. Scat seems confused, distracted by some unidentifiable interruption before a gradual rumbling becomes apparent, steadily increasing to a crescendo. The ground on which he stands begins shaking, increasing, mounting, it reverberates against the cliffs, and as it appears to culminate, a massive explosion, a deafening crack of lightning, rocks the ground. Pandemonium ensues. A part of the cliff gives way and in slow-motion slides down while the rock-face alongside it miraculously remains intact. The slide jerks to a stop, it holds firm for some seconds then resumes its downward thrust in a jolting fashion. Ahead of the collapsing crag, a mound of rubble mixed with fallen trees and debris accumulates to form an ever-increasing obstruction to its headlong progress down the slope. Tusk, flanked by two cliffs, saddled between the mountains, stands in insignificance as the tremendous forces release their energy. Powerless to act and with fate caring little for his earlier bravado, it takes its toll at will, metering out punishment on the landscape and anyone who stands in its way.

\* \* \*

Moraine wakes to Slate's movements as he prepares for their departure. Stretching, she shakes off the last vestiges of sleep and begins to bundle her belongings. Soon Quill, Fern, and Broach do likewise, but a sound interrupts them. Turning to each other in questioning confusion, they stop their activities to listen. A distant rumbling sound grows louder, then a trembling underfoot confirms their imaginings. It is real. The thunderbolt crack shakes the earth, they see the rock-face supporting the cliffs begin to slide, down, down towards them. The sight of it is beyond comprehension, rooting them where they stand, helpless, defenseless but to wait for what seems like certain death. Slate is first to react, shoving them closer to the boulder that provided shelter for the night, pinning them there in the hope that this will protect against the advancing debris. Large loose rocks and stones dislodged from the advancing maelstrom, strike the protective boulder, shattering in a spray of particles or bounce off at a tangent to continue their passage across the meadow below. At length, as the reign of terror abates, they cautiously venture to peer up from the side of the boulder. A mound of soil abuts the upper edge of the boulder, where it faltered in its downward advance. The once picturesque meadow lies below them, shredded of vegetation, strewn with the detritus of some evil force bent on destroying everything in its path, complete carnage. To the left and right of the now non-existent stream which moments before gurgled its pleasurable passage from the mountain top, a remnant of trees stand looking on the scene like spectators of a crime.

As their spirits lift with the realization that they have been spared, Slate urges, "Gather your things. We must leave before it starts again. Hurry!"

* * *

Unfortunately, one terror does not another dispel. Shocked and confused, in amongst the trees that escaped the landslide at the foot of the meadow, Runt struggles to stand, shakes off the dust from his clothing, and inspects the wound on his foot where a stray rock struck him. Testing it, he concludes that it is not severe and stems the flow of blood using his hand. After a while, with the flow stopped, he glances about for other members of his group. Scat lies near at hand, still disorientated by the events muttering incoherently to himself. On the ridge between the two buttresses, he can see

79

some movement where Tusk was. The fugitives seem unharmed in the shelter of the boulder that protected them. They appear to be preparing to depart in his direction. Diagonally across from them, he can see no sign of Rasp and Wart nor Grunt and Grate on the other side.

"Scat, get up, focus, we need to hurry, they are coming towards us. Moraine and her group."

Still disorientated, Scat blankly looks at Runt and stumbles over to him.

"There, up there, you can see them getting ready to come down this way."

"Ye, oh, okay, I see them. Should we re-signal the attack? Where are the others?

"I think we can handle one or two of the women, but that man looks to be a brute. Maybe we should get Tusk to close in from the top. Darn, where are Wart and Rasp and the other two? We need them. They were supposed to attack from the sides."

"Look, Tusk seems to be signaling to us to attack. He has both his arms raised, like before the landslide."

Exasperated, Runt reaches a decision having second thoughts since the fugitives seemed so harmless, and says, "There is no point in attacking from here. They have the advantage of coming down the slope. Let's hide here behind these boulders and surprise them as they pass. You grab Moraine, and I'll fend off the others. Tusk will see what we are doing and start down the hill. When the man sees him coming, he'll know he is outnumbered and run off with the boy and the two women. We can always track them again and catch them later on."

"Okay, sounds good."

Still unseen by Slate's group, who remain oblivious of the imminent attack, the two take up positions alongside the route the group will likely take.

Runt sees Slate picking his way over the rubble-strewn meadow, which is barely recognizable from before. Clearly, the going is treacherous. He has to stop to help the boy and the three women to negotiate the obstacles. Looking further up to Tusk's position, he sees that the stretch leading down is even worse. A cloud of dust still hangs in the air, and the incline is likely to trigger fresh slides if he proceeds. Reverting his gaze to the group, he watches, mesmerized by the care they take of each other. There is a bond that holds them as a unit. The gentleness of their interaction is at once intimate as it is carefree while the man in the group is continuously alert to the possibility of danger. His concern is for the boy who, judging by his thin frame, ails. Moraine's acceptance into the group is absolute, receiving and giving of consideration as they are wont to do. It throws Runt into comparing himself in his position in his clan. He, too, is underdeveloped physically and constantly at the receiving end of the temper of others. His name alone is a constant reminder of his inferior status in the group. These thoughts preoccupy Runt as he and Scat prepare to attack.

Runt vacillates, torn between attack and disrupting the contentment of the fugitives, then realizing the folly of his decision, whispers, "Scat. Hold still. Without Rasp and Wart and the other two, I don't think we should take them on. Look, the rubble is too bad, even up there, below Tusk. Better, we don't give away our presence and corner them further along when we can work as a group. Let them pass."

Having barely completed his instructions, they see the man and his group veer off to the side of the meadow just below where Wart and Rasp, who are still out of sight, were meant to be. With bated breath, they watch and wait as the group disappears amongst the trees. After a moment, they stealthily follow, taking care not to be seen. On reaching the edge of the forest, their first task is to find Wart and Rasp. A search reveals the two partially covered with sand and stones but still alive.

\* \* \*

Moraine and her group gingerly make their way through the fallen trees and the broken landscape. After a short while, they emerge at a clearing, previously an alpine meadow, flanked by another forest on the far side.

They stop, and Slate takes Broach from his shoulder, having carried him through the worst of the passage, speaking to them as a group: "What do you think? Should we keep going along the contour or head down and over that hill? On to the other mountains, we saw earlier."

Broach interrupts, pointing, "What is that moving there? Oh look, it's ... what is it?" Rushing over to an animal on the ground, "It's injured."

Moraine is soon with him and gently strokes the creature, offering, "It's a marmot. I think it is a marmot."

With its soulful eyes fixed on the boy, it stirs and tries to stand only to collapse as if accepting that it will be dispatched by these strange creatures.

"Quick, we need to clean that sore. Broach, get some water." He returns with a quantity in a leather pouch and Moraine, assisted by Quill, tends to the marmot, applying a balm after drying the wound. This seems to calm it as if it realizes the intention of the benefactors and minutes later, relaxes into peaceful rest.

Trine, the field mouse, just feet away from the activity with the marmot, still lying in a dazed state, tries to distance herself from the danger but slumps back, unable to coordinate her movements. This attracts Broach's attention, who gathers up the mouse, "I know this one, it is a mouse. It has three stripes along its back."

Moraine joins him, looking over his shoulder as he gently places it in his pouch, "You are right, Broach. It is a field mouse. Usually, they have four stripes. Come, there may be other animals that were injured by the rocks, let's have a look."

Broach and Moraine look about for some time but to no avail. Meanwhile, Slate, who remains alert to danger, whether from a fresh landslide or a concealed enemy, continues to scan the forests lining the clearing and scrutinizing the mountainside for risk of further slides. Periodically he glances over at the group and the sun, and judging the lateness of the day, eventually says, "We must be moving along. We need to find a safe place for the night."

With that, they carefully place the marmot in a large pouch. Fern and Quill take turns carrying the patient. They ford the river at the foot of the slope and set out in the direction of the distant mountains.

* * *

By late afternoon, the band tasked with the attack struggled up the incline to Gramater's position at the main camp. She and the rest of the clan felt the tremor but were never in danger of falling rocks. As they assemble, Tusk, again in a foul mood, complains of the circumstances that conspired against their plans, "Gramater, just when we had them, this stupid landslide or whatever it was, started. Rasp and Wart have been injured but this stupid idiot," giving Runt a cuff, "decided not to attack just when the enemy was caught off guard. If I was further down, I could have brought them in single-handed."

Sarcastically she responds, "Yes, Tusk, you are so brave. So brave. Now I want you to get another party together to get after them." Drawing closer to him, she taps her gnarled finger on his chest and whispers, "Mess up again and you will be castrated. Got that?"

Early the next morning, minus Rasp and Wart, they set out. The going is difficult in the broken terrain. Runt and Scat lead the way along the route they last saw the group take. On reaching a clearing, they stop to examine a trampled area where the group, for reasons unclear to them, spent some time. Telltale signs in their tracks indicate that they proceeded down the slope, and on the other side of the river, further footprints confirm this. They are on the right track. Moving at a pace, by nightfall, they catch a glimpse of the renegades, Moraine and her group, in the distance. Under cover of darkness, they close the gap despite stumbling over obstacles in the process. Fortunately, the topography had given away to rolling hills with none of the effects of the tremor there to delay them. Settling for the night, Scat is assigned to take the first watch, followed by Grate, then Grunt, two replacements for Wart and Rasp, with Runt taking the last watch.

This time Tusk is less confident and spends the night mulling over Gramater's last words, muttering to himself, "Someone needs to get rid of her."

At the first signs of twilight, the pairs move to encircle their target with Tusk taking up a position on the far side near the top of the incline. Tusk signals the attack and moves to a concealed position behind a large tree. In the murkiness of the half-light, he sees his four attackers burst out of the bushes and rush at their quarry, who had just begun stirring from sleep. The man of the group moves with surprising agility, grabs a club, and with a single blow, floors Grate. This gives Grunt time to close the gap and use his spear to repeatedly thrust at the man who seems immune to the injuries he is suffering. Scat and Runt crowd the man. As he parries their blows, he keeps gesticulating to the rest of his party to run, run in opposite directions. Moraine and Quill take the cue and rush up the incline. Fern grabs the boy and runs in the opposite direction. Slate manages to maneuver onto a mound, and a stalemate arises with him in this more dominant position despite being outnumbered by the four men. Holding his position, he manages to delay them long enough for the rest of his group to disappear into the forest.

Tusk, from his hiding, watches the unfolding drama. With dismay, he sees his men's ineffectual attempts at taking down the man. Then, not twenty paces to the right of his position, he sees Moraine with another female appear from behind some scrubs. They stop momentarily to look back with concern to see how Slate is faring. This is his moment. With the spear at the ready, Tusk closes the gap and lunges at the woman next to Moraine. The weapon strikes with deadly force penetrating her body to emerge on the other side. She falls to the ground without a sound. Tusk leaves the spear embedded in the woman, grabs Moraine, and drags her screaming and thrashing about violently, away from the scene. She is no match for his strength. In his lust and sense of power over his victim, he attempts to rape her. With tigerish fury, she bites and scratches until Scat and Runt appear, and he abandons his attempt with a punch to her face and kicks her in the midriff as she lies on the ground.

Slate meanwhile continues to hold his attackers at bay. Estimating that his group has built up sufficient distance to be safe, he moves on the smallest of his attackers, Runt, rushes him knocking him to the ground and breaks out of the circling foe. They set about chasing him as he leads them away from the routes that his friends took. Unable to maintain his pace and agility, they soon abandon the chase. Slate circles back and down the slope. After some time, he picks up the trail of Fern and Broach and is soon united with them. Finding a place of concealment for them, he sets out to look for Moraine and Quill. Approaching the site where they spent the night, he finds it abandoned as they left it. Recovering their belongings, including the pouch with the marmot and the mouse, he sets out up the hill. Near the top of the rise, he stumbles on the prostrate body of Quill, his cousin. Grief-stricken, he attempts in vain to resuscitate her. Unsure of what to do, pursue the attacker, or return to his party where he left them, he feels immobilized. The senselessness of the attack leaves him drained. Downcast, he eventually decides to bury his cousin in a shallow grave and slowly descends the hill to Fern and Broach.

As he approaches their concealment, Fern, concerned at his slow approach through the bushes, immediately senses something is wrong. Moving to meet him, they embrace. No words are necessary, distraught she says, "Is it, Quill?"

"Yes. I found her with a spear in her chest."

Unable to say more, Broach, Fern, and Slate stand in a close embrace, sobbing for long moments. Broach is inconsolable.

"They have taken Moraine. I, I must go back to find her. She can't be safe."

Proceeding up the hill, he leaves them at the side of the grave and, with instructions on where to conceal themselves, sets out in the direction of the tracks left by Tusk and his band.

* * *

With a leather rope around Moraine's neck and Tusk taking pleasure in jerking her to follow, they make their way back towards their basecamp.

As they go, he reprimands his fellows, "Idiots, how could you let the man escape? What have we got? Just this slut, and where are the slaves we were supposed to capture, gone? Gramater is not going to be happy."

Scat challenges, "Shut up, Tusk. Be careful who you call an idiot. I'm getting tired of your constant blaming. Clam up."

With that, Tusk goes silent but for occasional mutterings as he sullenly anticipates Gramater's response.

A crowd awaits them as they enter the encampment. Gramater barges through to the front, with her hands on her hips, she silently looks them up and down then with rising anger, she directs her question at Tusk, "Where are the rest of them?

"We, -- they escaped."

"What do you mean, escaped?"

"They got away. I killed one and captured Moraine."

Screaming, she shouts, "You were meant to bring them back here, alive! Alive. Do you know what that means? We need those animals as slaves. Who is going to do the work now, you?

What use is Moraine? She just does whatever she wants. She needs disciplining, learn to toe the line."

Tusk stands in embarrassment.

"Before you left, I warned you not to mess this up. Well, here is what we are going to do. You and this, this creature, you are banished from this camp. I don't want to see either of you for three nights. You can fend for yourselves out there.

As for you, Moraine, you will learn to submit to this man. These creatures that you followed, they have no brains, they are animals that are there for one purpose only, and that is to serve us."

Turning to the men in general, "Tie her up to that tree," pointing, "there for the night."

"Moraine, you will use the time to think about the stupidity of your ways. Tomorrow morning, before first light, I want both of you to be gone.

86

Tusk, do you understand that? Now get out of my sight. I don't want to hear a word from you."

Moraine is bound hand and foot and tethered to the tree in the center of the compound. She has been silent throughout Gramater's tirade.

As night sets in, and the cold of the approaching winter seeps in, Moraine, feeling despair at the loss of Quill and separation from her adopted family, steels herself for the long night. The thought of three days with Tusk, his groping arrogance now with Gramater's license, will be unnerving. She will have to fend him off from the outset.

In the early hours of the morning, the cold becomes unbearable, her singular concern. Lapsing into semi-consciousness on the verge of hyperthermia, she loses track of time as numbness inches up from her feet and arms into her torso. Held up by the bonds that bind her, the essence of life she so briefly shared with her new friends fades, and all hope of enduring drains for her. For some while, a recurring image of Slate surfaces, sustaining her through the gloom of her thoughts, his steady hand that holds their group together, and the gentleness of his care for Broach. What will his reaction be at the loss of Quill? She knows the devastation he will suffer and feels the pain that he surely is enduring. It drags her down into a dark pit of despondency. The cruelty of Tusk, Gramater, and the thugs that make up the clan, they stand in contrast to the man she holds dear. As the night drags on, overcome with despair, she slumps forward into the cords that hold her as all thoughts are dispelled by the blackness that fills her.

With no concept of the passage of time, she becomes aware of a pair of hands that take hold of hers, rubbing them and breathing on them to provide some warmth. She stirs and looks up. To her surprise, it is Runt. Their eyes meet, and she sees in them, apologetic sorrow. No words are necessary to convey the guilt he feels for his part in her predicament. Gently loosening the straps that hold her to the tree, he lays her down and covers her with the warmth of a pelt. Still, near lifeless, she falls into a deep sleep, a black void of nothingness.

The gentle twitter of birds heralds the new day. She senses the presents of a person. Wearily she realizes that it is Tusk. He leans over her, wondering where the fleece covering came from and how she managed to detach herself from the tree. Fastening a cord to her neck, he wakes her. At once alert, she quietly rises, and he leads her away. Stumbling through the gloom, they walk up the incline, over the rise, and down the other side. No words are shared as they separate themselves from the camp. In a daze, Moraine urges herself to focus, focus, and prepare for the inevitably evil that Tusk will unleash.

\*\*\*

Slate peers from the seclusion of a thicket at the rustic scene of the encampment. Smoke, from the remnants of a fire in the sleeping quarters built from long reeds with mat coverings, lazily rises in the still air. He regrets not arriving earlier. If a rescue was to be launched, it would have been better to do so during the twilight period. Already there is some activity as people begin emerging from the shelter. Taking care to have a path for a quick retreat, he watches.

At length, he sees a person of smaller stature than the rest of the men appear at the dwelling entrance. Recognizing him from the confrontation of the previous day, with interest, Slate observes his behavior, which immediately seems odd. The man glances, unsure of himself. A wizened old woman appears next. She walks over to a tree in the center of the clearing, looks about, and seems satisfied with what she was looking for. She begins barking instruction at some women who also emerged from the hut. Intimidated, they immediately obey her commands. All the while, the smaller man cautiously follows the old woman's actions while trying to avoid her presence. As time passes, Slate comes to realize that the old woman dominates life in this community. Her presence instantly transforms all discourse into subservience and to follow her bidding as she issues instructions, periodically reprimanding some unfortunate person. Surly aggression is evident between all members of the band as they go about their daily business. The overall result is a toxic blend of short-tempered, strutting self-importance in everyone's attempt at dominance.

Slate's mind turns to Moraine, realizing the incongruousness of her nature to life under this regime. His mind struggles between the throbbing

88

hurt of trying to understand a life without Quill and concern for Moraine and what her apparent absence foretells. The unbearable thought of harm having been brought to her requires all his will to quell the possibility.

At length, he sees the man of underdeveloped stature move to a secluded area within the encampment, looks about, and when sure that he is not being watched, unobtrusively disappears into the forest up a rise. Slate is torn between following him, suspecting a connection to Moraine, or continuing to hope that she will appear from one of the shelters. Deciding on the latter, he continues to observe the scene before him. As the day stretches on to early evening, the little man reappears from the forest and blends with the people.

\* \* \*

Tusk strides forth, yanking Moraine along as she struggles to maintain his pace. The meager warmth of the sun is unable to entirely dispel the cold of the night, even with the exertions from the march. Cold shivers rack her as her mind returns to Quill's last moments. The fear in her eyes and the pitiless cruelty on Tusk's countenance starkly counterpoint the morality of each. Then the callous, self-serving injustice metered out by Gramater. These thoughts weigh heavily on her dragging her energy down as she trudges after this brute before her. At around mid-afternoon Tusk suddenly stops, looks around, and is still treating Moraine as a nonentity, extracts dried meat from a pouch, and eats from it, giving her none.

Sated, he pulled her along to a stream and, bending over, drinks from the icy water with Moraine doing likewise. Tusk sits at the side of the river, pondering what to do next while Moraine considers how to react to an advance from him, which will likely occur sooner or later. Time stretches as hunger gnaws, and the sun sinks to the horizon. Then, a movement in the brush on the opposite side of the stream. Looking over Tusk's shoulder, she can make out the silhouette of a man. Looking closer, she makes out Runt, who immediately moves to better concealment. Alert for a possible rescue attempt, she averts her eyes to disguise her sudden attentiveness. The moment drags, drags, and with bated breath, she waits but nothing, nothing comes of it. Despondency eventually sets it. To comfort herself, she pulls the pelt, a poncho-like garment with no sleeves, over her, quietly thanking Runt for providing it during the night. In doing so, she discovers an object in an inside pocket of the fur. Through the lining, she can feel the outline of a sharp object. Careful not to disturb Tusk, she reaches inside to find a bladeless spear-like article tapering to a point at one side, the whole less than an outstretched hand in length. It feels like bone.

Wondering to herself, "Did Runt put this here?" Looking about for Runt again proves to be fruitless. Somewhat relieved at having a weapon to protect herself, she positions it for quick access and waits. At length, with darkness beginning enveloping them, Tusk begins preparing for sleep. To emphasize his dominance over her, he takes hold of the rope still tied to her neck and forcibly drags her to a tree. Still smoldering under the humiliation at Gramater's hands, he secures another rope to her foot, leads it around the tree, loops it through the knot at her neck with exaggerated roughness fastens it to his foot. With a parting kick to her midriff, he settles down to sleep at the extent of the rope, feeling sure that she cannot escape.

Moraine silently endures his meanness, waiting for an opportunity to strike back. He soon begins snoring loudly. Taking this as the signal to go on the offensive, she examines the object in the gloom, confirming that it is made of bone. Considering its lightweight and short length, the blow would require considerable force and be directed at vital organs to achieve any measure of success.

Attempts at losing the ropes prove to be futile. Trying to move closer to Tusk to allow some slack in the rope merely disturbs the cord sufficiently to partially wake him, judging by a break in his snoring before he settles down and the heavy breathing resumes. Frustrated, she decides to wait for an opportunity during the day and falls asleep, listening to the rumbling of her stomach. A blustery wind picks up, and as the cold sharpens, wakefulness returns under the inadequacy of the pelt and her clothing while Tusk continues asleep. The dawn breaks to the first sprinkling of snow. Tusk stretches, sleeps a little longer, then rummages through his backpack to produce more dried meat and begins loudly eating. Satisfied, he rises to urinate nearby with his back turned.

Returning to the backpack, he takes out more of the food and, while chewing, says, "I know you are awake. Ha, feeling hungry ... hmm, yes, probably?" After a pause with emphasis, "When you are ready to submit, you may just get some. Think about it, woman."

* * *

Concerned at Moraine's continued absence, Slate reluctantly moves to a safer distance with the intent to sleep and return before dawn to continue his surveillance of the camp. A cold wind brings overcast morning. The sky hangs heavy with clouds forecasting snow later in the day. Belated activities start in the encampment with the inhabitants emerging from sleep, much like the previous day. The simmering hostility towards each other continues unabated. Observing he sees a subtle hierarchy with the small man at the lowest level in the pecking order, taking the brunt of jokes and assignment of menial duties. The man again tries to detach himself from the general activities and, at the earliest opportunity, slinks off into the forest as he did on the previous day. This time Slate decides to follow. Keeping at a safe distance, he soon realizes that the man is following a pair of tracks in the forest. With rising optimism, Slate feels sure they are on the route taken by Moraine with another person. The smaller of the two footsteps show signs of uncoordinated dragging of the feet with the ground disturbed between each step by something being carried.

Over the rise and on down the other side, they proceed. By mid-afternoon, they reach a clearing next to a stream with a tree in the center. By now, snow begins lightly covering the ground and trees. Slates watches as the man inspects the ground, which, even at a distance, the crumpled vegetation is visible, maybe as a result of them having spent the night there, but increasingly the snow is covering everything with a white blanket. The man completes his scrutiny, circles the perimeter a few times, then crosses the stream to search further. Not long and he takes up a new path alongside the stream moving upward in the direction of the base.

Slate allows time for the man to distance himself so that he can inspect the clearing more closely. The vegetation is more disturbed than he anticipated, with some drag marks leading down to the stream. The tree bears the signs of scuffing with remnants of rope fibers on the bark.

91

On the far side bank of the river, the track continues with intermittent stops at the water's edge then resuming. Keeping at a safe distance, Slate stops to examine the footprints in more detail. The tracks show a labored pace. Something is being dragged along, and the strides are shorter than earlier. Then alarmed, he sees what looks like a trail of blood beneath the fallen snow. Anxious for an explanation, he steps faster but almost reveals himself to the other man who had abruptly stopped. Fortunately, the man is absorbed with a scene before him and is peering ahead from behind concealing bushes. Sounds, muffled by the snow which is falling in droves, reach Slate. Strangely the snow is speckled with black particles. Unsure what to make of it, he edges forward to find the source of the noise.

* * *

By now, Moraine is fully awake, steeling herself, she turns in her prone position to face him. His bravado has returned, gloating at her as he struts about satisfied with his strategy to weaken her to submission. Fixing her eyes on his, with deliberate slowness, she begins removing her clothing. Mesmerized, he stops and stands transfixed with his mouth half-open as he was about to speak. Moraine continues until naked, then turning she bends over with open legs, presenting her rear in an exaggerated invitation, luring him to partake. Luridly, with his eyes glued to the temptation, overwhelmed with lust, Tusk fumbles to remove his clothes, casting them aside in his eagerness. Like an animal stalking its quarry, its weapon, an oversized protrusion, leads as he closes the distance and mounts her, locking his arms around her neck in a chokehold. Her meager frame, dwarfed by the size of the man, is helpless but to submit to his will. Premature ejecta confounds his thrusts, forcing him to adjust as he seeks penetration to consummate his lust. Gasping in the stench of it, hesitating for only a moment, Moraine strikes. With the knife hidden close to her chest, she turns, thrusts the dagger into his midriff, and withdraws it for a second lunge at him. This time it penetrates his groin next to his manhood. As his grip around her neck eases, she completes her turn to face him. Face to face, with alarm and shock registered on his face, she shoves the weapon deeper, until it disappears into his body. Extracting her bloody hand from the wound, she falls back. Tusk too falls backward, pinning his left leg under his body in an awkward angle, eliciting a scream of pain. Even then, under the force of adrenaline coursing through his veins, it holds his erection aloft in a macabre obelisk before subsiding. As he struggles to right himself, Moraine, still naked, jumps up, fastens the other end of the rope that is still around her neck, to his neck. She ties it to his left wrist with an extension of the cord and jerks his arm up his back locking it in position. With him immobilized, she dresses while he moans in pain. Taking hold of the rope around his neck, she drags him wide-eyed to the stream, shoving him into the fidget water and shouts, "Wash your wounds, you will have some explaining to do ..."

Rummaging through his discarded clothes and backpack, she finds and eagerly eats the remaining food then throws the clothes to him with a shout, "Dress!"

Whimpering, he cleans the oozing blood, every move stabbing pain anew. Finished, he reaches for his garments, but they slip from his grasp into the river. Lunging for them in the torrent, he retrieves some, but his loincloth languidly floats away in the rushing water. With tears streaming, he slowly puts on his jacket and stands to move away from the water, his lower torso absurdly exposing his indignity.

"Come, it is time to go." She drags him back to the stream, enters, and wades through the waist-deep water pulling him with her. The snow now falling heavily blankets their passage as they slowly proceed upwards along the bank towards the camp, stopping periodically for him to stem the flow of blood in the water. Every step he makes becomes more labored as he limps on his injured knee, swollen to a large balloon.

The luminescence of the white landscape disguises the enveloping darkness of evening as the day draws its curtain. Finding a shelter next to a boulder and cluster of trees, they settle for the night. Taking Tusk's cue from the previous night, Moraine binds him to the tree, securing him from launching a surprise attack during the night. Tusk ceases his whimpering as he lies in a prone position, which brings some relief to the pain of the weapon embedded in his midriff and respite from walking on the injured knee.

\*\*\*

Startled by the man's abrupt stop, Slate watches as the man moves forward again. In the failing light, Slates edges towards them and sees Moraine on the far side of the clearing near a boulder and tree. She is engaged in securing a person to the tree with a rope fastened at each end to their necks. The man appears to be injured.

The approaching man runs to close the remaining distance to Moraine, startling her, he speaks in a language foreign to Slate, "Moraine, are you okay?"

"What! Runt, Runt, it is you."

Reaching her, "Are you alright?"

Recovering, she says, "Yes, I am okay."

Turning to the man still prone next to her, he says, "What happened to him? Tusk, where are your coverings? You look injured."

Tusk remains silent and immobile, staring up at Runt, disbelief in his eyes.

A rush of words from Moraine, "Runt. I don't know how to thank you. That knife or bone stick, whatever it was, saved me. He attacked me, and I used it on him. It is still in him, and he lost his loincloth - washed away in the river."

At this, Tusk splutters between the anguish of his pain and his humiliation. "You – you betrayed me, you, you ... it was you."

Ignoring him, Runt says, "Moraine, I must apologize. When we were watching you, before attacking your group, I came to realize how content you all are, peaceful, and present no harm to us. So much happier than life in our camp. I could not go on with the attack. Can you forgive me?"

Before Moraine can respond, Slate approaches. Overwhelming relief flows through Moraine. As tears stream down her cheeks, she reaches out to him, and they embrace. Slate holds her firmly for long minutes, whispering gentle, calming words. He cups her face in his hands. They look deep into each other's awareness, exchange affection, and share emotions in a wordless dialogue. She sees his struggle with the pain of losing his cousin and his relief at finding Moraine safe. Within her, he sees the desperation felt at the hands of Tusk, the determination to overcome the malice and cruelty of his intent but also the void and longing for Slate and his companions. At length, their attention returns to the situation at hand.

The finality of Tusk's degradation is writ large on his face. His enemy, his slave to-be now under the spell of his chosen woman. Runt, the underling, his menial underling now lording it over him. He, who is the supreme leader of men ... but the pain and his indignity interject in his thoughts to remind him of his fallen stature, and he whimpers, capitulating, surrendering his will. Like a dagger to his heart, a slow realization dawns on him, reducing him to inwardly grovel, tomorrow he will face the clan and Gramater's wrath.

By morning snow covers the forest and their temporary resting place. Moraine, now free of the tether around her neck and Slate having prepared a meal of an unfortunate rabbit over a crackling fire, they quietly eat and ready to leave. Tusk wards off all attempts at extracting the knife from his groin when the pain is too severe and disconsolately, with the rope still around his neck, they set out. The bleeding has stopped, but the agony of the object in him elicits cries of pain by jerks in the uneven passage they follow, as does his inflamed knee.

Progress is slow and increasingly difficult as the snow mounts. They curiously wonder at the dark specks in the snow, but by late afternoon the camp comes into view from the rise that they emerge over.

# 11   Correspondence

Proceeding along the escarpment, the terrain becomes increasingly rock-strewn. The cliff shows ancient landslides with house-size boulders further down where they came to rest after tumbling down the slope. The partial collapse of the higher portions provides a testament to nature's force with vegetation taken root in shale like slides of soil mixed with stones and boulders of varied size.

Michel remarks, "I wish Enrico was here. I am sure these are not just localized disturbances of the cliffs. My guess is that it resulted from a tremor of sorts."

Taking up his train of thoughts, Käthe expands, "Do you think it resulted from the shocks that must have accompanied the volcanic eruption 39,000 years ago?"

"Not specifically that, but you may be right. It seems a long way to Naples from here, though."

Jane adds, "Give him a call. Try to get him over here. The seismic effects on the bird population are well documented."

"Well, let me try." Calling Enrico, who promptly answers, Michel says, "Hello Enrico. This Michel. We spoke a while back."

"Yes, yes, I remember. Michel Brenner, is that right? Did you get hold of Käthe?"

"Yes, we did, thanks. Enrico, we are on the southern flank of the Pyrenees. The part that is in Spain. We have hiked over from France and ultimately are still heading for Gibraltar."

"Sounds exciting. I wish I was there."

"Well, here's your opportunity. We found a series of landslides along the ridge of mountains. They are obviously ancient. We are trying to correlate them with the migration of animals and birds, and from that, the possible effects on the Neanderthals. We need to know whether this may be caused by tremors because the slides are not localized to one area only. Could tremors associated with a volcanic eruption as far away as Naples, have this effect?"

"Hmm, yes, it could. The African tectonic plate is pushing against the Eurasian plate and eruptions and tremors, even earthquakes can and do result from this."

Jane interrupts, "Quite aside from 39,000 years ago. We are currently right now, seeing changes in the migratory patterns of birds. Michel has found a shift in the magnetic lines that birds are following in their migrations. I don't want to go out on a limb here, but something is not normal. These signs could point to an imminent eruption."

"Let me discuss this with my colleagues. Maybe I can find an excuse to join you. I will get back to you."

*  *  *

Not long, and Enrico is back, "Good news. I can come. It didn't take much convincing. I am long overdue for a holiday."

After agreeing on logistics, they settle on waiting where they are for his arrival. Otto will pick him up at the local airport to drop him off at the nearest trail from where he can hike the remaining distance to their location. No sooner than Michel ends the phone conversation than Käthe's phone rings with Ulrich from the cave site on the line, "Käthe, you won't believe this. We found skeletal remains just a few meters away from the entrance to the cave."

"This is amazing, tell me more. Can you estimate the age?"

"Well, it is definitely associated with the cave. It also shows distinct signs of intentional burial. There is a pit with rocks to cover the hole. It appears to be the complete skeleton of a Neanderthal."

"First things first. You must preserve the area. No tampering. This must be done according to the book. At some point, we will have to select the best of the bones for DNA analysis."

"Käthe, the most amazing thing is that we found a piece of slate with a drawing on it that matches the symbol in the cave. Listen to this; on the other side, there is an engraved drawing of a pair of intersecting flowers. There are colors embedded in the markings. It is only about two inches in diameter, like a medallion. It has a hole in it as if it could be worn on a necklace."

"Was! Bestimmt unglaublich, incredible! Ulrich, we are expecting a volcanologist or tectonic expert here in a day or so. I will ask them to take me back to the cave. Wait for me before you do anything."

\* \* \*

A day later, Enrico arrives, trudging up the incline with a heavy pack on his back, after exchanging seats in the CAV with Käthe. Otto wastes no time accepting the pre-existing destination coordinates and an instruction to hurry. The vehicle turns and speeds back down the track to return to the cave on the other side of the mountains.

Even as he unpacks his gear, Enrico glances at the rock slide reaching down to their location, intrigued by the repetition further to the left and right of their position. Finishing the unpacking, he turns to Michel, "Just a quick assessment. I think you are right. This is the result of a tremor, there is no doubt. Also, judging by the vegetation and trees, I think these are second or third growth trees. They have been here for a long, long time, certainly many thousands of years.

"Yes, that is what I thought."

Jane interrupts, "Greg, show him the magnetic deviation. Also, look there, the birds that rely on the magnetic paths in the sky, they are in full migration now, which is a few weeks late."

Michel indicates on his computer, "See here. Two magnetic South Poles. The deviation is already quite clear here in the Pyrenees."

"Okay, I see that. I have brought along a seismometer so I can measure the intensity of micro tremors. I can soon get a picture of what is going on. But first, we need to move further down the slope to where the ground is more stable. I need a solid base underfoot to take measurements."

Michel asks, "Will you set up your equipment down there and return here?

"My advice is to move everything. Any further disturbances could set off another slide, and we would be directly in its way. No, we should relocate down there."

With some reluctance, they begin disassembling the tents. On reaching the edge of the stream, Enrico looks about and after consideration, "You know. I think we need to move to the other side of the river. That way, I will have a broader view of the cliffs, and the ground looks to be less undisturbed."

With that, they set up camp with a panoramic view across the valley. Enrico's first attempt at taking readings from the seismometer gives poor results. Relocating the equipment further up the hill improves the readings but still not good enough. Moving even further up, he finds a suitable spot with a large boulder with a cluster of smaller stones to one side and an open space with firm ground underfoot, ideal for his purpose. Here the results immediately show a series of micro tremors. Satisfied, he leaves it in recording mode and returns to the camp.

The afternoon is spent hiking along the contour of the escarpment with Enrico expounding on the geology of the landscape.

"These mountains are definitely unstable. Not altogether unexpected, being at the interface between two tectonic plates where the movements will always be more pronounced. The upheaval of one and the subduction of the other below the mantle is a continuous process but tends to happen in sporadic bursts."

Michel asks, "But can this be related to what happens in Naples?"

"Oh, definitely. It is all part of the same system. We tend to think of these things as separated by great distances, but from a tectonic perspective, this is not far, just around the corner. A tremor here can be related to a volcanic eruption there. Either before or after. Conversely, an eruption there can trigger tremors all along the fault lines."

"And what about the magnetic field?"

"Well, you are the expert on that, but I would say that the magnetic field is a direct consequence of the magnetic dynamo in the Earth's interior. So, yes, they are related."

Returning to the seismometer, Enrico is somewhat satisfied with the readings but for gaps in the recording. Looking about, he finds a suitable place and begins to reposition the device closer to a large boulder in the hope that the ground will be more compacted. Driving the sensor into the ground strikes buried stones requiring a retry. On extracting it, he finds that the sensitive leading edge has a problem.

"Darn, the end of the probe has come loose." Cursing, he takes out his field spade and begins excavating the soil to find the probe.

Michel, sitting on a nearby log, observes his activities then ambles over, "Can I help?"

"No, this shouldn't take a moment," and he shovels the soil into a heap alongside.

As the heap grows, Michel sees some white objects mixed in the soil, "Wait, what is this?"

"Just some loose sticks and stones."

"No, wait. It looks like bones to me," and examining them more carefully, exclaims, "yes, definitely bones. I wish Käthe was here. She would know whether they are significant. Let me call her."

"Käthe, its Michel. You won't believe it, we have found some more bones. I told Enrico to stop any further digging until you tell us what to do."

"You are right. Don't do anything. Are they in a cave?"

"No, just out in the open next to a large boulder. It is definitely not the remains of an animal, that's for sure. They look human to me."

"Okay. If you have a tarpaulin of some sort, the first thing to do is to protect the area from the elements, then wait for me. I have just arrived at the cave site, and we are busy mapping out an excavation area. What a coincidence; if they are archaic remains, it is like striking the jackpot twice over. But we have to eliminate the possibility that it is a recent burial, in which case the police would have to be called. Just wait, don't do anything for now. I will come over right away or send one of my experts."

\* \* \*

Being late in the afternoon, the decision is to move all the equipment and camping paraphernalia nearer to the site after updating Jane. That done, they settle for the night, and on the following day, Käthe arrives and excitedly inspects the remains and soon proclaims them to be archaic. With her usual diligence, she maps out an area with small guideposts with connecting strings to mark off the area to be excavated. She begins sweeping up the sand and stones for removal using fine-haired brushes, leaving a progressively exposed skeleton. The process is laborious and will take weeks to complete because many related artifacts stand to be uncovered. Under her direction, Enrico, Michel, and Jane soon learn the process and contribute to the uncovering while Käthe secures additional resources for the work. Once a fully functional team is at hand and at work, Käthe reverts to a supervisory role, and the attention returns to the original objective, questioning whether to continue the hike along the planned trail into the heart of Spain and on to Gibraltar, or focus on the discoveries.

Käthe says, "Well, we should be okay to move on. I have given the team strict instructions to leave whatever artifacts and bones they find, in place, before moving them so that we can photograph them and document their positions relative to each other. This means that we may have to bring a halt to our hike at any time. I could be called back to have a look and provide direction. In fact, I may have to split my time between the Cave Site, this Boulder Site, and the hike. Is that okay?"

Jane agrees with Michel and Enrico, nodding, "Yes, we understand. This is very exciting even for us as observers."

Enrico adds, "For my part, I have seen what there is to see here in the Pyrenees from a geological perspective, so I am happy to join you in the march if you don't mind."

"Yes, of course ... okay then, tomorrow first thing, we can set off. Is that all alright?

Käthe adds, "The walk should get easier as we move into central Spain, which is not as mountainous. Then we skip Madrid and continue on the other side."

# 12    Settlement

Runt leads the way into the settlement with Moraine following with Tusk in tow. Slate walks alongside Runt as they stride into the central clearing. Prior, while still on the crest overlooking the commune from the concealment of the vegetation, additional attempts at removing the bone weapon from Tusk are met with squeals of pain, resulting in the abandonment of the effort. After a discussion with Moraine interpreting for Slate, Runt convinces them that he will take the lead in convincing the clan and Gramater in particular, to spare Moraine from further punishment and allow Slate to depart unharmed. Runt inwardly has newfound confidence bolstered by a conviction that these strangers are peace-loving people and in the belief that they should be awarded respect. Steeling himself, he commits to this conviction knowing that despite his meager shape and standing in the community, he is not deficient in his ability to convince and lead through a keener understanding of the underlying motivations of the people.

Stepping into the open, a gasp spreads from the first to another and another as the word spreads, and they gather to silently gape in disbelief at the spectacle before them. Gramater emerges from a shelter to stand dumbfounded in shock.

Runt moves forward with confidence rising as he directs his attention at Gramater and says, "Yes, you can stare. The injustice you metered out on Moraine has been met with a just outcome. She single-handed brought Tusk to submission. You effectively sentenced her to his evil attempt at the rape. She retaliated, with righteousness on her side, to wound the man with a knife, which even now is embedded in his body. You see his knee, swollen in pain. That he did to himself in his attempt to escape the harm that he attempted on her. His genitals are bared for you to see the humiliation he intended on her. Providence had him lose his loincloth in the crossing of a stream. That too was providence metering out its justice, not Moraine's doing. The rope around his neck should not shock you because that is the same injustice you condoned when Tusk led her out of here three days ago."

The bystanders stand frozen by what they hear and see, unaccustomed to Runt's authority. All eyes turn to Gramater as Tusk grovels in complete dishonor and indignity, still whimpering to add to his shame, but no words escape her.

Runt continues, "For too long, you have brought unhappiness to this congregation, pitting one against another until all suffer under your caustic rules."

With a rising voice, he proclaims, "No! That will end now."

Allowing silence to emphasize his ultimatum, he waits while Gramater struggles to gather her composure, but before she can speak, Scat steps forward from the crowd, and everyone turns to him as he shouts, "Runt is right. We put up with Tusk for too long, the coward that he is. He is exposed for what he is!" Scat's towering bulk adds emphasis to his words. For moments the crowd holds their breath, then a ripple of agreement spreads through the throng, and a shout goes up, rising to a crescendo, "Moraine! Moraine! Moraine!"

Runt holds up his arms, and silence returns, "This man Slate is good. He has taken no vengeance on Tusk for his treatment of Moraine. He is deserving of our trust. He has a sister and a young boy who wait where Tusk murdered his cousin. Even for the death of his kin, he has withheld any punishment of Tusk for this evil. We can learn from this man's kindness and ask him to forgive us for the harm we have brought on his family."

The authority with which Runt speaks dispels all condescension they previously directed at him. It is like he is another person, awoken from a spell woven by Gramater, that is now broken. The spell Gramater held over the people lies shattered, its force of no consequence. She, her mind racing, realizing her predicament, understands that dissension now would be to no avail, bows her head in acknowledgment of her fallen stature, and retreats to the back of the throng as they move forward to embrace Runt.

Runt speaks as they approach, "Gramater, you have one last task to perform, and that is to heal the wound on Tusk."

With that, Moraine releases the leash to Gramater, who takes him to her work shed, the space reserved for her apothecary potions and midwifery functions.

Like a curse lifted, the crowd senses a release from the bondage by Gramater. There is a new freshness in the air as they hug each other and crowd around Slate and Moraine with welcoming embraces. All vindictiveness between each other dissipates under the healing smiles and emerging happiness they all feel. Even the often surly Scat, whose formidable strength held even Tusk at bay, smiles at the transformation wrought on the community. Standing next to the small figure of Runt, the power of his physique seems to be dwarfed by the deference he holds for the wisdom of the little man so newly transformed from runt to ruler in kind.

An air of optimism pervades the camp, and life takes on a new vibrancy with the freedom they now inherit. Moraine cannot hide her affection for Slate, and him for her, which even their previous adversaries find charming.

With the evening approaching, their anxiety returns to Fern and Broach, who must be wondering where Slate is. In the morning, with confidence that the clan has fully adopted their newfound freedom, Slate, Moraine and Runt set out for Fern and Broach. Runt adamantly insists on accompanying them in seeking a way to right the wrong that he participated in.

Under Slate's urgings, they hurry along and down the southern flank of the escarpment, cross the river in the valley and soon arrive to find Broach and Fern waiting alongside the boulder where he left them. An emotional reunion brings tears to everyone's eyes, accentuated by the absence of Quill in the group even at that moment, a void that is difficult to breach. Runt, who stands aside to allow the union to proceed unhindered, becomes the center of attention at Fern's questioning look.

Slate responds, "This is Runt. He was a participant in the attack on us but has come to understand that we offered them no harm." Wrapping his arms around Moraine, he continues, "He helped my dear Moraine escape the leader of their group who meant to harm her. Runt also freed his clan

105

members from the evil of the woman who controls them. We are indebted to Runt for welcoming us into his people."

"Runt, this is Fern, my sister, and Broach, my son."

Runt moves forward, and Moraine interprets for him, "Please, please forgive me for wronging you. I am sorry for my part in the attack. Already before the attack, when I observed you, I was struck by your kind gentleness towards each other. I began to realize that I was wrong. I am especially sorry for the loss of Quill, who lies buried here."

It is Fern who first reacts to his words. She steps towards Runt, takes his hands in hers, and without words looks into his face for a long time, then draws him near, and they embrace. Broach, too, comes forward and takes his hand. The silence of the language gap speaks for itself, and reconciliation and forgiveness are apparent.

Slate turns his attention to the shallow grave and proceeds to dig a better burial place alongside the other. He gently moves Quill's body, breaks the shaft of the spear still embedded in her, and lays it alongside her. In the absence of flowers, they lay a wreath of pine needles around her head, and Broach places one of his engraved slate stones in her hands. Taking a last look at Quill, who appears as if peacefully asleep, they cover her with soil.

In the glow of a fire with the stars spread overhead, the evening is spent in subdued conversation with Moraine interpreting for Runt, who increasingly feels included in the group, a feeling not experienced in all the years in the clan. The stillness of the shroud of snow from the storm of the previous day lays to rest the fear-filled days that preceded and raises the prospect of a more peaceful future. As the fire dwindles to ash, they begin preparing for sleep, prompted by Broach, who can barely keep his eyes open with weariness. Moraine helps him with a fur covering for warmth and gently pries lose the marmot, still in its bag where it too is fast asleep and secure for the night. The field mouse has snuggled into the warmth of his Broach's coat pockets safe from escape.

In the morning, there is an unspoken understanding to return to Runt's clan, where they will spend a few days before continuing their journey to the south. Taking up their scant possessions, they set off. Runt and Fern walk alongside each other with Runt probing to understand her language. By the time they reach the camp, he can articulate words to describe some features of the landscape. Fern's naturally bright and joyful nature intrigues Runt, who responds with carefree laughter as the bond between them grows.

* * *

Gramater's descending from rank of matriarch to commoner is complete as she attends to her once favored person, but Tusk can only cry in pain at any attempt at removing the object from him. Even with the pain suppressed by an intoxicating brew administered by her, she cannot extract the weapon without bringing further harm. The result is that Tusk is left to endure the pain with the only position that brings some relief being to lie motionless on his back.

Wondering what to do next, Gramater resolves to disguise her mounting anger at her predicament under a façade of stoic blandness, demoted as she is from a position of absolute control to the recipient of derogatory glances from those who previously trembled in her presence. It is too much to bear. Every aspect of her plans lies in tatters.

Muttering to herself, "I will have to rebuild. I am still, midwife and medicine woman. They will have to come to me. Yes, I will use my position. Undermine that Runt and complete by vengeance on that woman, Moraine. As for Tusk, the useless individual. What an idiot. Yet, just maybe, maybe I can still get him to carry my bloodline."

Fang, a wiry woman with a habit of cringing self-deprecation and obsequious servility towards Gramater, intuited the old woman's precarious position. Sensing an opportunity to advance herself, she stays near at hand while the disgraced matriarch attends to Tusk. Hearing the woman muttering to herself in her enclosure, she waits then sidles into the entrance and offers to help clean the man. Startled, Gramater looks up, "What? Yes, okay." From that encounter is born a self-serving partnership with neither of them declaring their motives.

Observing Fang, a plan begins to formulate in Gramater, but as they work, the mood outside perceptibly changes by a disturbance. Everyone stops what they are doing to watch the approach of Runt with Moraine and Slate through the snow-covered incline. The curiosity is for two new people that accompany them, a boy and a woman. The boy has a bag with him from which the snout of a marmot can be seen. It comically peers about with intelligent eyes scrutinizing the gathering crowd. The woman has a shock of straw-colored hair matching Slate's and appears unconcerned by the unfamiliar surroundings. As they draw nearer, a sparkle in her eyes is apparent, and her confident bearing elicits a welcoming response from the crowd. The admiration for Runt is also still undimmed in his transformed standing in the group. The people gather closer, and Runt, holding Fern about her shoulders, introduces her as Slate's sister.

Turning to Broach, he says, "This is Slate's son and with him is Elle, an injured Marmot. Broach rescued her from the rubble after the landslide. Have a look. She is already quite tame."

Broach, understanding his meaning, opens the bag for some to press closer for a look.

Gramater and Fang, having ceased their attendance of Tusk, join the throng around the boy. Gramater has motivations other than curiosity over the creature in the bag. She sizes up the new woman and notes her comfort in the proximity to Runt. Then there is Moraine. Her apparent nervousness at being encircled by so many people is evident. She clutches Slate's arm as if for security while he appears to be intensely aware of every move around him. His eyes roam to the broader aspects of the settlement taking in the temporary structures erected for shelter and utility. Gramater watches him, taking care not to expose her interest, noting how keenly aware he is of his place relative to everyone else. He strikes her as a formidable opponent. One that cannot be ignored in any plan she may hatch as he intuitively absorbs the undercurrents of intentions without understanding a word of the clatter of sounds in the foreign language. For a brief moment, their eyes lock, and she feels as if he penetrates her inner thoughts laying bare her malevolent intentions. All she can do is avert her gaze to avoid the interrogation of her mind. Retreating to the safety of the enclosure with Tusk still prone and exposed for the half-completed cleaning, she beckons Fang, who reluctantly stops staring at the scene and returns to Gramater's side to complete their work.

At Moraine's insistence, on the pretext of not wanting to overcrowd the communal sleeping quarters, a separate shelter is erected for her and the guests with Runt joining them. This provides them with a semblance of privacy even during the day. The day is a dismally cold with a curious haze in the air.

It is Slate who observes, "Notice the snow. The black dust has been increasing since the tremors. The sky is dark with it, and the air smells strange. What can it be?"

Moraine answers, "Yes. It is strange. What does it foretell? I noticed that the birds that migrate at this time are confused by the early cold."

"Yes, Moraine. I want us to follow their passage. It leads to warmer areas so we can over-winter there. You are right. They are confused, but we cannot stay long. I know the route to take even if the birds are stranded here."

Broach, content to play with his two pets and periodically interrupt Runt and Fern as they teach each other their languages, shows an uncanny ability to quickly understand Runt's language. To their delight, he corrects Fern's attempts at articulating the sounds correctly, only to mispronounce the words, needing Runt to reiterate the correct manner of speech.

Encapsulated in their separate shelter under a blanket of snow the five, share a growing commonality of understanding and kinship that is new to Runt and dear to Moraine since tying her lot with these extraordinary beings led by Slate. Painful in its tenderness, Moraine cherishes every moment with them, and as she observes Runt, she sees in him a growing mirror of her feelings, as he and Fern bond in shared affection for each other. Broach, too, basks in the adoration of the adults around him. Most dear to Moraine is the unspoken language of shared emotions and thoughts that passes between them that renders the spoken language as superfluous. So deep is the understanding of the intentions that it is seldom necessary to talk to be understood.

In the days that follow, Runt and Fern are inseparable, taking frequent walks along the nearly frozen river banks.

\* \* \*

The meanness of Gramater is like a growing cancer in her. It tears at her being. When the foreigners, with Runt, appear from their seclusion, the contrast of their contentment juxtaposed on her grasping desperation for a return to dominance, consumes her. "I must act and act soon!" she mutters out loud. In constant earshot, even Fang is alarmed at the malevolence of her intent, but she understands, "Be ready. A chance will come."

The days pass under darkening skies and falling temperatures. The blanket of black snow deepens to the alarm of the residents. Though their store of food from the most recent hunt is still adequate, a continuance of the cold foretells a lean period ahead. Replenishment from the forest increasingly devoid of animals and berries to meet their hunter-gatherer lifestyle means rationing the existing supply. Generally, this falls to Gramater to organize, but in her obstinacy, she refuses to take the responsibility, and it falls to Runt to take control. With Fern in assistance, the people willingly follow their suggestions under Fern's cheerful engaging ways as she quickly learns the language.

Slate, however, urges Moraine, "We need to leave now. The forest will still provide enough for us until we reach the plains, and the warmer reaches."

Moraine answers, "Yes, Slate, you are right, but Fern's work with the rationing will leave a gap. I will speak to her."

Fern is reluctant, asking for a few more days, but Moraine sees that she is torn between going and leaving Runt with whom there is an ever-deepening relationship.

The days pass, and in the quiet of their separate shelter, Moraine broaches the subject yet again, "Fern, we cannot delay any longer. We need to leave tomorrow."

"Yes, Runt and I have given it some thought, and I have decided that my place is here. Runt and I are partners. We cannot separate. The village also needs Runt for a while before he can leave." Taking a breath, she says, "You see, I think I am pregnant."

Aghast, Moraine questions, "Fern, are you sure? You barely know each other."

"Yes. I am almost certain. Moraine, we love each other, and I cannot leave him. It would tear me apart, but you need not worry. We will be safe here. People love and respect Runt. If he leaves with us now, I fear that Gramater will again take control. For the sake of these people, Runt feels we must wait a little longer. He will coach Scat to take control, and when I have had my baby and our child, and it is old enough, we will follow you."

On sharing this with Slate, he says, "I don't trust Gramater. She is not the sort that will easily hand over to another. I feel that my sister will be in danger. I am certain Gramater will harm both her and Runt ... and, and I will miss my sister."

Despite their urging, Runt and Fern remain firm in their decision, albeit sad at the prospect of possibly not seeing each other again. With no alternative, the day finally arrives when the three prepare to leave. News of their departure has become common knowledge and in a show of gratitude for their part in the changes to their community, all but Gramater, Fang, and Tusk are present to bid them farewell. Slate is particularly downcast at losing a sister.

Fern says, "Wait," and taking Runt's arm, "we need to get some of the potions from Gramater for Broach. He will need them."

Entering the shelter, Gramater stands with her hands on her hips in a questioning stance. Fang stops attending to Tusk's needs and waits to hear Fern's explanation.

Using the rudiments of the language she has learned, Fern says, "We need some of your potions to help Broach. Do you have any?"

Gramater replies, "What is wrong with him?"

"He has a cough and sores on his skin."

"Can you wait a moment? I will see what I have got."

With exaggerated reluctance, Gramater takes some from a shelf, pauses over one to think, then decides on a mixture which she prepares. Adding a few more to the selection, she hands them to Fern, who thanks her and exits with Runt.

Moraine adds the remedies to her backpack, along with the supply of food they provided earlier. They hug Fern for the last time as Slate and Broach struggle to contain the emotions at the departure. Waving a final farewell to the gathering, they step out into the driving snow.

* * *

Gramater, while pleased with their departure, regrets that Moraine has escaped the reprisal she longed for. Turning her attention to Tusk, who remains incapacitated in the work shelter and alternates between groaning with pain or loudly snoring as he sleeps, as is her habit, she grumbles in a low murmur, "Useless individual, every day he becomes fatter and more useless ... what good is he to me?" Then, holding her nose, "Fang! Come here. He has soiled himself again. Clean him."

She dutifully carries out the task with mounting resentment. "The old baggage expects me to do all the dirty work. What for?"

The next day Gramater, having exhausted herself during the night, wracking her brain for a solution to her predicament, wakes to feel a little better having formulated a semblance of a plan, which gives her a sense of control. With Tusk apparently still asleep, she calls Fang to the shelter, "Fang, I have this one thing I want you to do. Get this right, and I will teach you all you need to know to lead this motley group."

With renewed interest, Fang listens intently.

"I want you to service Tusk. Seduce him, bear a child."

"You mean ... but he can hardly move."

"Yes, yes, I know. But he is a man. Arouse him."

Tusk, disturbed by the sounds, stops breathing heavily. The women, sensing his wakefulness, hold quite. Tusk turns onto his side to resume sleeping, but in a dreamlike state, he is vaguely aware of what was said. They wait a while and continue.

"When you clean his wounds, you can take it a little further. Okay?"

"I see ... hmm ... okay then. I will need some privacy."

"When it is over. I mean, when you have had the baby, I will see to Tusk. I just need to be sure."

Tusk turns on his back and resumes snoring loudly.

\* \* \*

The next day Gramater prepares a brew of fermented fruit, and with Fang's help, they encourage him to drink it. After waiting a while for it to take effect, Fang lays him bare and begins cleaning the wound while massaging his groin. He is soon aroused but turns aside in indignity. Undeterred, she persists. Mumbling in his drunkenness, he eventually submits. She mounts him, and the union is consummated.

\* \* \*

As the intoxicating brew wears off, Tusk stares at the straw mat covering the roof of the enclosure. An overwhelming sense of having been defiled pervades his senses leaving him destitute of pride and self-worth at having plumbed the depth of his humiliation. The thought of him as a vassal of this evil old woman is unshakable. He ponders all the events leading from when he first followed Moraine out of the camp at the old woman's command. His inability to ford the confluence of the two rivers, the chase, and ultimately the capture of Moraine. Every step was egged on by Gramater in her condescending way, maliciously appealing to his insecurities, now left wallowing in the depth of self-loathing. Try as he may, to dispel the awakening to his faults, his mind invariably returns to the inescapable fact of his arrogance and egotistical boasting. Through the fog of his misery, the image of Moraine insistently returns. Pushing it aside for fear of its accusatory pointedness, he repeatedly suppresses it, but return it does, until his denials can no longer be sustained. Though his attempt to subdue her failed, his intent was clear, nothing less than the rape when she was at her most vulnerable. Finally, finally, the fact of it is indisputable, undeniable. Recoiling in horror at his discretions, he tries to shut his mind to the admission but to no avail. It stands as a stark outline of the character that he is. It does little to obfuscate the mounting guilt that, only now, that a parallel has been committed on him as the victim that he should arrive at this realization. His actions mirror the treatment at the hands of Fang, at the direction of Gramater, they raped him when he too was most susceptible.

A full day passes before he gradually emerges from the haze of a deep depression. Fang enters the enclosure to begin her routine of cleaning him. Stirring to wakefulness, he brushes her aside and indicates that she must leave. With her gone, for the first time since his confinement, he staggers to his feet and holds a post to steady himself. With dizziness threatening, he takes a step, then another as the pain in his groin pierces through his body. Calming himself, he opens the flap to the enclosure and steps out into the glaring white of snow. Thankfully, there is little activity at this hour. Taking a deep breath, he strides out and into the forest area where he relieves himself. Returning to the work-shed, he feels satisfaction at the small independence achieved and resolves to dispense with the assistance from Fang and Gramater henceforth.

\* \* \*

The blizzard persists for a few days. Emerging from the shelter reserved for Fern and Runt, Runt looks about at the frozen landscape. The inhabitants are still in the communal sleeping quarters where the first sounds of activities stir for the day. The sprinkling of black dust mixed in with the snow remains an unexplained curiosity. Even with clear patches between the clouds skidding along the sky with the fresh breeze, the sun is strangely obscured by streaks of haze.

Wondering out loud, "Can it be to do with the tremors? Something must have happened over the distant horizon."

114

Returning to the shelter, he says, "Fern, the sky still has that dust from a few days ago. It must be causing the cold, surely? The sun is quite cold."

"You are probably right, dear."

"Fortunately, we have enough food for the winter. I have not seen any animals since the cold started, and there are no berries. The late berries will be frozen and not edible. We should move from the mountain to the valley where there will be less snow and maybe more animals. We cannot depend on the store of food. We need fresh food as well."

"Runt, if you want us to move, we should go soon, before the baby is much bigger."

Later in the day, Runt calls a meeting of the members, and there is immediate agreement. They will move back to the valley where they came from before the chase, hoping that they will again hunt for deer and other animals. With that, preparations are started for the move. In a couple of days, they congregate to begin the march. At Runt's instruction, stretchers are prepared for Gramater and Tusk, who will otherwise not complete the distance.

The momentous events of the last few days are soon forgotten. They leave the mountain pass to its previous desolation.

A period of sadness follows, but the understanding and compassion they have for each other surmounts the loss, and they return to the more pressing need to provide for themselves. With mixed feelings, where their love blossomed and where they faced the loss, they decide to distance themselves from the sorrow and seek warmer regions.

Skirting the mountain to the West, day after day stretches into summer, and still, the iciness persists in disdain for the solstice, insistent on an inverted season. However, imperceptibly by degrees, the temperatures do rise, challenging the frostiness. Plants take the cue to cloak the landscape with a sheen of green, and animals, though scarce, return from the brink to feast on the unfurling vegetation, a promise of better times to come and the child within Moraine shows renewed vigor. Even Elle shakes loose the hibernation to emerge hungry and ready to explore the world. She and Broach are inseparable, as they playfully fill the void of the companionship of their age. They dart about and squeal with pleasure, then when tired, curl up together to doze in the meager warmth of the failed sunshine.

In a land where animals are weak from the long winter, a pair of eagles circle overhead to prey on the frail, for they too require sustenance. The animals they find are usually dead, their carcasses frozen in grotesque shapes, and impossible to feed on. Lured by the summoning warmth, they take to trailing the creatures below, three who stand erect and one, a marmot that stays close and out of reach of their talons. As the mountains recede, the nomads strike across the vast plain, to an uncertain destination, confident, as the beckoning warmth confirms their chosen path as the correct one.

In the absence of herds to follow, the promise of a life free of the shackles of ice guides the wanderers. Each day Ayrial and Eyther rise to great heights to scan the distant vista seeking pastures that offer the reward, but it remains elusive.

Slate, pointing up, says to Moraine, "Look, the eagles. Look up there. There are two of them. I have been watching them these last few days. With no robins and finches to follow, I think they will guide us to where we need to go."

Moraine, always aware of the birds in the forest, says, "Yes, I have seen them too. It has been so dismal without all the usual birds."

"True. The eagles seem to be following us, and we are following them. I think we have the same destination in mind."

Broach, hearing the conversation, ceases playing with Elle and comes nearer. In concern, Broach asks, "Will the eagles catch Elle?"

Moraine answers, "Yes, my boy. You need to keep her close to you. They won't attack while you are near."

Elle tilts her head, seeming to understand the conversation. Standing on her hind legs, she reaches up to hold the boy around his leg. The adults smile at the scene and also join in the embrace, laughing. To their delight, the little creature darts around them in circles.

Each day it becomes a routine to look to the birds of prey to guide them.

By their habits, Moraine sees that the eagles struggle to find prey in the frozen landscape and suggests, "We have some excess. We should feed them."

With that, they routinely every morning leave the less edible portions of the food out for the tailing pair. At sunset, the two eagles take to roosting in nearby trees, and in the morning, they hesitantly approach and hungrily devour the portions, then soar high in the sky, gliding on thermals or coasting to nearby rocky protrusions to silently watch the progress of the wanderers.

On a particular day, the two birds rise to an elevation that is higher than usual. Looking to the east across an expanse of the sea, beyond the horizon, they see the persistent column of dust has diminished to a small column of smoke. Turning southwards, they see that the land ahead ends abruptly beyond a rocky mountain that protrudes above the surrounding terrain. There the sea curves around the horn-shaped massif and disappears in the far distance. This, they know, is their destination. Dropping to the height of trees near the travelers, they give a cry as they alight on the bare branches, calling, calling to follow. Slate and Moraine watching, look at each

119

other quizzically. Can their strange behavior be a sign, they wonder. Days later, the top of a mountain shimmers in the distance, and the air leaves a salty taste in their mouths. Stepping out, they walk with increased speed. A sense of anticipation drives them as they suspect that something is changing in the landscape ahead. With Moraine large with the child, Slate anxiously watches over her, and with the change in the air, hopes that their destination is near. Over the following two days, the mountain looms more massive, and for the first time, they see water stretching to the horizon, an immense lake of a size they have never before seen. Patches of blue in the sky reflect the light in an azure aquamarine that entrances them with wonder. Spellbound, they take in the scene. The sheer size of it leaves them amazed at the expanse of water. Never before did they contemplate such a sight. Even the eagles that wing their way ahead of their passage seem unusually demonstrative in the way they playfully circle each other, touching wings, then sweeping down to loop back up and repeat the spectacle. They lead the way around the cliff face that drops to the water's edge, leaving a shallow beach of pebbles and reeds in the lapping water. Raucous seagulls and cormorants in abundance swoop and dive for fish then return to rocky ledges where they consume their catch. Following the tide around the curvature of the mountain to the farthest edge of the land, they stop. This is the end of their journey. Looking around, the first and most apparent feature they see is a cave at the foot of the cliff. The absence of footprints in the sand and the undisturbed vegetation signals that it is uninhabited. Despite this, Slate cautiously walks along the cliff face until he reaches the entrance. Peering inside, he confirms that it is unused. With Moraine and Broach following closely, they penetrate the darkness to find that a fine layer of windblown sand reaches the far interior. Somewhat relieved at finding it deserted, they relax and inspect it closely.

Broach is first to exclaim, "Look, a drawing on the rock wall. See here!"

They gather around and scrutinize it. It shows a pair of parallel markings that intersect.

Slate observes, "It looks so much like the scraping I do when I sharpen the edge of the slate arrows."

Broach fumbles in his bag and extracts one of his painted stones and turns it over. On the other side, there are two similar intersecting grooves. Excitedly he compares them, "Yes, they match. I do the same when I sharpen the stones. I sharpen the stone to a point on one side then use it to scratch a design on the other side. Except these on the wall are much bigger."

Surprised, Moraine exclaims, "You are so clever. And, you know what that means? Someone has been here before us."

Slate joins in, "Yes, I do that too when I make the points for the spears. Remember, I left the same markings on the cave we escaped from." Turning to Moraine, "You are right, someone has been here, but if you look at the marks, they are not recent. There are dust and even some moss in the markings."

The remainder of the day is spent scouting further around the curve of the cliff, looking for any sign of activity, but nothing is found that is of concern. Feeling more relaxed, they settle in the cave with Broach reserving the deeper reaches for himself.

As evening approaches, they gather dried reeds and branches scattered on the beach to make a fire. Slate hollows a patch of the sand sheltered from the wind in a corner of the cave. Below the surface, he finds the remnant of a previous fire. The coals are unmistakably from a frequently used fire pit from some distant time.

As the summer sun sets to a day that marks the end of their long journey, a sense of homeliness brings contentment with the realization that the journey required a continuous state of alertness that can now be shed. For the first time, Slate and Moraine find themselves comparing their lives prior to their meeting. Moraine explains how they followed the herds of roving deer. Their trek across the land was entirely dictated by the animals they followed as they moved to richer pastures as the seasons changed. In a full year, they only once met another group of their kind, and before that, it was many years prior.

Slate describes a life of dwindling numbers as they too followed the herds. "We were once attacked by a group of people that looked different. They were smaller in stature, more nimble, and able to run for long distances without tiring. They captured some of our group, and, being outnumbered, there was nothing we could do. They had lighter spears with bone tips. Much lighter, not like ours, which have slate stone tips. They speak and shout a lot. They have a way of signaling when to attack as a group. We are more solitary and good at tracking individual animals, whereas they corner whole herds and slaughter more than they need."

Picking up Tusk's club, which he has carried with him all this way, he points, "See how it is made of bone. It has these carvings on it, which is easier to do than on stone. It is quite clever."

"After the attack, we decided to follow the birds to warmer areas and not return to face these other people. You found us a full summer later when my partner was sick. We stayed at that cave for many moons as we tried to heal her, but she died there. Being late in the year, we decided to stay there for the winter, but then you came to warn us. We did not want to be captured like our other friends and relatives. That is why we decided to leave with you. Dear Moraine, you saved us from slavery. We know that because we saw how they bound and treated our kind."

"It is strange how your kind is so aggressive, even to each other, yet we met, and I could not love anyone more. My chest pains me with joy when I think of you, Moraine."

Moraine quietly listens to Slate, recalling the terror she felt when it dawned on her that Gramater intended to enslave these people as she had seen done before. Now, here is the man Gramater would harm. This man, who is everything to her. The man in whom she has complete trust and who shares intimacies beyond what was conceivable before its birth.

"Slate, my dearest Slate, my chest too pains with the joy of you. I cannot excuse my kind. Their ways are strangely discontented. They feel they must control everything. They never cease to strive for some unfathomable goal while their happiness lies within, there to accept without question. This is why I love you. We communicate without speaking, yet we understand each other's thoughts and desires better than they do. Your kind has harmony with nature, a sharing as equals without goals, and the need for control. You are

122

one with the forest, the birds, the animals, the land, the rivers, the sky, and the stars. When I met you, I met all of this, and I feel you and all this in me. My life is full, and I do not need more, just you."

"I must also confess. When I decided to warn you to leave, it was because I knew Gramater intended to enslave you. She said so. You see, when I was younger, we met another group like ours, and I recall that there was a man and woman of your kind, tied to a pole as slaves. I remember their unhappiness. They had a child by their slave master of that I am certain. I could not bear the thought of anyone being treated like that. When I saw you and Broach at the edge of the river and your loving concern for him, I had to act. It was clear to me that your ways are so different from those at our settlement. I yearned to escape and be part of you."

"Thank you, Moraine. You are a very special person. It must have taken a lot of courage to break with the group that you had spent all your life with."

Immersed in their new life at the water's edge proves to be sheer bliss as the memory of their loss fades. All three become adept at spearfishing in the tidal pools where Brock and Elle enjoy splashing in the shallows while offshore schools of porpoises frolic in a display of their swimming, leaping, and diving prowess. Sea turtles leave their eggs in the sand, which provides a steady source of food. On occasions, they explore the wider area around the peninsula, where food is increasingly in abundance. Returning to the cave, they have a view of the broad seascape, and in the distance, another land that rises out of the ocean, enticingly close, and they wonder what secrets it holds.

Broach often asks, "What land is that? Can we go there?" But neither of the adults can answer. Their excursions along the coast always veer away from that land no matter how far they go, leading to the belief that it is separate and apart from their homeland.

As fall approaches, Moraine once again finds herself in child. By late winter, the pregnancy is quite advanced, and Slate and she begins planning for the addition to come. Even Broach shares in feeling the life in her belly as it moves. As winter draws to an end, alarmingly, she experiences pains across her abdomen, and after a few days, they find themselves once again burying the child. The grief, though profound, Slate in consoling her, says, "Moraine, you must not be hard on yourself. It is just not to be. This land has no people other than ourselves. The child will outlive us, and only loneliness will follow for it. We are happy, the three of us, but even Broach will be left on his own when we are old and die. No, we must be happy with what we have. I cannot have anyone better than you to share this time with."

Moraine understands and comes to terms with the loss. Despite this, when they need to pass by the burial place near the cave entrance, a piercing reminder tears at her heart as she thinks of what might have been. Invariably other matters intercede to distract from the pain, and life goes on. But, despite the pristine environment, loneliness lies under the surface of their bliss, intruding now and then as they consider what life would be like if they shared the world with others of their kind.

Evenings are usually spent watching the ebb and flow of the tides and gulls diving into the sea to retrieve their last meal for the day before settling on the cliffs for roosting. Some are seen carrying twigs picked from the flotsam of logs and branches washed up on the shore, to construct their nests on the ledges as spring approaches. The eagles have become permanent residents taking prime position on the highest ridges above the cave where they too begin their nesting habits.

"Look, Slate, something is moving on that log. Can you see it?"

"Where, oh there, I see it. It's floating on a log. You mean that?"

"Yes. Can we catch it? It looks like a mouse?"

"Okay, come, let's get closer ... careful the water gets deep."

Moraine, looking down from the cave entrance, curious at the excitement, walks down the sloping beach to the pair. Slate stretches out into the lapping waves and, after a few attempts, pulls the log nearer to the shore. The exhausted mouse sluggishly moves to the far side of the log to escape being caught, but Slate throws a soft fur pelt over it, bundles it into a ball, and wades to the shore where they carefully open the covering to examine it.

Moraine joins them to look at the little creature, "Oh look, it looks just like Trine but has four stripes on its back. Slate, do you think it is the same breed?"

"Yes, it looks like it."

Without a word, Broach darts up the slope to the cave and returns with Trine, "Let's see whether they like each other," gently placing Trine next to the timid newcomer. They sniff each other, and Trine nudges it, as the other responds in kind. After a little coxing, Broach soon has it eating seeds, and drinking water from his hands, which quickly revives its spirits, and Trine seems invigorated by the friend, which they determine to be a male.

"What can we call him? Can we call him, Drift?"

"Yes, that sounds like a good name. Hello Drift."

* * *

With the addition of Broach's pet, life on the edge of the sea continues with many interests occupying their time. Spring brings the sight of many birds crossing from the far land across the waters to fly in flocks of many thousand. Waves of different species take turns in the crossing with Slate and Moraine, watching them and calling out those they recognize.

Moraine remarks, "So that's where our Rollers and finches go in winter. I often wondered. It must be warmer with forests and fields there."

"Wouldn't it be nice to go there? If we did, we could see what it is like. It may be an island."

"We should climb to the top of our mountain. From there, we may see how big it is."

"Good idea. Broach ... hey Broach, would you like to climb our mountain?

"Oh, yes, yes. When can we go?"

"Let's pack some food, and tomorrow early, we can go and spend the day there."

After circling back along the coast and then walking up the incline, they reach the top. Partridges and rabbits share this domain peering at the intruders from a safe distance. As they approach the precipice, the azure sea spreads before them, and across the waters, the land on the far shore rises to a range of mountains on the horizon stretching far to the left and right. The legacy of the cold still blows up here with a fresh breeze at their backs. Finding a comfortable rock sheltered from the wind, the day passes as they watch the tide flow through the strait. The cormorants take to the air to dive for fish as the flow pauses, and the water begins flowing in the opposite direction. Intrigued by the lure of Farland with the sun sinking to the horizon, they descend to their cave. Over the days that follow, they frequently return to the subject of Farland. Its temptation draws them into an imaginary world, a fantasy of an Eden where all strife is absent and where they are part of a community of shared dreams and aspirations. Farland becomes the focus of all that is good and desirable that this shore does not offer.

Slate's mind returns to the day they rescued the mouse off a floating log, and gradually the idea takes root. What if he strung a few logs together, would they be able to cross the expanse to the other side? During their evening time, when watching the ever-changing scene before them, he takes to watching the tidal flows, how they change from morning to afternoon.

Slowly a pattern emerges that corresponds with the rise and fall of the tides. Then, throwing a log into the sea, he watches its movements. Sometimes it drifts out to sea to be lost to sight. At other times it hugs the shoreline and eventually circles back to where it started. At other times it remains motionless for long periods before being swept along by a current.

Moraine watching Slate's curiosity, she says, "And what are you thinking so deeply about?"

"I just wondered, if I tie some logs together, would we be able to paddle across to Farland? It seems so near."

Intrigued, Moraine suggests, "It could be dangerous, and if we fall in, we will drown. We can't swim like porpoises."

"Well, what if we learn to swim?"

Thrilled at the prospect of doing something different, Broach and Moraine join in the planning for a trial. The swimming lessons are fun. At first, they splutter and splash about making little headway in the shallows, but after a while, they relax, and the fear of the lack of buoyancy dissipates as they become proficient. Soon they can swim some distance from the shore and confidently return.

Next, Slate recruits them to help build a raft by tying a few logs together. As a test, they stand on it to see whether it will hold their weight, and with some modifications, they achieve success. Using the platform, they paddle out a short distance and take turns to swim back to shore. As they build confidence, they venture further out. On such an excursion, Slate is alarmed to see that the current is incredibly strong, pulling them along at a faster pace than they can counter. After a long struggle, exhausted by the effort, they manage to reach calmer waters further along the peninsula and stay close to the coast to make their way back to the cave.

That evening as they discuss the experience, it is clear that they need a better understanding of the currents. Slate says, "I have noticed that the current changes during the day and some days the water is quite still. We need to learn more before we venture out too far."

Moraine suggests, "Why don't we float some logs out and watch their path from the top of the mountain. We can attach a white pelt so we can see it from a distance."

Thus, they start a series of trials over many days until they can predict how fast the log will travel and what its route will take.

"Moraine, I feel quite sure that we can safely do this, but we don't know what happens to the currents near the other side. If we want to do this, we have to take that risk. What do you think?"

"We can do it, but we will need to take a reasonable supply of food in case we can't reach land."

Their final preparations take a day or two, during which time they secure the logs with new bindings and prepare a few paddles. Broach finds his best stone picture and attaches it to some protrusions on the cave wall with some twine taken from the reeds on the beach.

Watching the tides, Slate finally determines that conditions are right, and they set off. It is early in the morning, and a clear sky forecasts fine weather for the expedition. By noon they are well past the midpoint. As the Farland terrain comes into focus, they see trees lining the edge of a rocky beach, extending up a hillock. Paddling against a strengthening current, they manage to maintain their course for a while, but the closer they get to the land, the stronger the flow.

"Keep paddling, come on, we need to keep paddling." Slate shouts. With aching muscles, they keep going, but they cannot counter the current. Allowing the raft to drift a while, they see a bay area protected by an extension of the land.

Pointing, "One last try. If we can get closer to that strip of land, we may find a calm area." Redoubling their efforts, they soon see the end of the turbulent flow of the current, marked by a stretch of still waters. Tired, a bay unfolds before them as they enter a safe harbor. The exposure to unpredictable dangers and the release of tension at having accomplished what they set out to do, brings a sense of euphoria. They approach the shore with eyes wide in anticipation until the raft grinds to a halt on the gravelly beach. Seagulls greet them as they wade through the shallows to the beach, not realizing that they have set foot on a continent, the cradle of their humanity. The two eagles, Ayrial and Eyther, languidly circle overhead, then gracefully turn and, with a cry, swoop low as if in congratulation before heading back across the strait. The landing party watches as they disappear in the misty haze of their emotions, recalling, as it does, the epic journey that brought them here. The subconscious burden of the two children lost before birth lifts under the spell of a new beginning.

By nightfall, they secure an adequate shelter with the intent of exploring for better in the morning. The next day, their dream of the possibility of a welcoming party to greet them soon evaporates. No footprints in the sand, no sign of human activity, quickly dismisses that with certainty, bringing both disappointment and relief. The unspoiled surroundings provide freedom, otherwise not there if they had to share it with others.

Moraine helps Slate construct a shelter using the stems of long reeds, branches, and layers of broad leaves. The site provides a view across the bay and back to the chain of mountains on the other side of the strait with the towering outcrop below which they lived in their cave. The next day's exploration of the area reveals that they landed on a spit of land projecting into the strait. Their settlement is near the end of the peninsula. A slope leads to the top of a nearby mountain with a sheer drop off the one side. From here, a range of mountains is visible far inland. Returning to the beach and wandering along the shoreline brings them to a series of low cliffs that lead into the water at an angle. Near the point where the edge of one of the cliffs meets the water, a shallow cave provides the ideal location for a home with access to a nearby stream that brings fresh water from the mountain, small trees for shade, and a beach from which they can fish. By nightfall, they relocate to this place, feeling pleased with their decision to cross the waters.

* * *

Initially, their happiness knows no bounds, but as time passes, Broach's skin condition worsens, and his cough returns with severity. The potions that Gramater provided continue to bring relief, providing spells free of the ailment. The salve for the skin works wonders, and drops of the

129

menthol mixture help with the cough. To Moraine, a new concern arises as Slate too develops the same symptoms, and they too progressively but gradually worsen. Days of bright sunshine seem to exacerbate the problems for both of them. With two of them needing the potions, her concern grows with the rapid depletion of medicine.

Eventually, Broach cries with the pain and becomes bedridden. At this time, the potions provide little relief. Slate, distraught with concern for his son, spends many hours at his side comforting him. In the end, a fever takes hold of the boy, and he periodically lapses into semi-consciousness. Elle seems to understand his predicament and stays by his side until he finally succumbs.

Gently cradling the child, Slate takes the boy to a patch of soft earth not far from the cave entrance and lethargically begins to dig a grave. Each shovel of the earth extracts profound sadness as he weeps for his cherished child, then placing him in the resting place, he carefully closes his small hands around the two of his painted stones and covers the boy with soil.

Many days of mourning follow with Moraine sharing in his grief.

\* \* \*

Without Broach to play with the field mice, they decided to release Trine and Drift, the other field mouse, into the grasses near their shelter. The two quickly begin building a straw nest nearby and fend for themselves. In a little while, squeaks coming from the nest confirm the arrival of a litter.

Elle is not so fortunate. Being an alpine marmot, the warm conditions bring problems for her with her thick fur. Chunks of it begin falling out, and she loses all appetite. The types of food in the area are also foreign to her. As winter approaches, her condition deteriorates to the point where she is not ready for her usual hibernation, which requires her to begin the period in peak condition. She passed away in the fall, and Slate and Moraine buried her alongside Broach.

\* \* \*

Each day Moraine anxiously tends to Slate, who rapidly deteriorates. The once robust man withers under the onslaught of the malady with both his skin and cough worsening. In a temporary respite, the coughing ceases as he rests, but his skin festers with painful sores. In a desperate attempt at arresting the downward spiral, Moraine uses the remains of the salve for the skin, leaving the last jar of menthol for when needed. The lotion works its magic, and Slate improves to the extent that he can walk about, even remarking on the beauty of the view from the cave entrance. After several days free of the throbbing sting and with the cough abated, just as hope of recovery begins to grow, the cough returns with a vengeance. Helping him out of the glare of the sun into a corner in the cave, there Moraine watches over him, dampening his fevered forehead and feeding him with soft foods from berries and melons. Fearing the worst, she takes out the last of the urns, confirms the rich smell of menthol, tilts his head forward, and gives him a few drops. The reaction is almost immediate. He turns deathly pale, coughing to clear his throat, and speaks his last words, "I love you, Moraine." He closes his eyes and becomes still.

Aghast, Moraine staggers backward from his prostrate form as if struck by a blow. A violent shiver passes through her body as the realization penetrates her consciousness, "The urn, the potion, Gramater, what have you done?"

The container still in her grasp, sears her skin, its evil presence white-hot to the touch. Desperately she prizes it loose, and it falls to the ground, tilts on its side, its contents smoldering in the soft sand of the cave.

Rushing back to her lover, she holds him close as violent sobs wracked her body, "Slate, Slate, Slate, oh Slate! What have I done?"

Even as his body turns cold, she cannot leave him. The anguish of releasing him is unbearable. Her mind in a turmoil of torture cannot hold to what has happened until exhausted; she collapses alongside him, staring at the roof of the cave. For how long she cannot tell, the darkness of the night passes over and through her, and even as the glow of dawn lights the space, her mind fails to come to terms with the loss. The noon sun passes over to late afternoon and penetrates to shine on her from an angle. The cold of her torpor warmed by the rays stirs her. She looks about in a daze, and her worst fears are confirmed as Slate remains still, unmoved in death, next to her. Her mind turns to Gramater, and she cannot dismiss the image in her mind of the vessel on the shelf in her shelter with the red X marked on it. "Why, oh why did I not check it myself, destroy it. Why?"

A wave of guilt overwhelms her, and her anger at the evil of the old woman mounts, but as she turns to look at Slate, she sees the peacefulness of his kind face and realizes that there lies his power. She cannot allow the old woman to consume her with her evil.

A new certainty overwhelms her. Rising, she finds the urn and turns it upright. It still contains a small quantity of poison. Taking one of the paddles from the raft, she begins to dig a pit next to the grave of Broach. Slowly but surely, she heaps the soil alongside the hole, then, when satisfied with its depth, she places the body of her fallen partner in the grave. With deliberate care, she drags the raft over the grave, leaving a space at one end. Then, heaping the soil on top of the raft, she places all their belongings next to him and enters the space left open and lies alongside her man. Taking the last of Broach's painted stones, she places it in his hand. Raking some of the remaining soil through the opening, she partly covers their bodies. Closing her eye, she relives in her mind, the time from when she first set eyes on Slate, their attempted escape from the chase, their capture, and the joy of the union of Runt and Fern. With a smile on her face, she recalls the love Broach and Slate shared with her, their daring crossing of the waters, and the moments of joy they shared here on Farland. With her mind fixed on the brief but enduring happiness from when their paths crossed, with her hand on her chest, she listens to the pain of her love for Slate beating in her breast, and she swallows the last of the potion. A profound stillness envelopes her, and death draws its shroud over her.

# 15    Gramater

Gramater wakes to a sense of euphoria. An inexplicable elation suffuses her being as if a foreign force is flowing through her veins to invigorate her aging body. This mounting sense of accomplishment has been rising for some time, but now, like a wave from a distant source, long in coming, it has arrived. It instills in her a certainty that her plans will bear fruit. The happenings that demoted her stand, many moons in the past, appear entirely surmountable under this new energy. Plans that faltered and lay in tatters crystalize into a strategy, a scheme that will right previous wrongs.

Gramater muses, "I need a man. A strong one ... hmm, maybe Rasp, no Wart. Yes, Wart. Wart, it will be then, okay?"

A day later, sidling up to Wart, she probes, "You are looking strong, young man. What have you been doing?"

"Huh, old woman ... None of your business."

"Scat would stand no chance against you. You have grown so much," she lies.

Left to his thoughts, the suggestion begins to work on him. At every opportunity, Gramater reinforces his superior physical appearance until he reluctantly at first then more seriously considers the possibility that she may be right.

When the time is right, he happily responds to her, calling him for help with demanding tasks. Her undisguised admiration for his proficiency bolsters his ego, and with that, she feels he is ripe for the next step in her plan. "Wart, you know you should be appreciated more by everyone. I can see you have really good leadership qualities, and you know, I have seen how the women admire you. You should do more. You are born for more. You know that, don't you?"

"Well, I don't know, Runt is a good leader, and everyone likes Scat."

"True, but you could be so much more. It is unfortunate."

Left to consider her meaning, Wart cannot fathom how he might fulfill her ambitions for him. At a loss, he increasingly depends on her for guidance.

In her next step, she plants the seeds of her vengeance, offering him the control of the whole community if he should follow her instructions. Calling him to her work shelter, she whispers, "Wart. Only Runt stands in your way. He is such a weakling. He is just all mouth. Mouth, mouth, mouth, that is all he is. You shouldn't stand for it."

With that, Wart skulks off, sullen, in a confused state, but firmly in the web of Gramater's revenge for those that stand in opposition to her. Unsure of why he feels like he does but sure of his unhappiness, he feels assured that others seek to oppress him and rob him of a place of power. Gramater allows the wound to fester, amplifying the malevolence in him at every opportunity until, like a taut string, he is ready to release the building tension when commanded.

Feeling satisfied with her plans, Gramater opens the curtain that serves as a door to her shelter, revealing a scene across the familiar settlement they previously occupied. Stretching in the unaccustomed warmth of the sun, the day promises to shake loose from the grip of winter held steadfast for so long. Their journey from the mountain to this place extracted much from her frail frame. Then, closeted in her shelter struck down by debilitating depression, it now seems that it will lift, realizing that as she wallowed in self-pity and anger, the embryo she planted silently germinated and grew.

Fang, advanced in her swollen state, will be part of that plot, the means to Gramater's end. Superficially, ever attentive to Gramater, Fang annoyingly exercises her indispensability to Gramater's plans with smirks, sneers, and side glances that give away her disloyalty. Caught in the act, she quickly averts her gaze to hide her true intentions, leaving Gramater uncertain of her dependability.

Tusk, in the meantime, remains immobile in his separation from the community, moving only to accept proffered food and to relieve himself. To Gramater, he serves only one purpose, insurance for if the first impregnation fails and a second is needed. After that, his purpose will have been served, and he can be discarded like useless garbage. In the work shelter with

Gramater's medicines arrayed on shelves along one side, he spends his days snoring loudly while daily growing fat from inaction.

Runt and Fern, on the other hand, daily depict their irritating happiness, infecting the community as they too await the birth of an offspring burgeoning inside Fern. Observing from her enclosure, Gramater watches the pair in the central clearing of the settlement. Suppressing a wave of rising anger, she mutters, "Your days are numbered" and returns their greetings with a joyless smile masking her inner hatred.

The two mothers' due date rapidly approaches with Gramater spending time in her medicine shack toying with the potions and muttering a mix of suppressed anger, self-encouragement, and fragments of her emerging plan. Tusk, in periods of coherence, listens to her confused ramblings catching only snippets of her intent that carry no meaning. Dismissing these as one in the throes of dementia, he turns his back and covers his face to blot out the noise, but her rattling noise takes on more urgency as the days pass.

Following the sighting of a small group of reindeer by their scouts, under Runt's direction, Scat, and a band of his fellows, set off on the hunt. Concerned at the rapidly dwindling supply of food under the severity of the climate, Runt urged Scat to lead the hunt. With Fern's child due any day, Runt excuses himself from the expedition in favor of staying with Fern to await the birth. Scat questions Runt, "Who will be helping Fern with the birth? I hope you are not trusting Gramater to do it. She is still filled with vengeance. Who knows what she will do?"

"I spoke with Fern about that. We decided to let her do it. She is the only person who knows what to do. The other women don't have experience as midwives. You know how she kept that to herself. Anyhow, the old woman has been trying to be friendly lately, so we decided to let her do it."

"Well, be careful. Okay?"

With the hunting party absent, fate conspires to lend a hand to Gramater's plans when both Fang and Fern simultaneously go into labor, Fang being premature in her season, whereas Fern is at full term.

Crowded in her work shelter with Tusk to one corner, surprised at the events, Gramater hurriedly prepares her usual midwifery routine for delivering the babies. She takes in a deep breath and turns to the two prospective mothers, "Okay, I want you to stay calm, breathe deeply, and follow my instructions."

It seems that Fang will deliver first while Fern moans in her agony alongside. Outside, Runt anxiously paces back and forth and stops periodically to draw the curtain and check on Fern's progress. Addressing Gramater, he says, "Gramater, don't you need someone else with you to help? You can't do this alone."

Ignoring him, she continues fiddling with the potions and utensils. A few moments later, with rising tension in his voice, "Gramater, please, can I help. You can tell me what to do."

"Look, mister. Shut up, I need to concentrate."

For a third time, Runt interrupts, but before he can speak, she says, "You are useless to me. Go and call Wart. He can help with removing the mess after it is done. Go!"

Runt runs off and with Wart by his side, "I have got Runt. Must he come in?"

"No, just wait there. I will call when I need him."

By this time, Fang is crying aloud as the pain comes in waves. Tusk, wide awake in his corner, pulls the covering over his head to shut out the noise. As Fang reaches the climax of her agony, Fern's pain rises to a pitch. Working methodically, Gramater issues calming commands to Fern while tending to the child that is emerging from Fang. Moments later, the infant is born, and a weak cry confirms its first breath and the severing of the umbilical cord. Gramater inspects the baby and with some concern for its prematurity and color. Faintly worried, she double-checks then shrugs, satisfied that with some care, the child will survive. Carefully placing the baby in her mother's arms, she says, "You have delivered me a boy. Well done. He is small, so you will need to feed him well."

While Fern's struggles with the contractions and Fang lies exhausted and semi-conscious, Gramater, feeling satisfied with the first step in her unfolding plan, turns her attention to the more difficult next steps. Muttering to herself, she says, "Now to finish off the rest. First, poison for the bitch, Fern, and her baby as soon as it comes out. Let her suffer first. Easy to make it look like a failed birth. Hah! Then kill that runt, Runt … Wart, you had better be ready!"

Taking up a bone knife, she stabs it into a nearby log where it remains quivering to emphasize its menacing purpose. "Last is this sorry misfit, Tusk. Wart can do that dirty work too, and dump the bodies, who cares, Wart can take the blame. Who cares?"

Alarmed at what he is hearing, Tusk remains motionless, holding his breath, drenched in sweat, wondering what to do, thinking, "I must do something … don't care much for me but, but not them. I have wronged them. Oh, what to do. I don't have the strength."

Anticipating a long birthing process, Gramater calls Runt, who is quick to open the entrance, "Your wife is in trouble. I expect the birth to take a long time. Leave us, and I will call you when I need you. Tell Wart to remove this mess. Fang has had a boy."

"No, no, I will wait here. Wart! Gramater wants you."

"I don't want you hanging around here. Go. It will be night before anything happens. Besides, it is bad luck for a man to be present at the birth. I am going now. I need to rest for a while and return when it is time."

Sensing something wrong and unsure what to do, Runt decides to return to his shelter rather than test the veracity of her warning.

Time stretches into the night, and still, Fern struggles with the contractions. At length, with the pain at its peak, Gramater responds to her heightened cries and returns to her side. By the dim light of a flame in a wick floating in animal oils, not long and a baby emerges. Gramater examines the infant, curious about its small size, wondering, "Small devil, must have inherited it from Runt," and continues to clean up the afterbirth, but when the contractions continue, she realizes that a second child is on the way. The exertions extend for a long time, and ultimately the child is born, with Ferns exhausted and on the verge of unconsciousness. Gramater looks about; all is quiet. Fang is quietly feeding the child, and Tusk is motionless in the corner. Speaking softly, she murmurs, "Now is as good a time as any ... one at a time." Taking the child from Fern, she wraps it in a covering then gently smothers it. A tiny jerk confirms its death. She lays it next to the other child next to Fern, where its small eyes stare up at Gramater in accusing innocence. Gramater shudders and turns her face from the grim indictment. She dispels the guilty charge with an evil glint and bends over the first child to administer her twisted judgment on the hapless infant. As she bends over to carry out the foul deed, a movement in Tusk's corner catches her eye, and she stops and pretends to attend to its comfort. Deciding to defer the act to a later time, she resumes cleaning up. With a last glance around the scene of her crime, she emerges from the shelter to find Runt at the door.

With a flash of angry surprise, she blurts out, "Fern, has given birth. Two children. One is dead."

"Is Fern alright? Can I see her?"

"No, she is asleep. Leave her alone, she is okay. Go!"

Taken aback by her attitude, Runt ignores the command and opens the flap to peer into the gloom where the last of the candle still burns. In the dim light, he can make out the form of Fern, Fang, and Tusk. All is quiet. Satisfied, he backs out and returns to his shelter.

Tusk, rigid with fear, his heart racing, cannot believe what he just witnessed. As the old woman leaves the enclosure, he stares up at the thatched roof. Certain that the fright that induced him to move may have saved the other child, his mind turns in a turmoil, "What can I do? What, what. I can't move ... the pain. But I must! Runt, Fern, then me. We are all in danger."

As time passes, the candle dwindles while Fang still exhausted from her ordeal, fends off sleep, the child suckles feebly at her breast. As weariness begins to overwhelm her, she jerks awake and drinks some water to stay awake. Gramater is absent; otherwise, she would ask her to move the baby so she can rest without sharing the space with the child. In the gloom of the night, she redoubles her effort to stay awake until Gramater returns and decides to move the child herself. Surprised at how small it is, she lifts the bundled child as she sits up. Moving the covering aside to look at his face, she sees no movement. It is still. Clearing more of the soft fur for a better view, to her alarm, it remains limp and motionless. Feeling for a heartbeat, she finds just the faintest throb. Falling back, she lies, looking up, wondering what to do. At length, a decision begins to formulate in her mind. With Tusk's clear abhorrence of her, she understands that a repeat at conceiving him is doomed to failure, and with that, her life under Gramater will be unbearable and potentially fatal. In the failing light of the candle, she takes up the child and feels her way to Fern's sleeping place. Guiding her hand over the prostrate forms, she can make out Fern's shape and the two children. Careful not to disturb Fern, she delves into the bundle of one of the children, feeling for its heartbeat and finds it quite vigorous. Slipping the child out, she exchanges it for hers and returns to her sleeping mat, feeds the child, then places it at her feet and, exhausted, falls asleep.

Day breaks to the sound of activity in the settlement. Gramater soon appears at the entrance, looks around, and sees Runt at his hut door. Ignoring him, she enters to find Fang asleep with her child contentedly gurgling little noises, at her feet. Moving to Fern, she examines her intently, dispassionately like a spider hovering over its prey. The color has returned to her face, and she seems to be sleeping. The baby next to her stirs, its dry mouth opening and closing, looking to suckle. The other child lies cold and stiff in death. Gramater stares for long moments at the scene, her mind churning with choices; when to act, what to do? Startled, she averts her gaze as Tusk repositions himself murmuring in a semi-wakeful state. Deferring a decision, Gramater takes up the deceased child, wraps the covering tighter, and then shakes Fern, who wakes with a start. Immediately turning to look for her newborn child, she sees it and grasps it to her breast to begin feeding. Gramater, standing over her, allows a few moments to pass then coldly breaks the news, "You had twins. Here is the other one ... dead."

For a moment, Fern fails to grasp the import of her words. As Gramater watches, her face turns from an expression of joy at feeding her child to anguish, "What, where ... no ... no ... is that my child? Give me my child," she shouts, grasping the swaddling clothes but momentarily recoils in

139

horror at the stiff, cold form in her hands. Overcome with grief, and with returning composure, she holds the child close and cries bitter tears, sobbing quietly.

"Runt, where is Runt?" she shouts, and with that, Runt enters, ignoring Gramater, he goes straight to Fern and holds her with the children in his arms. Feeling her despair, he looks from the immobile form to the other. Mirroring her anguish, he struggles between joy and sorrow then quietly to Fern whispers, "Fern, I love you, and we can be thankful that one survived. We will give him a name, I see it is a little boy, and then when you are ready, we will honor him with a burial. I am proud of you, Fern. When you are ready, I will take him to our shelter and wait for you to recover. Okay? Now rest and get strong. We need you."

Gramater interrupts, "Both children are very small. Fern will have to stay here so that I can see to her. The birth was difficult, and she needs rest. Come back this evening, and you can see her again."

Taken aback by her abruptness, Runt answers, "I will wait a while, thank you."

Gramater shrugs and exits the work shelter leaving the two mothers with Tusk and Runt. As she enters her hut, she signals to Wart to come to her. In the shelter, she says, "Wart, I want you here as the sun is setting. Are you ready for the work that you are destined for?"

"Yes, yes, Gramater. What is it that I must do?"

"Runt has had a boy, and his head is swollen with pride. The boy is like his father, small, sick, and pathetic, he won't last long. Runt thinks he is sooo important. It is time for you to take command before he starts bossing everyone around. You will see he will pick on you because you are so strong. He'll give you the worst work to do. You can't let him do that, can you?"

"No, I'll show that little ... what must I do?"

"Bring along a heavy club. Runt will be there to visit Fern. When he is in the work hut, I will distract him, and you can put him out of his misery with that club. Can you do that? When I bend over Fern to give her some medicine that is when you must deal with Runt."

"But, do you think we should … yes, I can do it. YES, I can do it," he says, trying to convince himself of her expectation.

"That's it. I can see you are strong. You can do anything. Now look, I will take care of Fern, so don't worry about her, but I want you to come back around midnight and remove the body. Bury him somewhere where no one can find him. They tell me, there is a sinkhole down near the river and along a bit, throw the body in the pit. That would be the best. They say it is very deep. Okay, you understand, no one must find him. Say nothing, and in the morning, I will tell everyone that you are in charge. Oh, also, when Scat returns from hunting, he will think he is in charge. Play along, and in a few days, I will see to him as well."

$$* * *$$

Gramater feels that familiar wave of euphoria sweeping over her again. "Today is my day. Justice will be done. That little man and his foreign slut. They will be no more. Hah. Just Tusk and Scat, then things will be back to normal."

Eager for the day to pass quickly, she spends the day checking over the concoctions she brought with her from the work shed, fondling them like precious jewels, going over in her mind the plan, and visualizing the outcome. "Once again, people will respect me and obey me. Most important will be the new child, my child, by Fang. Hmm … What name to give my heir? Let's see, Bull or Beast? No, something with strength, and that commands respect. Auroch, yes, Auroch. He will be Auroch!" From then on, she refers to the child by this name.

The day drags respite her efforts to urge it along. By nightfall, a sense of frustration builds on her impatience, translating into mounting anger as her mood swings from the earlier euphoria. Finally, the time is right, and she takes up her staff, bundles the potions into a wrapping, and hobbles her way across to the shed. Inside the gloom, all is as she had left it. Fern is feeding the child, Tusk has his back turned, and Fang is asleep with her baby at her feet, contently sleeping.

She walks to the corner where her medicines are stored and arranges the ones she brought with her in a pretense of business. Outside, the light of day seeps away as the veil of darkness spreads. Taking this as the signal, Wart nonchalantly takes the club, nervously weighs it in his hand yet again as an assurance of its suitability, and steps out into the open. All is quiet. He sees movements in Runt's shelter as he too prepares to visit his companion and offspring. Retreating into his enclosure, Wart decides to let Runt proceed first. Not long and Runt emerges, strides across to the work shed, opens the flap, and disappears inside. Wart follows and enters. Runt turns to him in surprise and opens his mouth to question his presence when Gramater says, "Thank you for coming Wart. Just wait there. You can help me when I am done with these medicines."

Inside, with six adults crowded in the enclosure, Tusk now fully awake but with eyes closed, listens, and waits. An intangible tension pervades the atmosphere, mounting with time, as no one speaks. Taut like a trap about to be sprung, he waits. Increasingly he feels a building certainty that an evil deed is about to be perpetrated. Mobilizing his inner reserves, he decides he must act, but wonders what from the menace will manifest itself. Then it happens!

Gramater takes an urn and shuffles over to Fern and says, "Set aside the child, I need to give you your medicines."

Runt moves to help, but Gramater intervenes, "Runt, stay back, I can manage." Fern stops feeding the child, wraps the boy up carefully, and places the child next to her with her arm around the infant.

Gramater extends the urn to Fern with a gesture to drink. On cue, Wart strikes. Pandemonium breaks loose as Runt slumps noiselessly to the ground, the blow to his head, instantly fatal. Surprise and horror spread across Fern's face as the import of the event penetrated her disbelief. In her alarm, she jerks the proffered urn aside, which shatters on the floor, spilling its contents. The noise snaps Tusk out of his inactive stupor, surprised at the suddenness of the attack. With a burst of adrenaline-induced energy which suppresses the pain in his groin, he launches himself at Wart and, in doing so, knocks Gramater to the ground. Wart, caught in the act of raising the club for a second blow, is violently thrust to the ground dispersing the assorted urns

142

in a crash. As he struggles to his feet, Tusk grabs Fern by the arm urges, "You are in danger, mortal danger. You must escape. Hurry, you must escape. These people mean you harm."

Fern, confused by the turn of events, questions, "But, I don't understand."

"You don't have time, take the baby, come!"

Combined with her maternal instinct to protect her newborn and the undisguised urgency on Tusk's face, Fern is moved to trust in him. She takes up the child in a single motion, and with Tusk still holding her arm, they exit the shelter.

Meanwhile, Wart slips on the spreading potions on the floor mat of the animal hide and falls to the ground only to slip and fall again before righting himself. Gramater, nursing a painful hip from her fall, struggles to stand until assisted by Wart. By this time, the darkness of night has cast its shadow over the settlement. To avoid attracting attention from others in the settlement, Gramater urges in a loud whisper, "Get them! You can't let them get away."

In groping to find the exit, they stumble over the prostrate form of Runt, wasting time until when they emerge, there is no sign of the pair.

# 16    Grotto

Stumbling in the darkness with the ghostly whiteness of the snow providing some visibility, Tusk leads the way with Fern following closely. Taking care not to trip and fall and injure the infant, Fern tries to slow the pace as Tusk urges her along. They soon arrive at the edge of the frozen river and follow its course upstream.

Unsure of the wisdom of fleeing, Fern asks, "Are you sure we should be doing this? Others in the settlement will come to our help if we appeal to them. I need to go back to help Runt. He may need help."

"No, we can't do that. It would be suicide, Fern. Runt is dead. Please, you must understand, he could not survive a blow to the head like that. Also, I overheard Gramater. She intends to kill Scat when he returns. I think she will be poisoning him."

Breathlessly she asks, "Why did you decide to help me? I thought you disliked us."

Panting and interspersing his words with agonizing pauses as he tries to minimize the jabbing hurt in his midriff, "I am so sorry for all I have done ... to you and Runt and especially ... Moraine. I have no excuse for my actions, but Gramater had me in her spell ... Everything I did was to satisfy the hold she had over me."

"I can see what you mean."

"I don't care about myself now, I deserve whatever happens to me, but Gramater planned to kill me as soon as Fang gave birth. You see ... I am the last in Gramater's family line. Now that she has had her baby by me, I am next in line for discarding. Fang forced herself on me. It would be easy for her to get rid of me ... I am helpless with this injury."

They silently trudge along at a steady pace. After a while, Tusk says, "If you want me to take you back to the camp when Scat is back, I can do that."

"I don't know what to do. Where are we going?"

"There is a cave up the next tributary. You may remember it. You stayed there with Slate. Remember?"

"Oh, yes, I do."

"We can rest there, and you can decide what you would like to do. Okay?"

"Yes, yes, that is a good idea."

* * *

Wart returns to the work shelter where Gramater has a candle burning, "I can't find them. It's impossible in this dark. I don't know which way they went."

"Idiot! How could you let Tusk get the better of you? He is only half a man." Giving the prostrate form of Runt on the ground a kick, she adds, "Take him. Find that pit I told you about and dump him in there. The ground is too frozen for you to dig a hole, so find the pit. I don't care if it takes you all night, find it! Also, go to Runt's shelter and take the dead child. Throw him into the pit with Runt. Understand?"

Fang remained silent throughout the ordeal. Surprised beyond measure at the extremes to which the old woman is prepared to go, she trembles in fear, realizing that she will have to toe the line in the future. Her mounting confidence and sense of indispensability may be an illusion. The woman could turn on her at the slightest provocation. She must safeguard the guarantor of her life, the protection granted by the stolen child. Without it, she is surely lost.

Tired, ridden with guilt and unsure of his future, Wart returns to find Gramater absent from the work shed.  He staggers over to her sleeping quarter and calls her name.

The response is curt, "Did you find the pit?"

"Yes ... what must I do now?"

"Go, sleep, and say nothing. Do you hear me? Nothing! I will deal with it in the morning."

145

Turning, he shuffles to the communal quarters, feels his way to his bed mat, lies down, and stares at the darkness until exhaustion overwhelms him, and he falls asleep.

Gramater too lies in the pitch blackness, staring with blank eyes, her mind circling through what to do. The day started with promise, now this, what to do? Periodically cursing out loud, she discards one choice for another until left with one, she decides. Do nothing. They are gone. Where to? "I don't know."

\* \* \*

Day breaks with more snow. Unhurried, Gramater rises, puts on another pelt against the cold wind, and steps out into the open, the first to do so. Wandering over to the work shed, she enters to find Fang wide-eyed looking at her. Noting the look of fear, Gramater feels reassured that the woman has not and will not counter her again. "You Fang, it is your job to bring up that child in good health. Say nothing about events from last night. Let me do the talking."

"Y ... yes, okay, okay."

Stepping back out into the drifting snow, she walks to Runt's shelter, opens the door, peers inside, then walks to the communal quarters, enters, and shouts, "Do any of you know where Runt is?"

Silence greets her. "If you see him, tell him I need to speak with him."

\* \* \*

Thankfully the water at the confluence of the tributary and the main river is frozen, making it easy to negotiate the bend and proceed along the embankment lining the tributary. Staying close to the edge of the icy stream where the path through the undergrowth is more visible, they steadily make progress. Fern's ordeal with giving birth to twins and Tusk's discomfort and periodic stabbing pains gradually slow their passage. With some relief, Fern is first to point out that they are opposite the location of the cave at the foot of the cliff. The snow begins falling heavily as they walk up the escarpment and enter the cave. Fern looks around in the gloom and sees that it is as they left it months ago. Relieved to take the weight off their feet, they sink to the soft sand. Fern, without hesitation, begins feeding the child while Tusk stretches out to reduce the piercing pain.

Fern says, "The walk hasn't been kind to the baby. He is suckling very weakly."

Finishing the feeding, she asks, "What are we going to do for food?"

"I will see what I can do in the morning. I have nothing to work with, so I will have to start from scratch. The reeds by the river would be a good start to make a spear."

A fitful night brings the dawn, and Tusk sets out to equip himself to hunt for food. In the meantime, Fern finds dry brush, leaves, and sticks in the cave to start a fire. As time passes, she increasingly becomes concerned at the absence of Tusk.

Around noon, he finally limps up the incline, despondently slumps to the ground, exhausted and without food. "I think I wounded a rabbit, but it got away. Tried to follow it but, in the process, twisted myself. I think I worsened this injury. I had to give up the chase."

"Rest awhile. You may feel better later. Is there anything I can do to help?"

"No, no, you also need to rest. You don't look too good yourself. Is the baby alright?"

"Yes, the birth was not easy on me, and the baby is terribly small. So fragile. As long as I have milk, I think the child will be okay, but we will need food and also water."

"I can get some snow and melt that for you."

*　*　*

At mid-morning and Gramater sounds the alarm; Runt and Fern have disappeared. A search is launched, but without success, the snow blanket makes it impossible to find tracks. As the people return from the woods, rumors begin circulating, some suspicious of Gramater. Others talk of the possible return of Slate and Moraine and that they enticed Fern and Runt away. This finds traction, which Gramater amplifies by reminding everyone of Moraine's original disloyalty in choosing to desert the clan.

Under Gramater's direction, Fang disguised the spot that Tusk occupied to feign the form of a man asleep to avoid questions about his absence. Two days later, Gramater announces Tusk's death resulting from the dagger in his groin and that Wart has buried him. As a distraction from the events, Gramater retakes responsibility for preparing for the smoking of the meat from the hunt. Ice chests are ready, and fire pits dug and covered from the persistent snow to await the hunters. By the conclusion of these activities, Gramater once again feels in control of the situation and prepares herself for the return of the hunting party. Feeling secure with having duped the clan with the story of Runt's disappearance with Fern and the explanation of Tusk's demise, she decides to continue with this narrative.

Three days later, Scat and his troupe arrive. Curious as to the subdued welcome, as they deposit the deer at the side of the fire pits, Scat queries the absence of Runt. In disbelief, he hears the explanation, "Surely Fern wouldn't leave with a newborn baby," he questions.

Gramater remains silent, allowing the people to voice their belief, but Scat increasingly becomes adamant that the explanation is not valid, finally saying, "I don't believe this one bit. Who first noticed their absence?"

All eyes turn to Gramater, who calmly says, "I went to the work shelter in the morning, and they were gone. Ask Fang, she was in the shelter all the time."

"Where is Fang?"

Fang, who has been listening to this exchange from the shelter, emerges with the child at her bosom.

"Fang, did you see Runt leave."

"I ... I was asleep. Resting after the birth," rocking the baby for effect, I heard some noises but didn't think much of it. I presume ... I presume it was then that they left."

"And where is Tusk, call him. I want to hear from him."

Gramater answers, "Tusk died yesterday from the wound that he had. It has been festering for a while."

"Where is he buried?"

"You can ask Wart here, I asked him to bury him."

"Wart, where is he?"

"I ... I threw him in the ... the pit."

"Is Runt in there as well?"

Trapped and unsure what to say, Wart hesitates and looks at Gramater. An "aaahh" spreads through the crowd as their original suspicions begin to take root, prompting Scat to say, "Take us there. I think you must show us where he is buried. Runt is buried there? Right, Wart?"

Gramater gives him a withering look of anger to which Wart lowers his head and remains silent, the color drained from his face.

"Won't answer? Okay then, come, let's go and see for ourselves," and he starts to go. Gramater turns to go back to her shelter, at which Scat says, "Gramater, you must also come."

With that, led by Scat, the crowd follows as they make their way to the river's edge, along with and up an embankment, to the pit.

Here Scat says to Wart, "Is this the pit that you threw him into?"

Wart remains silent. Peering over the edge, Scat makes out the form of a body in the dark shadows. Righting himself, he says, "Well, Wart, is that him?"

Wart moves forward then stops without looking into the pit, "I ... I ... I don't need to look." Turning to Gramater next to him, he blurts out, "It is Runt! I don't know why I did it. I killed him."

A gasp of surprise spreads through the gathered crowd as they press nearer.

149

Breaking down, he confesses, "I was taken in by Gr ... Gramater promised me ... we planned it. I am sorry. I should never ..."

Silence grips the congregation for moments, then he continues, "Fern had twins. One died, and Gramater was going to poison her."

Scat asks, "Where is Fern, then?"

Speaking more coherently, looking down in shame, he resumed, "It was Tusk who stopped Gramater from poisoning Fern. He stopped me from hitting Runt again. I hit him from the back on the head. We were in the work shelter."

Standing next to Wart, Gramater turns pale with each word uttered. As her world falls apart, she seems to become frailer with each passing moment and begins shaking uncontrollably, aging perceptibly before their eyes.

Wart continues, in a low voice, "Tusk took Fern and the child. They escaped in the dark. I could not find them."

A murmur of astonishment ripples through the audience as they turn to each other, realizing that Tusk's confinement had changed his very nature. Pressing closer, someone says, and others repeat with anger rising, "They might still be alive" questioning. "Where are they? We must find them. Where are they?"

Scat interrupts, "Where did they go?"

"I ... I don't know. It was dark. I think they went to the river."

One of the group begins barging forward, shaking his fists in anger, demanding to know where they went. As he draws nearer, the press of the crowd pushes Wart, Gramater, and Scat closer to the edge of the pit.

Scat shouts, "Stand back, stand ..."

Before he could complete his sentence, Gramater teeters at the edge of the pit and loses her balance. Wart, lunging to arrest her fall, he too loses his footing. She disappears down the shaft, and he tumbles in after her with

150

a despairing cry. Everyone looks at each other horror-struck. Scat, shading his eyes, staring into the depth, says, "Surely, it's too deep to survive ... I don't see any movement, listen ... there is no sound!"

After a while, with no sign of the pair, some of the people begin to return to the camp,

Scat says to Rasp, "You know, the only place they can be is at that cave where we first saw Slate. We need to go there in the morning. Can you be ready? You and I can search in that direction. It is too late to start now."

*  *  *

As the sun sinks to the horizon, Tusk sets out again with a pair of pointed reeds. "I will try again before the sun sets. With some luck, I may find something."

Again he returns empty-handed and much worse for wear and barely able to stand. Fern is not much help, experiencing persistent abdominal pains, and the child lolls weakly in her arms, unable to feed. The night exacerbates their problems with a cold draft even in the depth of the cave, relentlessly exposing their unprepared state. Only the fire provides some relief but needs frequent stoking to keep it going. By morning, cold and despondent, Tusk offers, "I think I will have to go back to the camp. If Scat is there, he will help. If not, we will be at the old woman's mercy."

"Yes, I think that is all we can do. How long before you get back?"

"Tomorrow morning. If I can't make it, I will send one of the other men with food."

"Okay, Tusk. Take care of yourself."

Around mid-morning, Fern is surprised to see Tusk struggling up the incline to the cave, even crawling on hands and feet for the last stretch. Collapsing at the entrance, he says, "I just can't go. Sorry but the fall I had chasing the rabbit yesterday has done more damage than I thought. I bleed from the backside. The pain is unbearable."

Comforting Tusk, whose face is pale and drawn with pain, Fern says, "You have done your best, Tusk. There is nothing more you can do. We will have to hope that Scat remembers this cave and sends someone. That's our only hope."

Tusk, moaning quietly, lapses into a semi-conscious state while Fern, feeling equally bad, tends to her child who has not moved for a while. Urging the baby to wake for feeding fails, and her only resort is to provide comfort and warmth against her body. Fearing the worst, she sings a gentle calming song to the child, and after a short while, it succumbs. With tears streaming down her cheek, she resolves to bury it in the morning. One last night in her arms provides her with a measure of comfort.

* * *

Scat and Rasp set out early, making quick progress along the river and tributary. By noon they climb the incline to the cave. All is still as they approach. Entering the cave, they find Tusk in a seated position leaning against the rock face. He is cold in death. Fern, lying in the far end of the cave with the child wrapped close to her, is in a fetal position, looking at the child's face. Approaching, Scat shakes her. She is warm to the touch, but, like the baby, she too is dead.

No words are spoken as they silently consider the scene. Had they arrived earlier, she may have been saved. Taking their time, they hollow out a depression in the cave and place the bodies in the grave. Standing over them, they quietly offer their respect, then cover them with soil and sadly make their way back to the camp.

The news is greeted with sadness by their fellow villagers. On the following day, Scat suggests that they break camp and depart from this unhappy site.

# 17    Later

Ten years later. The mountains from where they embarked on the new dispensation under the leadership of Scat lies on the far horizon under a pale sky. Undulating hills are now their nomadic home, and the once dark skies, having dissipated with time, have returned the land to its former warmth and abundance.

Within the brutish outer appearance of the man that led them from the events of mountains lies a gentle disposition with a profound sense of fairness. These, the hallmarks of a good leader, serve the clan well. Learning from the lessons of caring and joy, so briefly experienced with Fern in their midst, instilled in them happiness, which Scat nurtures at every opportunity. The wisdom of Runt becomes the model on which they measure their values. The resulting cohesiveness is cherished each day. They help each other, share duties, and, most of all, embrace the pristine world, at one with nature and its bounty.

Of all the people in the community, Fang stands alone and at odds with the prevailing kindnesses shown by everyone, but she has learned to disguise her inner vindictiveness to achieve a measure of acceptance. As Auroch, Fern's child stolen by Fang, grows, his resemblance to Fern becomes apparent. His straw-colored hair and happy demeanor so closely mirror Fern's that people begin to question his parentage. When approached on the subject, Fang adamantly defends her stance that Tusk was the father. Rather than allow a wedge to form, Scat intervenes to quash the divisions. Emphasizing the importance of the moment they live in, rather than delve into an unchangeable past, he points to the rich daily life that Auroch brings to the community. At this time, Auroch is the center of everyone's pride and joy as his open zest for life infects everyone. He truly is the product of everyone in the clan.

With time, a realization begins to dawn on the people. Slowly by degrees, they and Scat realize that they owe their contentment to the people from 'the mountains' as they refer to them. Moraine's name takes on a mystical aura with Slate, Fern, and Runt making up a quartet for reverence with Broach and his vulnerabilities, being an addendum that unfurls the inherent goodness of his former caretakers, Slate and Fern, for everyone to see. Stories abound around Moraine, Slate, and Broach's possible fate, with fictional elaborations becoming the staple of stories told to the young. Folklore of adventure, heroism, and endurance arises around their characters with even Elle, the marmot, having a role to play. Songs are sung, and dances danced in their honor. Theirs is a society built on truth and honesty.

As the herds of reindeer move to new pastures, the band follows. The occasion of these moves draws great excitement as new terrain is explored. Rivers, forests, lakes, and all manner of creatures are encountered to their wonder. Scouts, whose responsibility it is to reconnoiter the unfolding world ahead, becomes a much sought after responsibility. They have to locate the herds and find suitable sites for setting up camp with a source of water nearby and natural features that offer shelter from the elements. Growing children under the guardianship of an assigned adult teach them hunting, tracking, and reading the habits of the birds and creatures of the land. Dangerous animals such as sabretooth cats and woolly mammoths regularly present danger, and lessons on avoiding them are part of their instruction.

With Auroch having reached the required age, it is with great excitement that he prepares his spear and packs a quantity of dried food. Scat leads the group, and Rasp is assigned as his mentor. For days they walk with Scat, always checking his bearings against the distant mountains, the hills and the sun during the day and the stars at night, to ensure that he can retrace his steps to the camp. On the fifth day, they find themselves at the crest of a hill with a view overlooking a wide valley and a broad meandering river, curving its way around smaller undulating hills.

Scat calls a halt, "This is about as far as we should go. See that sheltered alcove where the river turns, at the foot of that bank? That looks as good as any place for a camp. Let's have a closer look, and if it is good, two of you can remain here, and the rest of us can return to help the others move."

Nods indicate agreement as they take in the verdant expanse of trees and the picturesque landscape with the blue sky reflecting off the winding river. Rasp observes, "Yes, the river should attract animals, and there will be fish as well. It looks like a good choice."

As they descend the gentle slope through stands of trees and meadow clearings, a profusion of birds, small and large mammals, and various insects that crawl or fly, from ants to butterflies to moths and bees, greet them as they make their way in the gentle breeze. A succession of smaller hills intervenes, and at each hilltop, the vista draws them in as they approach the river.

It is Auroch who first notices it, excitedly pointing, "Look, look, there!"

Everyone stops to follow his indicating hand. There, on the far side of the river, obscured by some trees, smoke curls lazily in a column, then, caught by the breeze it drifts away."

Scat is first to react, "Take cover ... hide. Quick get out of sight!

Rasp grabs Auroch's arm as they melt into the surrounding foliage, glancing about to the rear, sides, and front, with practiced purpose, to ensure that they are alone. After some moments, Scat steps out of hiding to proclaim, "Okay, we seem to be safe but be alert. We don't want to be taken by surprise."

Edging into the open while maintaining a defensive posture in readiness for an attack, they surround Scat in a loose group and move forward.

"It has been many years since we crossed paths with another group. We need to make sure that they are friendly before approaching them."

After exchanging some ideas on how to proceed, Scat says, "Okay, Grate and Grunt, I want you to stay here with Auroch. Make sure you are well hidden, stay out of sight. If anyone comes, try to move away before they see you. Your job is to keep Auroch safe."

Tapping Rasp on the shoulder, he says, "You and I will go nearer to see how many we are dealing with and whether they look dangerous. The rest of you form a perimeter around Rasp and Auroch, just within shouting distance, but no shouting, just whistle the usual warning signals to Rasp. Okay?"

Scat and Rasp disappear into the forest in the direction of the column of smoke. From the observation point, Auroch watches the open area leading to the river. After some time, he sees Rasp and Scat appear in the clearing at the water's edge. Their greatest danger lies in being exposed while crossing the river. They spend some time checking before safely wading across the waist-deep water. Keeping obscuring bushes between them and their target, crouching low, they approach cautiously, stopping now and then to check that they are still undetected. Finally, they reach close enough to watch the activities. Observing the movements around the fire for a while, satisfied that they have seen enough from that vantage point, they circle to the left to get a view from that angle. In a while, they retreat, re-cross the river, and return to the waiting group.

Scat explains while his party listens in rapt attention, "There must be about twenty people. They were not aware of us, so they were going about their business without showing signs of being watched. There seem to be more men than women, and the men are quite well built and in good condition. It would not be easy to overcome them if it came to that. There are about four wolf-like dogs tied up in the center of the clearing. They look quite fierce. They were fighting over scraps of food thrown there by three men busy roasting meat over the fire. The curious thing is that three people are tied to a pole on long leashes just out of reach of the dogs. From our distance, the three looked in bad shape."

Rasp asks what the others probably wanted to know, "The compound, would it be safe to enter? Should we go there? You know, to greet them?"

Unsure Scat vacillates, "Well, I don't know. Something tells me they won't be friendly. Look, I know that it has been many years since we have seen anyone, and you want to exchange news and even join forces with them, but it could turn bad. We have to be careful."

Grunt grumbles, "What do you want to do now? We were going to explore this area to set up camp for the rest of us."

Scat replies, "Well, clearly, that is not possible. This area is taken by these people. We will have to start back to the camp and find some other place along the way. But before we do that, I think we should spend more time observing them and make a decision after we are more certain about whether they will welcome us."

The next day, on a signal from across the river, Scat motions to the rest of the group to join him and Rasp. This time they approach from above until behind a large boulder with dense foliage surrounding it. The view is better and offers more vegetation to camouflage their presence. The activities in the camp are again routine, although, after a while, four or five of the men seem to be preparing to leave, apparently for hunting purposes, given the spears, long straight branches, and plaited thongs to bind the animals for carrying purposes. They also have sleeping mats, implying at least one night out. Sure enough, they soon depart for the river and walk along the bank, heading upstream. The routine in the camp resumes with the woman performing more of the work while the men laze in the warmth of the sun. The three tied to the central pole still languish in their discontent. At this distance, it is apparent that two are older, a man and a woman, and the third is a young man. An unusually large male strolls around the central area barking instructions at the women. One points to the three bound to the pole, at which the man takes a whip and administers a few painful lashes on the older man who silently endures the ordeal.

Auroch speaking to Scat, whispers in alarm, "Why is he doing that?"

"He must be punishing him for something he did."

"But why would he whip him?"

"You are right, Auroch, it doesn't seem right."

"Those three look different from the other people. They are very dirty."

Scat looks closer, his curiosity aroused. There is something familiar about them. The overseer, in particular, reminds him of someone. The more he looks, the more certain he is. Then it dawns on him, "You know, you are right, they are dirty. If you look closer, you will see that the older man and the woman have yellow straw-colored hair like yours. It's just that the dirt makes their hair look brown. ... Yes! Now I remember. When I was a teenager, we

157

came across a clan, and they had two people, like Slate and Fern, as slaves. There was also a young boy tied up. Yes, that's it. These are the same three, except the boy is now grown. I also remember the overseer, the one doing the whipping. He is the same person. I'm sure of that! Yes, definitely."

Rasp interjects, "They remind me of Gramater's days. These people are not friendly."

"Rasp, I think you are right. They are not people we want to meet. They could turn on us."

Auroch asks, "But we can't just let them treat those people like that. Can't we rescue them?"

"Well, boy, now that we know what Fern and Slate were like, I agree, we can't just leave them."

Grate points out, "Scat, if you are thinking of rescuing them, we should do that while those other five men are away."

"Good thinking, Grate. Come, let's see what we can do? Let's go back to the other side of the river, and we can talk further."

Silently retreating, they return to the promontory across the river where they resume their exchange.

Scat says, "We will have to act soon because they may return at any time."

Rasp offers, "I have been thinking, It would be quite easy to do it at night because they seem to leave them there, tied up, all the time. The problem is going to be the dogs. They will set off the alarm. The only way around that is to be very quick; in, cut the ropes and out."

"You are right, but we could create a diversion? Something to attract them to the other side of the compound."

After considering various options, Scat says, "Okay, I will be the one to free them while the rest of you attract their attention to the far side. The problem with this plan is that the three will probably not understand our language, and I must admit that I am not the friendliest looking person. Why should they just come along with me? They may think they are just exchanging one problem for another. The only way around this is for Auroch to come with me."

Rasp begins to interject, but Scat cuts him short, "Yes, yes, I know, we can't put a child in danger but do you have any better ideas? We can just walk away from the problem. That would be the easiest."

Grunt reminds them, "We owe it to Moraine, Slate, and Fern to do something. Look, you can see that Auroch is like them. We must do something."

"Well, without a better idea, do you all agree with my plan? I must insist that we only have one chance at this. If we fail, we can't try again. So, I will take Auroch with me, but I will leave immediately if there is any danger to him. It is up to you to create a big enough distraction to lure them away from us. Okay – everyone in agreement? ... Fine, well before dawn. Fortunately, it is a full moon, so we can see what we are doing. Those of you that have safely shaken off anyone chasing you, you must come here, to this spot, and wait. Okay? Okay."

* * *

With the moon sinking to the horizon, the light illuminates the encampment. From this vantage point, Scat and Auroch have a clear view of the three captives huddled together against the cold in the center of the camp. The dogs, too, lie prostrate unaware of being observed. After a short while, Rasp with Grate and Grunt appear at the far side of the incline. An answered signal between Rasp and Scat confirms their readiness for the next step in their plan. Scat, taking Auroch by the hand, leads the way, keeping their approach as silent as possible. Slowly, step by step, they draw nearer to the sleeping group. Moving at an angle to obscure their presence from the dogs by keeping an intervening shrub between them, they manage to approach within a few steps from them. Stopping, Scat takes a pebble and throws it at the sleeping forms. Nothing ... a repeat stirs one of them, who turns over and resumes sleeping. The third attempt is successful. It is the older man who sits up and looks about. Scat gestures to Auroch to attract the man's attention by waving from a crouching position. The man is at first startled and looks closer. Auroch waves again and quietly mouths the words, "come, come, come," urging him to come.

The man seems to grasp the boy's intention and looks around for any danger. Then holding up the tether indicates without a sound that he is tied up. Scat then moves from a concealed position, which again surprises the man, but when Scat shows a knife and motions a cutting action, the man understands. He gently nudges his sleeping companions, who, by his movements, remain quiet but alert. Pointing, he indicates to Scat and Auroch, and after a subdued exchange of words, they gather up their things to prepare to leave. Now and then, the dogs, sensing the disturbances, growl deeply, but when the group ceases activities and stays still, the dogs quieten, allowing the captives to continue their preparations. At length, they signal their readiness to Scat, who approaches keeping low to the ground. Once there, he gently strokes the man to show his non-aggressive intent and begins slowly, methodically slices through the tough ropes that bind them. To free all three individuals without disturbing the dogs takes considerable time and explains their inability to escape without the use of a sharp object like a knife. Finally, free to move, in the darkness before the first light of dawn, they shuffle quietly to the edge of the site. The dogs snarl, but being accustomed to the three captives near to them, their agitation does not rise to the level of barking, and the escapees manage to exit the encampment without disturbing the inhabitants.

Once out of earshot, Scat turns to the three. Bows, and while looking each in the eye, says, "Are you okay? Are you okay? Are you okay?"

To his surprise, the younger man responds in a dialect sufficiently similar to Scat's, enabling him to make out his meaning, "We are okay. We thank you."

Gesturing them to follow, the group descend the slope to the river and ford the fast-flowing water. The three briefly stop midstream to splash water on their faces and hair and emerge on the bank with the crust of dirt removed, somewhat clean, their features distinctly resemble Auroch.

As the twilight takes over from the moon, they see Rasp, Grate, and Grunt negotiating the river further upstream, clearly happy with the outcome, waving in congratulation. Having barely reached the protective forests lining the river, a cacophony of noise erupts from the camp. The dogs let out loud yelping, howling, and snarling noises while the men shout angry commands to each other. Without waiting to hear more, Scat and Rasp's group run to distance themselves from the enemy. At the top of the promontory, they regroup and press on down the other side. Once well out of range of potential pursuers, they slow their pace and walk until they reach a secluded area with a view across the shallow valley to the other side. No one is following.

In an awkward exchange in their differing languages, they manage to introduce each other. The Older man's name is Stag, the younger one is Linna, and the woman's name is Moss.

Auroch listens, enthralled by their manner, curious language, and the obvious relief at being freed. A shadow passes over his face as he looks more closely. They appear malnourished, and the clothes they wear are worn and broken in many places. Scars show on their arms and legs where the skin is visible under the animal skins they wear. In a heartfelt gesture, he approaches the young man and hugs him around the waist. The whole group silently watches his demonstration of concern, which removes the last vestiges of unease as Linna ruffles Auroch's hair, kneels beside him, and holds the boy to his chest. Even Scat swallows hard to remove the knot in his throat.

With their scouting excursion in disarray without a suitable place to set up camp for the main group that is to follow, Scat decides to return via a circuitous route in the hope of finding an alternative site, one that is sufficiently far from the adversary to reduce the possibility of crossing paths with them in the future. Three days of steady march takes them to just such a place with running water, a nearby herd of deer and is secluded while offering a sweeping view to watch for the foe. By the time they reach the main camp, the newcomers have fallen into the routine of the group, and their assimilation is near complete. Enamored by Auroch's charming ways, they joke with each other over their propensity to wolf down the food that was so rare during their captivity.

161

## 18   Fang

Their arrival at the main camp is greeted with curiosity and sympathy as the newcomers are introduced, and the story of their enslavement circulates. Some of the older generations recall meeting the captors many years prior. The appearance of the newcomers engenders much debate about their likeness to Slate and Fern. The similarity to the older man Stag is so striking that they wonder whether there can be a relationship, and the old question of Auroch's parentage resurfaces fueled by the coincident ramblings of Fang. While the scouting party was away, Fang fell ill, suffering from a fever and delirium, during which she repeated relived a nightmare that centered on Gramater, her child, and Fern's baby. By this time, she had returned to sleeping in the communal quarters so that, to those who heard her disjointed obsequious, sometimes argumentative dialogue, in the middle of the night, it was apparent that something had happened to the children. Fang's condition deteriorated, and with it, her internal torment, so that she was moved to Gramater's old work shed where she would not disturb the people and could be attended to in private.

Preparations for relocating to the scouting party's new campsite gets into full swing. A couple of days later, Fang is placed in a stretcher made of animal hide and poles for carrying purposes, and the procession is underway. As they walk in a column with an advance party ahead looking out for danger, there is great anticipation at what lies ahead. On arrival, the new huts are set up in a pattern, long established as the best configuration, with adjustments for locational differences. By nightfall, tired but excited, they settle down around a campfire, happily talking about what adventures lie ahead in the new locale.

The march, unfortunately, has exacerbated Fang's condition. Her fever relentlessly alternates between cold shivers and profuse sweating as the illness takes hold while her ramblings only become more incoherent. In a moment of lucidity, she calls for Scat and Auroch. Entering the hut, Fang's rasping voice greets them, "I ... I don't think I ... ", coughing, "I don't think I will last much longer. Wanted to tell you ... ", more coughing, "Auroch" taking his hand.

"Yes, mother?"

"You are a dear child, Auroch. I ... I have wronged you, dear child. I am not your mother!"

"Mother, you are not well. You must rest."

"No, no, you are Fern's child. Fern is your mother."

Scat intervenes, realizing the significance of her words, "Auroch, what Fang is saying is that Fern is your mother. You never knew her. She died when you were just two or three days old."

"Yes, Auroch. I wronged you. My own baby would have died, so I exchanged Fern's baby for mine. You are Fern's baby."

With tears welling up in her eyes, she says, "I had to hide the truth from Gramater; otherwise, she would have killed you too. I ... can you understand? I am so sorry. My baby died with Fern. All these years ... oh the torture ... what could I do?"

Racked with a long spell of coughing, she lapses into her earlier incoherent ramblings.

Auroch takes her hand. Without fully understanding what has transpired, his inherent kindness offers her absolution, "Dear, dear mother." Leaving the distraught frame, they depart the enclosure with Scat leading the boy where he says, "Auroch, with time, you will understand what she said. If you need someone to talk to, anytime, we can talk. Okay?"

"Thank you, Scat," and with confused emotions running deep, he walks down to the river, where he pensively watches the water rushing by.

Some days later, Fang succumbs to her illness.

As they stand around her grave, Scat says, "Fang wanted it to be known that Fern is Auroch's mother. She confessed to this. Please don't hold this against her. It was one of the evil deeds that Gramater brought about. In the end, we are richer for Auroch, the child that survived her scheming, and for that, we need to be thankful. We will also remember the happiness that Fern brought to us."

Auroch, not having known his biological mother but from stories of the changes she brought to the community through her happy disposition, finds grounds for the pride he feels.

The news that Scat conveyed is not all that unexpected to the band members but having confirmation brings closure to the conjecture. Yet while the explanation closes one chapter, another is opened. Following the burial, Stag cannot shake the mention of Fern's name by Scat.

Dwelling on the description, he approaches Scat and, in his broken dialect, asks, "Scat, the person. The one … Fern, you tell me more of her?"

"It is a long story, Stag, but you will have noticed that Auroch is different from the rest of us here in our clan. He has yellow straw-colored hair, like yours. Well, Fern and her brother came here many years ago, and it is through them that this community changed from a lot of in-fighting between us to a more caring way of life. It was Fern who infected us with her happiness. She partnered with one of our men, a man called Runt. They had a child at the same time as Fang had hers, which was premature. And as you heard, Fang swapped the children because she believed that her child would not survive."

"I had a sister, also Fern. She very happy. Our brother, he try to rescue us from those bad people. They too many and too strong. He not listen, he fight. They injure him, and I tell him, go. I say, go … save Fern. He go. That be a long time ago."

"Was your brother's name, Slate?"

"Yes, yes, that be his name. You know Slate?"

"Yes, Slate stayed with us. He was a quiet man and very gentle. He was kind to one of ours. You will hear a lot about her. Her name is Moraine. They decided to go where nature calls, over the mountains, to a distant land."

Stag, both surprised and overjoyed, asks, "Then Auroch be my nephew?"

"Yes, Auroch must be your nephew."

Unable to contain himself, he runs to Auroch, who is surrounded by others. Beckoning to Linna and Moss, he says in their dialect, "Scat told me that Slate and Fern were here. Can you believe that? Slate may still be alive. He and another person, Moraine, left to go over the mountains. Remember we were going to go there too. Fern stayed here, and Auroch is her child." Turning to Auroch, he says, "Auroch, Fern, your mother, she be my sister. You be my nephew! Yes, my nephew."

The joy of the news spreads through the community. Their happiness knows no bounds as they dance and sing to the news.

# 19    Disruption

Enrico, Käthe, Jane, and Michel set off down the foothills of the Pyrenees. By the hour, the hills diminish to plains with the Pyrenees receding at their back, and the Sierra de Cebollera looms larger up front, and further along, the Sierra de Guadarrama rises near Madrid. Keeping these mountains to their right, they skirt them following the migratory birds as they head for warmer reaches. The days are distinctly cooler as winter approaches with a chill in the air in the evenings and at night. Unavoidably the terrain becomes steeper as they hug the eastern slopes of the Sierra de Cebollera. Progress is slower, but the vista across rivers, hills, and the mist-covered range is both relaxing and invigorating. All the carefully laid plans wane as the inspirational landscape dispels all worries and concerns under the spell of its beauty. Forests of wild pine, stands of beech, groves of white oak, lime and maple trees, mountain elms, quaking aspen and ash trees enchant their progress as fox, wild boar, deer, squirrel and mountain cats in the forests, and otter and muskrat in the rivers provide distractions to ease their tired limbs. Jane is enthralled by the forest birds of prey, goshawk, sparrow hawk, honey buzzard, and the booted eagle. The passage of migratory birds crown each day for her, and the common buzzard and ever-present eagles thrill at every turn. Nocturnal birds noiselessly fly seeking their prey, owls giving away their presence with haunting hoots at night.

Just as these attractions elevate their enjoyment to a sublime trancelike state, a rude awakening interposes to remind them of other realities that are present. Tremors, at first mistaken for the distant rumble of thunder and obscured by the rustle of leaves in the wind, leaves them wondering whether a change in weather can be expected. A recurrence during a cloudless spell with no wind leads Enrico to say, "You know, I don't think that is the sound of thunder. Listen, it is very irregular, and when it happens, it sounds more like a tremor. It's very difficult to feel it here, out in the open. If you don't mind, I would like to set up my seismometer, see whether something is going on."

Sure enough, the instrument confirms a series of tremors after waiting a while. A sudden distinct jolt puts the questions beyond doubt.

"That registered as a minor earthquake, 3.3 on the Richter Scale. I wonder what is going on."

Jane asks, "Can it be dangerous? Can you tell where the epicenter is?"

"Danger? No, not out here unless it is much stronger and if there are cliffs that may cause a landslide as we saw in the Pyrenees. I would need another instrument to triangulate the source. Let's see if I phone my office in Naples. They will have readings as well. That will enable me to resolve where the epicenter is."

"Can you do that?"

"Come to think of it, at 3.3, it is probably just above random background noise that happens all the time. Let's continue, and if it gets any worse, I will contact them."

Jane suggests, "Michel, why don't you take a magnetic reading. We can track the readings against the tremors – see whether they correlate."

"Not a bad idea, hold on a minute ... well, let's see ... the reading still shows the southerly divergence we saw earlier except that it is slightly more pronounced, but I would put that down to the distance we have walked since the Pyrenees."

"Are the birds following the path of the magnetic patterns?

"Yes, it looks like, or should I say, they are following one of the two streams. The path we are on. I can't say what is happening at the other stream."

Continuing on their way, there is no repeat of the tremor until the following day. This one is significantly stronger with an initial jolt and then lower-level rumblings. Enrico sets up his device with the aftershocks registering a steady 3.5 for some minutes. He concludes, "We missed the main shock but based on the strength of the aftershocks, I would say the main one must have been around 5.5 or even 6.0. It all depends on where the epicenter is. I am assuming it is here nearby, but if it is as far away as Naples, which would be a much higher reading ... I will call them."

By the expression on his face, a quick call and speaking Italian tells the others that something of significance has happened. Ending the call, he says, "Not good, the epicenter is in the Alps due north of Naples. They estimate it as 6.5 on the Richter scale. They don't yet have reports of damage, still too early but one of the vents of the volcano at Naples is now active. They say the two events occurred at the same time."

Michel says, "I have taken another reading, and the magnetic lines are still unchanged from earlier."

Enrico, with concern in his voice, "I think I should be going back to Naples. These events are likely precursors of more to come. I don't want to sound alarmist, but you never know with these things."

Käthe offers, "It will be about a day's hike to the nearest point at which Otto can meet you. Would you like me to arrange that?"

"Yes, sorry to spoil your fun, but it would be negligent of me to continue here with you."

"Not to worry, it is just a minor diversion from the path we would have taken. Let me call him."

Back on the trail, this time, they walk faster while Käthe continues to look out for features that may require closer examination concerning archaic potential. With the arrangement for Otto to meet them early in the morning, they manage to reach the rendezvous point and set up camp for the night. Enrico sets up his seismometer for the night. In the early hours of the morning, violent shaking starts with a rumbling sound that grows louder by the minute. Even the trees quiver and vibrate violently as the noise passes by. The peak of it lasts for a full five minutes, followed by shuddering every few minutes. After an hour, normality returns. Enrico's device recorded the start of the main event but got dislodged by the shaking during the latter stages. Checking the instrument for its readings, he finds a 7.0 magnitude.

Alarmed at the reading, he says, "I have never personally witnessed a 7.0 magnitude. This has got to be a serious situation if it is in the Alps. My guess is a magnitude of 8.0. At that level, they will have serious damage …

What time will Otto be here? They will need me in Naples. I just hope the volcano is behaving itself."

Michel interrupts, "You had better phone them."

"Yes, yes, I must do that right away," as he reaches for his phone.

There is no dial tone. Dead. Repeated tries with the same result. Käthe uses her phone to contact Otto, with the same problem.

Concerned, she says, "I just hope Otto gets here safely."

Settling down, they try to resume sleeping but with little hope of accomplishing that. At eight in the morning, there is no sign of Otto. Continuing to wait, and at ten o'clock, there is still no sign of him. Unsure what to do, they resolve to stay at their location until the following morning because there are two possible routes he may take to get there.

Käthe points out, "If we go left, he may come in from the right. I think it best that we wait here. Otherwise, it will just add to the confusion."

Michel asks, "How far is it to the nearest town?"

Käthe replies, "I would say it is a good four-hour march. What did you have in mind?"

"We could split up. Two of us could stay here and the other two walk there. It is the only way to find out what the problems are."

"Sounds good to me. If Otto arrives, he can head in that direction. If he doesn't arrive, whoever reaches the village can send for help."

"Käthe, I suggest that you and I do the walking. Jane and Enrico can wait here. When we reach the village, we will wait at the village center ... one more thing. Let me take another magnetic reading."

While busying himself with extracting the device, a series of aftershocks rumble through, disturbing birds that take to the air from a nearby tree, squawking loudly. A hare leaps through the vegetation, passing right between Käthe and Jane, eyes wide as it frantically tries to escape the unknown threat. When calm returns Michel proclaims that the magnetic paths are in disarray with no clear north/south pattern. A further series of aftershocks heighten their alarm.

With a concerned edge in his voice, Enrico says, "This is not good. I can only imagine that there will be widespread damage. The reason we don't have a cellular connection is probably that the relay towers are down."

Michel adds to the concern, "You know, you are right! That explains it. Otto is using his CAV. The whole thing about connected autonomous vehicles is that they depend on geo-navigation to get anywhere. Without the cellular towers, the CAV will be as dead as a doornail."

Jane questions, "But can't he use manual controls, surely?"

"No, that was done away with about ten years ago. It was thought that the network would be robust enough with many failsafe systems that kick in. When one fails, another takes over automatically. The satellite Wi-Fi system would be the third recourse to connectivity. This is a global system with multiple satellites circulating the world to give blanket coverage, no matter where you are."

With some skepticism, Enrico says, "I can't believe that there wouldn't be a way around that. The onboard system in the vehicle surely has maps cached for just such a problem."

"Yes, it would have, but for the vehicle to drive, it needs to get its bearings from the cellular towers or the onboard compass. If the towers are out of action and if the north/south magnetic fields are in disarray, basically the whole system is in the dark. The on-board compass can't find its bearings, and the signal to verify its location from the satellite system would also not work."

"Well, that is incredible. How long do you think this may go on for?"

"I am not an expert on this subject, but I can imagine that it probably depends on several factors. From my standpoint, the question is whether a polar magnetic flip is underway. We know that the South Pole has been in an excursion phase. This is the whole point of us tracking the birds. They have been confused by two magnetic South Poles. Quite aside from the birds, this is a known problem. It has persisted for decades already. Usually, a polar reversal or Laschamp Event, as it is known, can take two or three hundred years to transition. The excursion observed is evidence that a change is underway, but it is a change that may never happen, as in the case 39,000 years ago, it normalized after a while. The problem for us is that a severe excursion event can wreak havoc on electronics because the protective magnetic shield around the Earth is weakened, allowing harmful energetic particles from the sun to penetrate the atmosphere resulting in damage to electronic equipment. Satellites circling the Earth will be first to take the hit."

Enrico's voice echoes the alarm on their faces, "I don't know what to say. What we do know for sure is that there have been some rather serious tremors. Depending on where their epicenters are, they may be significant earthquakes. Earthquakes are one thing, but as I mentioned, they can coincide with volcanic eruptions. This is where my responsibility kicks in. There may or may not have been an eruption at Naples, and here I am, thousands of kilometers away. I need to find out what the situation is and urgently."

Michel suggests, "Why don't you and Jane walk to the nearest village to find out what is going on. Käthe and I can wait here. I would go with you instead of Jane, but that would leave two ladies here on their own. It would not be safe."

"Okay, Jane, are you okay with that?"

"Yes, of course. I just need a moment to gather my things, and we can go."

"Okay, then. Same arrangements we spoke of earlier. If Otto arrives, follow the path we take. If we get to the village before you, we will wait at the village center. If you don't arrive by nightfall, we will book in at the nearest hotel or leave a message at a grocery store or post office."

With that, the pair set off, leaving Käthe and Michel to wait for Otto.

As they settled down, Käthe asks, "Michel, you seem very knowledgeable about the effects of a potential polar reversal. Where did you learn about it?"

"It is related to my field of study. You know, the magnetosphere and the effects on our daily life."

"I am interested in the effects on the Neanderthals back 39,000 years ago. It is so difficult to prove anything. We know from the iron-bearing rocks from volcanic eruptions from that time that the magnetic fields changed. It is locked into the magnetized rock as evidence."

"Yes, that is well recognized."

"But, how that affected the Neanderthals is only conjecture."

"True, but is it possible that their remains, for example from the cave that you are busy excavating, is it possible that these remains contain a signature of the magnetic effect? Sort of locked in like the rocks?"

"You are right. We should explore that, but we would need a specialist in the field to help with that. We don't have that expertise in our lab at Leipzig."

"I would be interested in helping, but I would need a counterpoint person with knowledge of the bones. Aren't you that sort of person?"

"Well, yes, but it would have to be a case of exploring the possibilities. I can't just point and say, 'there it is,' it would need research, building on the unfolding logic."

"Precisely the same for me too. I would need ultra-sensitive equipment to detect that, something I would always want to add to my collection."

"Hah, ha, and here we are stuck in the middle of nowhere. Who knows if and when we get out of this mess?"

Returning to her backpack, Käthe says, "We need to eat something. It could be a long wait."

They silently consume their lunch, each deep in their thoughts until Käthe observes, "It is so peaceful here. This is the part of my job that I like."

"You couldn't be more right about the peacefulness. It sinks into one. It is good to get away from the daily scramble of life in the city."

"I like to imagine life at the time of the Neanderthals. Even if you take the tremors and the effect on our communications, at their time, if this happened, they would just continue their lives with nature around them virtually unaffected. I would exchange our time for their time, anytime."

"Well, you can't be too sure about the effect on them. I remember you saying that they may have suffered skin cancers because of the penetration of ultraviolet light without a protective magnetosphere. I agree with you. We have this longing to understand what we only perceive superficially and then explore and immerse ourselves fully in the subject. You have chosen an interesting study to do that with. It must be very fulfilling. "

"I did say that about them being so unaffected about tremors, but what I meant is that everything didn't come to a dead stop like we are experiencing now."

By evening, with no sign of Otto, they set up a tent and roll out their sleeping bags.

As darkness envelopes them, the sounds of the forest seem amplified. Exploring her inner feelings, Käthe begins to realize that this man, lying in the dark next to her, has much in common with her. Their careers, so different, yet underlying them is the quest to understand the natural order, present, and past. His endearing quality, his open-mindedness, viewing what she says with interest uncommon among the men she generally mixes with, so refreshing.

Michel feels strangely alive listening to Käthe's dedication to a distant past, her passion for understanding the Neanderthals, and the way she immerses herself in the subject to tease out their world view. It draws her in until, in her mind, she becomes one with them.

174

Thinking to himself, "While life goes on around us, Käthe lives in this other dimension separate from us. All this time, I had no inkling of the depth of her sentiments, just another person. It just needed a few hours spent alone with her to understand. What a revelation? So inspirational."

The warmth of the sun's rays on the tent wakes them to the twitter of birds.

"Good morning, Käthe, did you have a good sleep?"

"Yes, thank you, I hope you did. I woke up before dawn. The air is so fresh, I almost hope that Otto doesn't come."

"What do you think we should do? I know it is tempting to just stay here, but the others will begin to worry."

"Well, I guess we need to pack up and head towards the village. I was thinking, do you have a piece of paper and a pen. We could leave a note on the tree."

"Yes, good idea. Let's see ... here it is."

"Okay, 'Time is 9 AM. Have left in -> that direction to the nearest village. Meet at a hotel or Post Office'. Does that sound good?"

"Just perfect, there. He shouldn't miss seeing it on that tree."

Käthe and Michel set off in the direction of the village. A new sparkle enters their dialogue, as the enjoyment of each other's company, each attentive to the words of the other.

# 20    Turmoil

Two hours passed when a tractor towing a trailer rounded a curve ahead of them. Jane and Enrico, standing on the trailer, wave in their approach. As they step down, Jane explains, "This was the only vehicle we could find that did not depend on GPS and electronics. This is Rafael, he owns it."

"Pleased to meet you, Rafael," Michel says, shaking his hand.

Jane continues, "All the systems are down. Anything that depends on electronics, it seems."

Enrico elaborates, "We were able to hear from a local who listened in on a Spanish radio station. He told us that a magnitude 8.5 earthquake has struck northern Italy, and the Vesuvius volcano, which is part of the Campanian volcanic arc where I work, has erupted, causing widespread damage to Naples. Two other volcanoes have also erupted. Taupo in New Zealand and the other is the Yellowstone Hotspot, which includes some related volcanoes across Idaho, Wyoming, Montana, Oregon, and Nevada. These are supervolcanoes, and they estimate the Volcanic Explosive Index to be between 6 and 7 for these two. Eight is the maximum for this index. As an example, Pinatubo in 1991 was about 5.5. Some smaller dormant volcanoes are now partially active again, including at Bolivia in the Andes."

Käthe and Michel listen in alarm as Enrico continues, "It is unprecedented for two supervolcanoes to erupt at the same time. You can be sure that it will disrupt the climate for many years. Dust in the air will prevent air travel for some time."

Jane adds, "Our immediate concern is for Otto. There is still no sign of him. The roads are impassable, or he can't find transport or a means to get us a message."

Käthe says, "Yes, Otto is part of my team. I need to get hold of Leipzig and have them manage Otto's return. They need to get a message to him somehow. We can leave a message here at the B&B and other places in the village where he will likely enquire."

Michel asks, "Has there been any reports of the effect on the magnetic field?

"No, we haven't heard anything. It was difficult to understand the man. Enrico understands Spanish better than I do. Enrico, did you hear anything?"

"No, but it seems likely that it has been affected, given the communication difficulties."

Enrico adds, "My responsibility is to go back to Naples. Air travel will probably be suspended, and the roads may be a problem even if I can find a car that works. My suggestion is that we stay in the village. There is a comfortable B&B there. We can decide on the next steps when we have news."

With his agreement, the farmer turns the tractor around, and they soon arrive at the village. At their request, the owner of the B&B provides a battery-operated radio.

Tuning into BBC, which provides blanket coverage of the events, a commentator is heard expounding on the potential travel limitations, "Authorities recommend that all travel plans be shelved, pending a full report on conditions on the ground and from the airline authorities. Routes through the Alps are impassable, and Monaco has suffered severe damage. Italy is effectively isolated for land access. Rescue services from France, Germany, and Austria cannot get through, leaving only the Mediterranean Sea as an option. Many rescue craft from Greece and Spain are en-route to Naples, but these are limited to boats without integrated electronics that depend on GPS coupled to the navigation systems. We still have not heard from the authorities on the reasons for the communication difficulties. This is BBC World Services reporting from a temporary broadcasting facility at our Archive Center at Perivale, Ealing Greater London. We apologize for the poor quality of our service as we address the technical difficulties brought on by events."

Enrico is first to speak, "Well, that about sums up my problem. The only way I can get to Naples is by boat. My best bet is to try to get to Barcelona and a boat from there."

Michel echoes, "Yes, in fact, if the Alps, and for that matter, the Pyrenees, are probably impassible, our best route back would be into France along the coast from Barcelona."

Käthe responds, "We have to decide whether to call off this field trip. Remember, our destination was Gibraltar."

Michel offers, "The other option is for Enrico to take a boat from Gibraltar. The rest of us could try for a boat up the English Channel. Jane and I can disembark at Dover, and you Käthe, you could go on to the Netherlands and up the Rhine to the nearest point to Leipzig. Is that feasible?"

"Of course, that is feasible, but either route depends on so many unknowns. First and foremost, will our credit cards work, and are there any ferries or services available? Everyone will be thinking the same. The demand could be high."

Jane offers, "We have to take the option that has the least chance of failing. Also, don't forget Otto in all of this."

Käthe says, "Yes, it would help if we knew where he is at the moment."

Michel suggests, "Considering the options, let's vote on it. The majority wins."

Indicating their preferences results in a deadlock, Jane and Enrico prefer the Barcelona route, whereas Käthe and Michel prefer Gibraltar.

Smiling, Michel says, "So much for the majority. What about a compromise? I suggest we go to Valencia. It is about the same distance to Italy for Enrico, and the rest of us can either go north or south from there by road or boat."

With no dissension, Valencia is agreed to.

In broken English, Rafael offers, "I know someone who may be able to help. He has an old car. If you pay his expenses, he could take you to Valencia."

178

A day later, with the four cramped into a small Seat Ibiza car, they set out for Valencia on the east coast, a distance of about 350 kilometers along country roads. On arrival at Valencia and thanking the driver for help, Käthe assures him her office at Leipzig will transfer the costs to his bank account as soon as possible. A hotel near the harbor also kindly agrees to a deferred payment for a few nights.

Their search for a means to complete their respective journeys is not fruitful. All tourist-orientated trips are suspended, leaving freighters as the next choice. Enrico is first to secure a seat on a boat headed for Sicily. With this as the only choice, he accepts and, after a delay of three days, departs with the assurance that he will keep in contact.

All attempts at finding a road or boat transport to Barcelona for all three prove to be difficult. The best they can find is a single-seat as a passenger in a car destined for Paris. Given their predicament, the hotel guest offering the ride insists on no payment. After much discussion, Jane decides to rather stay, hoping to find a means to reach Gibraltar where she can continue with the geo-tagging project.

A week later, with communications still not restored, they offer themselves as work-hands on a fishing trawler destined for Gibraltar. The sign on the boat reads 'Temporary Workers Needed - Destination Gibraltar.' On inquiry, the owner speaking Spanish requires a deckhand, Rodrigo, to translate for them. He says, "The captain says that the other workers live in Valencia. They could not get transport back here from Gibraltar, so they decided to look for other work."

Michel explains, "We have no experience. Does that matter?"

"No problem. I will teach you. It only takes a few minutes to learn. You have to clear the nets and do some packing. You will be on the boat for three nights. You get one meal per day for nothing."

"Okay, we will try that."

Signing off at the hotel and relocating to the boat does not take long, and they soon find themselves streaming along, off the coast of Spain. Most of the trawling is done at night. Under the glare of lights focussed into the water to attract the fish into the nets that sweep up the catch to pour the wriggling mass onto the deck. Daylight is spent sleeping, and as the sun sets, they gather for the meal, which is mainly fresh fried fish with potato chips.

They use the time to catch up on the news with Rodrigo translating for Spanish, as he listens to a battered radio.

From what Rodrigo relates, the news is sketchy, but accounts are of continued widespread disruption. Clouds of volcanic dust, caught in the stratospheric jet streams, quickly circle the globe, bringing dense smog across Europe. Temperatures drop by as much as ten degrees for the time of the year. The expectation is of further drops over the next month.

Rodrigo is right about the smog. Even in the open waters, they plow through the water at a much-reduced speed, enveloped by a dense cloud of grey dust as the captain peers ahead for obstacles. Even during daylight hours, he trains the searchlights ahead of their passage as a warning to would-be craft venturing across the bow. Instead of three days, the trip takes four days when they finally pass the ghostly outline of the Rock of Gibraltar to birth in a sheltered harbor on the western side of the mountain.

Thanking the captain, they disembark and gather at the dock. Käthe is first to speak, "I have contacts at the University of Gibraltar. They have a campus at Europa Point, where the director is well known to us at Leipzig. They were expecting us as part of our hike. I will check in with them and see whether they can provide accommodation. Their Director of Life and Earth Sciences, Donald Stevenson, was the first to postulate that the Neanderthals finally became extinct here are Gorham's Cave. He is an evolutionary biologist and has many books published about them. Jane, you will be interested in his book, Birds of the Strait of Gibraltar."

Jane responds, "I can't wait to check on our geo-tagging now that we have this confusion with the magnetic field. It should be interesting."

Michel replies, "Actually, I just checked on the fields, and it is still a mess. Particularly in the south. The North Pole has also shifted but is still somewhat intact."

Hiking the short distance to Europa Point, they arrive and, on inquiry, are directed to Professor Stevenson's department. One of the lecturers, Craig Smithers, enthusiastically welcomes them and waves aside the need for a hotel, "Don't worry about accommodation, we have plenty of space here in the residences. You will be our guest. I heard about your find at the Foix Cave. The news spreads quickly, but everything has gone quiet since the earthquake and volcanism. We can't wait to hear more."

Käthe thanks Craig and expresses the wish to see the Gorham Cave. "Is there anyone who can direct us there?"

"We have a problem, though. The tremors have caused rock falls inside the cave. It is usually somewhat open to the public, so we have had to close it while the rubble is removed."

"Oh, what a pity. But you must have specialists doing the removal, right?"

"Yes, very much so. Some of the students are helping with that. We were busy excavating down to a new layer when the tremors started. We had to stop work. It was too dangerous, but it has been quiet for a while, so we will be starting again tomorrow."

"Well then, I would like to help if you don't mind, speaking for Michel and Jane. They can pitch in as well. I can direct them on the proper methods if you like." Turning to Jane, "What do you think? I know you will want to do some bird watching as well."

Jane nods, "My focus should be the birds, but I would very much like to help excavate as well."

"Of course, you can do both. We have experts on the subject of birds in this area ... It would be an honor to have all of you help with the clean-up. We have heard so much about your expertise, Käthe. I would go so far as to suggest that you should lead the recovery and discovery processes."

"No, no, I wouldn't want to overstep our welcome. We will be happy to work under your direction."

"Okay. Done. Tomorrow we will head out there, and I'll show you around. First thing, 9 am, okay?"

# 21  Gorham

The cave does not disappoint. Even with rocks scattered across the entrance and interior, Käthe is entranced by the imagery that comes to mind. Archaic people, their daily lives, nature around them, and in the distance, Africa, the cradle of our birth, mysteriously beckoning. What went through the minds of these people, the interactions between them, their hopes and desires, and frustrations? She pictures a life removed from the bustle of 21st-century life, an experience that can never be recaptured. The pictures on the walls evoke a past filled with the drama of the hunt, pastoral times, and the artistry of the person who captured these ideas.

While the calamities of quakes, eruptions, darkened skies, and communication difficulties abound around them, Käthe single-mindedly focusses on the excavations. With meticulous care, the rock-strewn interior is cleared, and work on the exterior begins. Her dedication draws Michel into her world, infecting him with the allure of a bygone era, he too finds his thoughts straying to the alter-reality as they enjoy their newfound comradery.

Jane, engrossed in the endless flocks of birds that use the strait at the southern extent of the Iberian Peninsula, the narrowest crossing to Africa, to channel their migratory paths. Soaring birds, eagles, buzzards, stork, falcons, kites, and many more stream across the waters to their wintering grounds. An array of divers and smaller birds like finches, larks, swallows, wagtails, wrens, warblers, flycatchers, tits, weavers, and waxbills delight as they swarm in their masses before noisily launching across the narrows. On returning at day's end, the subject invariably returns to the attractions that draw the birds across to the far land. The intrigue of seeing at firsthand what lies there grows to an obsession for Jane. When the radio link to her geo-tagged birds, Cyan and Zinnia, lights up, she excitedly tracks their passage to the water's edge, and with binoculars in hand, she sees them cross the water, solidifying her determination to follow them across the strait.

In her turn, Käthe, looking across the water, marvels at the coincidence of standing at this shore. In her mind, it invokes archaic man's circuitous route out of that land, Africa via the Middle East to journey across Europe and culminating in this place. Their speciation over so many millennia whittled them down to just us, the Sapiens, and how the poorer we are in our aloneness. It brings a measure of sadness to her. She dreams of visiting that land just to plant her feet there if only to complete the circle of man's journey.

Day five, with the rock-fall cleared, the excavation to the new layer begins. By this time, Käthe's methodology is in clear evidence, and Craig and his students gradually adopt her processes as they learn from her experience. With the more relaxed pace of work, they find time to explore the surroundings. In her eye for detail, Käthe is drawn to an area abutting the cliff face where the ground shows signs of disturbance. During work intervals in the cave, she exposes the top and under layers of the disturbed soil. By the day, the shape of a small depression is apparent. As she uncovers successive strata, excitement mounts as she anticipates that something must lie below. Her first confirmation comes with the uncovering of a small round slate object with markings on it.

After taking photographs of its position within the depression, she carefully removes it. Pouring water over it reveals its secret; two intersecting sprigs of flowers engraved into the slate and, on the reverse, the double intersecting striations. By this time, Michel is by her side, spellbound by the unfolding drama of the discovery, it resembles the description of the artifact found at the Foix Cave. Digging further reveals the remains of a child.

Looking closely, Käthe excitedly proclaims, "Judging by its size, I would say it is a premature baby. Maybe around eight months. On the surface, I would say that it is not recent. It looks prehistoric to me."

Michel questions, "Is there a way of confirming this?"

"Well, yes. We would have to take the remains to a lab for further analysis. Also, because it is not fully formed, I cannot tell whether it is a Neanderthal or modern man. Again, that would have to be determined by DNA tests. The first thing to do is to safely extract the bones, taking the usual precautions of recording the position and layout of the grave."

Craig offers, "We have elaborate DNA capabilities here at the university. They were able to build the entire Genome of a Neanderthal based on bones taken from Serbia."

Käthe nodding, "Yes, I have followed your work here. We, too, at Leipzig, have similar facilities."

After careful removal of excess gravel and dust from around the tiny skeleton, they lay it out on a board and carry it to the laboratory to select the bones that are the most likely to yield marrow from which to extract the DNA. While this work progresses, they return to the site for further excavation work.

With a lull in the activities, the possibility of transiting the strait surfaces again. On inquiry at the harbor, they find that the fishing trawler they worked on is still docked there. With Rodrigo translating, the captain agrees to ferry them across to Ceuta, the Spanish Enclave, at the tip of Africa. Being part of Spain, their visas are valid. Under grey skies and the cold imposed by the volcanic dust in the air, they cross the treacherous currents to land on the other side.

For Jane, Ceuta offers only a small glimpse of habitat for the birds as they continue their migrations in a south-westerly direction into Morocco. Somewhat disappointed, she joins a day trip with Michel and Käthe around the enclave, including the cave, at Benzu, where crowds of tourists throng the area despite the cold weather. Käthe suggests they have a look at the lesser-known cave on the shore to the east of Benzu. Walking the distance, they arrive to find archeologists busy working in and around the cave. After introductions, they are thrilled to meet Käthe, having heard of her find at Gorham's cave.

The lead investigator explains, "When we learned that you located the remains of the child, not inside the cave itself, but alongside it, we decided to do likewise and expanded our search to the adjacent area as well. It wasn't long, and we came across this, come along, let me show you," Pointing to a marked off area, he says, "You can see that the ground here is not as compacted as the area around it. It is roughly ten feet square. You can see, we have begun clearing the surface soil and hope to go deeper over the next few days."

Käthe, with her eye for opportunity, nods, saying, "You are right. It certainly looks promising. Can we help you with the work?"

"Oh, for sure."

With only a few hours of daylight left, they roll up their sleeves and begin working. To accommodate a more extended stay, they agree to continue the next day after confirming with Rodrigo and the captain that they will return in a week to ferry them back to Gibraltar. This affords Jane more time to track the birds, and Michel, now fully prepared to learn from Käthe, join as a recruit in the excavation.

As layer after layer is removed, excitement at the prospect of another find mounts. By the end of the week, the first bones are laid bare. The Spaniards working the dig began systematically working to Käthe's procedure. First, a female form then that of a male alongside, is found. Only a few inches to their left, there lies the remains of a young boy.

 When Käthe unearths another small flat round stone with the now-familiar pair of intersecting sprigs of flowers on one side and the two parallel markings on the other side, her amazement is complete.

She exclaims, "This is hard to believe. There has to be some logical explanation."

Michel enjoins, "Käthe, somehow this has to be related to the earlier discoveries. It can't just be a random chance."

"You are right. The secret must lie in the bones. We must do a comparative DNA analysis of all the remains we have found. We also need to carbon date their ages. Surely, there must be a correlation between them."

Over the next few days, a tentative collaboration agreement between the Ceuta group, the Gibraltar University, and the Max Planck Institute at Leipzig is discussed. With the telecommunication difficulties still frustrating contacts, the plans are deferred to a date when this barrier will be lifted. In the meantime, Käthe and Michel continue assisting the excavation, and Jane joins in, having exhausted her exploration of Ceuta.

As the cold deepens, compounded by the approach of winter, the three cross the strait with the trawler. By this time, the captain and Rodrigo are just as excited and proud of their contribution to the findings. They happily waive all costs and offer further services as required.

# 22    Return

As the season stretches into winter, Michel continues tracking the magnetic field, which shows a gradual normalization of the magnetic North Pole. The South Pole stubbornly remains in an excursion state divided into two strong forces and a third weaker magnetic pole. The normalization of the north brings some relief to the communication network, and combined with technical adjustments, certain channels become available for use. It is by this means that Käthe learns that Otto has returned to the cave at Foix where he is working with Ulrich. They have relocated their base to a more accessible site alongside the main river. A smaller group continues their work up the tributary at the actual cave.

Not far from the base camp, a sinkhole is being excavated, hoping that the remains of animals will reveal the types of fauna that frequented the area in bygone years. Not surprisingly, each layer shows a chronological record of the creatures that fell victim to the pit. On reaching what is assessed to be representative of 39,000 years ago, the remains of a woman, two adult males, and a newly born child are unearthed. After careful extraction, these skeletons are transported to Leipzig for further analysis using the transport infrastructure, which became operational as the GPS network came to life with improved communications.

Meanwhile, at the insistence of the captain of the fishing trawler, the three board the craft with Hamburg on the North Sea as their destination. Jane decides to disembark at Dover and proceed from there to London, her home. Having established an intimate relationship with Käthe, Michel chooses to accompany her to Hamburg, where they will find transport to Leipzig.

\* \* \*

The auditorium at the Max Planck Institute is filled to capacity. The din of the audience rises as they expectantly wait for the speaker to appear. At length, a man in a tailored suit walks up to the podium, and a hush falls over the crowd.

The speaker raises his hand, "Thank you for attending this special occasion. It is my honor to welcome Käthe Loeschke. Käthe, would you like to step forward?"

As she enters, the crowd begins clapping as they rise to greet her with loud cheers.

"It is my privilege to bestow on Ms. Loeschke, a professorship for her work on the Neanderthals. This cap and gown are our formal recognition of your outstanding work. Would you like to say a few words?"

"I would like to thank my colleagues, who assisted me in the work. Without them, we would not have accomplished what we did. I might add that the discoveries that we made were incredibly fortuitous. That we should stumble upon not one but four sites, so rich in remains from the past, is extraordinary. As I said to my colleague, 'it is like winning the jackpot four times in a row.' The only conclusion I can draw from the sequence of coincidences is that our decision to follow the migratory path of animals and birds improved our chances of finding the remains. To that end, I thank Jane Woodruff for her contribution concerning the migratory pattern of birds and Michel Brenner for steering us along the magnetic fields that certain birds use to visualize the magnetic fields in their migration. The coincidence of the volcanic eruptions in Italy 39,000 years ago and the magnetic polar excursion of that time as mirrored in the events over the last six months, produced the circumstances that led us to the discoveries we made. We continue to examine the DNA of the specimens we found and will publish a paper on our findings when the work is complete. It remains for me to also thank our counterparts in France, Spain, and Gibraltar, who made our journey possible. Finally, thanks also go to the captain of the fishing trawler who generously made his boat available to us to travel to Ceuta and all the way to Hamburg. Thank you."

\* \* \*

Generous applause sees Käthe leave the stage where Michel waits to congratulate her. En route to their apartment, Michel says, "I have some good news for you. I have been accepted into the faculty of Earth Sciences here at Max Plank."

Bringing the car to a halt in an avenue lined with trees, she hugs him, "Well, that is even better news than the professorship. I love you, Michel."

"And may I add to our happiness?"

"What is that?"

"Come here to this bus stop." Kneeling, he says, Will, you be my wife? Käthe."

"Oh yes, oh yes, dear, dear Michel. What a surprise. Oh, how happy I am at this moment. I will always love you!"

Their happiness knows no bounds, reliving their hike and learning from each other, each day is unique to them. In three short months, they are married. Not long after, Käthe proclaims that she is expecting a child.

While they continue in their marital bliss, careful extraction of the DNA from the many remains found in France, Gibraltar, and Spain continues, and gradually a picture emerges.

## 23    Paper

Käthe again stands at the podium in the conference center. The child in her, now in its eighth month, makes its presence known with movements as if it too is nervous of the occasion. The excitement is palpable as the audience settles down. Scraps of news of the findings seeped out from the faculty where she works, serving only to heighten the interest in the story of the distant past. Seeing her husband with Jane as a guest in the front row settles her nerves, and she begins.

"Good evening, ladies and gentlemen. Thank you for attending. As you probably know, a group of us conducted a field study last year. I will be presenting the information that we gathered during and after the field trip, in the sequence of the discoveries as they unfolded.

Broadly speaking, six sites produced artifacts of interest. I will present the factual details of each and conjecture on the meaning of the findings as we currently understand them. I will use the term 'Modern Humans' to mean the anatomically modern humans like us or, to be precise, 'Homo sapiens.' Also, for ease of reference, we decided to assign names to each of the skeletons we found, like the hominin Lucy found in Ethiopia dating back 3.2 million years.

The first site we excavated was within the cave near Foix. It uncovered the remains of two adults and a child. The remains of the adults were that of a male and female. These provided the first surprise. The male was a modern human while the female was found to be a Neanderthal. To everyone's surprise, the newborn child in the woman's arms was not her child, even though the infant was assessed to be only two or three days old and probably from premature. The maternity test results showed that the child was fully modern human to an unknown female and the man next to her was the paternal father. Most curious was the fact that the man appeared to have died from a wound in his groin. A sharp, carved bone knife-like object was found in him. Traces of scar tissue around the object indicated that it had been in place for about a year. Specialists determined that he must have been in considerable pain during the entire period. They speculated that he could only have survived that long if he was mainly bedridden. Prolonged walking would have been fatal, and for this reason, there is some certainty that he died as a result of just such a walk.

The knife made of bone instead of stone drew particular attention. It suggested it was made to the Aurignacian culture of the Homo sapiens of the time, where bone replaced stone in the tools they made. By implication, the man was not stabbed by a Neanderthal, unless one happened to have access to such a weapon. The Neanderthals used Mousterian stone tools, usually from flaked stone. The woman came to be known as 'Fern' and the man as 'Tusk.' The child, whose sex could not be determined, was given 'Ivory.' Some remarkable cave art was also present in the cave. The slide on the screen shows this and implies that this group or some other group spent a reasonable period in the cave.

Next was bones found a few yards from the cave entrance, at the foot of the cliff near a landslide, yielded a link to the female in the cave. The remains were of a female Neanderthal, and ancestry studies indicated that she was a cousin of Fern, the female in the cave. The adults were all in their twenties, and carbon dating placed them around 39,000 years ago, which is the Late Middle Paleolithic period age from 60,000 to 35,000 years ago. The presence of the Homo sapiens in Europe 39,000 was in itself unusual in that they were thought to only have arrived 35,000 years ago. By way of explanation, it was postulated that this group may have been a precursor to the main influx of modern humans into the area. It may be an anomaly that they penetrated that deep into Europe, maybe finding themselves isolated from the main group and continuing through either being lost or being more adventurous than those that followed. She was given the name of 'Dawn.'

The third set of bones were found on the southern side of the Pyrenees in Spain. This was a single Neanderthal female. She died from being stabbed with a spear. The spear had a bone tip which, like the bone knife-like object in the man at the cave, suggests that the woman was stabbed by a modern human. This woman was given the name of 'Quill.' She was a cousin to both Fern, the woman in the cave, and Dawn, the woman outside the cave.

The next site we will discuss is at Gibraltar at the southern tip of the Iberian Peninsula. We joined a group there to help clear a rock-fall inside the cave resulting from tremors. The tremors also interrupted an excavation of a new level down that was underway. The bones of the infant were found outside the Gorham cave. They proved to be most intriguing. The child, a male, was probably stillborn and was from the union of a male Neanderthal and a female modern human. The fact that the woman carried the child to term is remarkable because anthropologists generally believe that such a union across species would seldom be fertile. If it was viable, it would abort before the end of the term. It has been determined that a female Neanderthal can successfully carry a child to term from a male Home sapiens. This relationship accounts for the distribution of Neanderthal DNA in most Europeans. The striking aspect of this child is that it would have been a nephew to Fern, Quill, and Dawn. How the child came to be born at Gibraltar, 1300 kilometers from Foix in the Pyrenees, is staggering in its implications. It implies that the child's mother walked the distance during a period of extreme weather conditions brought on by the ice ages combined with the volcanic winter induced by the eruption of the volcano at present-day Naples. Another aspect that ties these two groups together is a small round slate stone with a pair of intersecting sprigs of flowers engraved on it found at the cave at Foix and in this child's grave. I have one of these here with me, see? We called this child 'Shine.'

Next, on an impulse, we decided to cross the Strait of Gibraltar to Ceuta, the Spanish enclave on the coast of Africa. We visited a lesser-known cave near Benzu, where the remains of three individuals were discovered. They comprised two male Neanderthals, an adult, a child of around ten years old, and a modern human female. This is the only evidence of Neanderthals on the African continent. More about that in a minute. The child we called 'Broach' had with him, not just one of the engraved stones but also a few of them. Some were incomplete. We think we found the artist that made them. It was Broach. The collection of engraved stones were grouped as if they were in a bag of sorts, which has long since disintegrated. Next to the boy was also a notched bone artifact, which we believe to be a flute-like musical instrument. Broach may have been a musician and the artist who prepared the stones that he carried with him and was responsible for the cave-art at Foix. If that is not remarkable enough, a maternity test revealed that Dawn, the person outside the Foix cave, was his mother. Can you believe that? To complete this incredible story, DNA analysis of the marrow taken from the bones of the male Neanderthal found at Ceuta, who we called 'Slate,' proved to be the child's father. You need to understand that Dawn and Slate were cousins. This corresponds with the known fact that the dwindling number of Neanderthals resulted in a certain level of inbreeding. This lack of genetic diversity, in turn, contributed to a weakening of their ability to withstand diseases and is another factor contributing to their ultimate extinction as a species. This seems to be a case in point, although marriage between cousins is a common occurrence, even today.

Judging by the layout of the graves, the child probably died days or weeks earlier than the adults. The mysterious modern human female found next to Slate, whom we called 'Moraine,' turned out to be the mother of Shine, the stillborn child near the Gorham cave. Slate was the father. The implications are so clear that I challenge anyone to claim otherwise; this couple was in love. After Dawn's demise, Moraine, Slate and Slate's child by marriage to Dawn, walked across Spain. Their attempt at having children was always doomed to failure, given the cross-species mating problems mentioned earlier. There were probably other failed attempts at procreation en route from Foix that we do not know about.

On the subject of this being the first evidence of Neanderthals on the African continent, my opinion is that the sadness they experienced at the loss of Shine while at the Gorham cave prompted them to attempt a crossing of the Strait of Gibraltar. Add to this the sight of a steady stream of migrant birds crossing to their summer breeding grounds in Africa. It must have led them to believe that warmer places existed across the water, especially as they had to contend with frigid temperatures brought on by a series of ice ages and the volcanic winter. You can also imagine their predicament: They were virtually alone on the European continent, being the last of the Neanderthals. Superimpose on this the magnetic excursion, which caused a weakening of the protective magnetosphere resulting in harmful ultraviolet rays reaching the Earth's surface, affecting their health. There is evidence that the boy and the man suffered from forms of cancer, which ultimately resulted in the boy's demise. His bone marrow showed extensive damage from ultraviolet light. He probably suffered from bouts of skin rashes, coughing, and general ill health for a long time. The cause of death of the man is a mystery. He did not die of cancer but rather of poisoning. Why or where he got the poison is uncertain. Indications are that flora in the vicinity at the time would not be the source of the ingredients for the poison. It was found to be an herb local to the area to the north of the Pyrenees. This implies that they carried this potion all the way from Foix. Why he took, it is unclear. The mystery deepened when we found that the female with him also died of the same poison and that they probably died on or about the same day.

The positions of the bodies imply that Moraine was the last to die. She must have taken considerable care to bury herself alongside Slate in such a way to discourage animals from disturbing their grave. She had Slate's hand in hers when she died. The only conclusion I can come to is that they had a stock of remedies for the boy's ailments, which they also used to treat the man. Maybe he incorrectly consumed the potions from an urn that contained the poison. When it killed him, she likely decided to join him in death and drank from the poison as well. The urn was found next to her body.

Just as an aside, the body of an alpine marmot called 'Elle' was found next to the boy. It was likely a pet. These marmots were common in the Pyrenees at that time, but this type went extinct in that location at about the Neanderthals' time in history. Today they are being reintroduced to the Pyrenees from Switzerland, where during the Middle Ages, traveling musicians carried them in bags and did tricks with them, including dancing to the music. I wonder whether their extinction in the Pyrenees was as a result of landslides covering their burrows. You see, they lived in burrows up to ten feet deep. If a tremor struck at night, there is a strong likelihood that many were buried alive, especially if this was during the winter hibernation period. This is compounded by the habit of forming tight-knit communities led by a dominant male and female pair. Juveniles seldom strayed from the protection of the community. The result is that a catastrophe like an earthquake leaves them with little chance of surviving as a breed.

The final site that I can tell you about is what we call the Foix Pit of Bones. This is not to be confused with the Sima de Los Huesos or Pit of Bones in northern Spain at the Atapuerca cave shaft. Those date back 400,000 years where the remains of 28 Homo Heidelbergensis or Denisovan's were found.

Our pit is near the cave at Foix that I mentioned earlier. This pit was near the confluence of a larger main river and its tributary. Two modern human adults, one a male and the other a female, plus a newly born child who was a cross between a modern human and a Neanderthal, were found. The female was quite old. We gave her the name 'Gramater,' and we estimate that she was over seventy years old, which is quite unusual for that time. The average life expectancy would have been in the lower thirties caused by disease, illness, and accidents. Her bones showed extensive symptoms of arthritis, and she probably walked in a bent-over posture. Given her age, she would have occupied a special status in the group. She was likely the medicine woman and midwife for the community due to her experience over many years. She would not have survived the fall into the pit due to her frail condition. One can only wonder how she came to be in the pit. The man with her was, as I said, a modern human. He was an unusually small man in his late twenties. His cause of death was a fractured skull administered by a blunt object struck from behind. It is not likely that this injury was sustained by the fall into the pit. He was already dead before being thrown into the pit. He was the biological father of the child with him, who probably died at birth given the size of the infant, which we estimate to be around 1.5 kilograms. In the absence of the mother in the pit, one can only assume the child was born elsewhere and then thrown into the pit with its father. We gave the man the name of 'Runt' and his child, 'Tutu' because we think he or she may have had a twin which was never found. The DNA revealed that Tutu is Fern's child, the female Neanderthal found in the nearby cave. I will leave it to you to figure out how Fern came to die with someone else's child, of the same age, in her arms. Maybe she swapped her child for another by another woman because hers died, but then, the question is, where is the twin of this one? A real mystery?

Käthe ends her presentation with an acknowledgment of the contribution made by her colleagues as well as Michel and Jane.

Stunned silence follows the conclusion. It takes a few minutes before the audience reacts with protracted applause. Innumerable questions from the floor follow until finally, she exits with Michel and Jane. In the parking lot, Michel instructs the CAV to take them home.

Exhausted, Käthe flops down on a couch. Celebrating with some light drinks, they relive the lecture with Michel's pride in her performance, obvious. As the evening draws to a close, Käthe says, "Time for my little one to sleep."

To which Jane asks, "Do you know whether it is a girl or a boy?"

Michel replies, "No, we decided we would prefer it so that it is a surprise."

Käthe adds, "You know, like in the good old days of the Neanderthals. They had to wait for the day. Just joking, but the doctor says he or she is healthy, and that is all that matters. Michel will have to rush out to find pink or blue baby clothes while I recover in the hospital."

"When is the day?"

"Let's see. We have exactly 30 days from today."

# 24   Birth

Jane returned to England the next day, and the next four weeks flew by as the day approached. The birth was without any difficulties, but to the surprise of Käthe and Michel, identical twins emerged, both boys. Even the doctor, Dr. Le Grange, was surprised at Käthe having twins, which she ascribed to the fact that both infants were relatively small, obscuring the twinning. Otherwise, they were in good health. This did not deter the couple from enjoying the unexpected doubling of their family, and with both on extended maternity/paternity vacation, they doted on their offspring.

As the months passed, the children showed signs of rapid cognitive development as the parents devoted time to them, encouraging their individuality as a contrast to being twins and the tendency to think alike. After two years, when babies typically grow thicker hair replacing the softer hair up to that stage, they were surprised at the emergence of a shock of yellow hair in both children when both Käthe and Michel have auburn colored hair. Their development in terms of size remained small compared to other children. Concerned that a congenital defect may impair their future, the parents decided to have them tested.

At the appointment, Dr. Le Grange says, "I don't think you have anything to worry about, but just to be sure we can have tests done. It would have to be at the genetic level. Have either of you had a genetic scan done?"

Käthe replies, "Yes, I had one done many years ago. Would that still be valid?"

"Yes, you won't need another one done if you can provide me with the report. Michel, what about you?"

"No, I have not had one done."

Käthe offers, "We have a genetics laboratory at my work. They use the lab for mapping the genomes of archaic man. Will that be okay?"

"Yes, I guess that they would need quite sophisticated facilities for that sort of study. We will also need your children's DNA. Can you do that too?"

Michel agrees, "We will arrange for that ASAP and get back to you. Thank you, Dr. Le Grange."

\* \* \*

A month later, back in Dr. Le Grange's office, she says to the pair, "Thank you for providing the reports. I spent some time on it and reached out to some specialists to understand an anomaly in the results. It seems that your twins have inherited a rare recessive gene that only expresses itself under certain conditions. Let me first say, there is no need for concern. Your children will be fine. First, you may be interested to know that you are actually related. There is a distant relationship between the two of you. Don't worry, it is too far in the past for it to remotely imply incest. What is unusual about this is that you both carry this gene, and that is why it has expressed itself in the form of children who are smaller than the general population that you are a part of. This gene only expresses itself when both parents carry the same profile. It is rare and made even rarer by the need for both parents to carry it. Another factor is that it is usually associated with twins. All this adds up to a very rare occurrence."

Allowing time for them to absorb her words, the doctor continues, "Have you found that they are very bright, quite intelligent?"

Käthe replies, "Yes, I think that is fair to say."

"Well, that is another trait of this recessive gene. As far as we can tell, there will be no health-related consequences. So, aside from being slightly smaller than normal, you will have two very clever kids. I don't think you have anything to worry about."

Michel breathes a sigh of relief, "That is good to know. I have no problem with their size. I just enjoy having them, and having two of the same size is a bonus."

Käthe adds, "Yes, at least that is out of the way. Dr. Le Grange, thank you for your trouble."

\* \* \*

As they drive home, Käthe says to Michel, "It is interesting. Do you have any small ancestors? I don't, not that I know of."

"You are right, it is curious. I also don't. I will say that I can only trace my ancestors back to my great grandfather on my mother and father's side. It must have been before that."

"Same with me. I think I will talk to them at the institute. They may have more to say. You don't mind if I talk to them about your genome, do you?"

"No, of course not."

\* \* \*

A few days later, in their living room, Käthe says to Michel, "Did you know that you also have Neanderthal genes in you, like me?"

"Oh, that's interesting, but then most of us Europeans have that, don't we?"

"Yes, true, but yours and mine are slightly more pronounced than most people."

Thinking about it, Michel asks, "You know what, it is curious that the kids have yellow hair. The doctor didn't mention that. Do you think that is also part of the genome?"

"You are right, I will talk to them at the lab, but I wonder whether that isn't just a standard part of the Neanderthal genome that many of us have. I think I need to ask them whether this is the reason for many Europeans having blond hair. You see, many Neanderthals were known to have fair hair."

The conversation ends with Käthe struggling with an inarticulate idea that refuses to surface. Wakefully tossing and turning in bed through the night, it steadfastly refuses to form into a coherent concept or plan, until she finally falls asleep. In a dreamlike state, she relives parts of the hike and her talk at the auditorium, then suddenly, with a jolt, she sits upright in the bed, fully awake.

*  *  *

Without saying anything to Michel, the first thing she does from her desk at work is to call up the genome of Runt, Fern, and their child Tutu on the computer. Having spent so many hours with the geneticists, she compares these three genes with hers and Michel's. With her heart beating rapidly, she sees it, the same recessive gene in Tutu. It seems that the child inherited the trait from the parents by some atypical means because they do not have the characteristic. It implies that it was a spontaneous mutation, possibly caused by ultraviolet damage to the genome. Tutu is probably the first to carry the gene, inheriting Runt's size and maybe his intelligence and Fern's yellow straw-colored hair.

Käthe wonders, "Is it possible that the deterioration of the magnetic field around the earth, caused by the polar excursion brought on the ultraviolet exposure and caused the mutation? It must be. But how would Michel and I inherit this? Tutu died as an infant, so he had no offspring."

Puzzled, Käthe closes the session and attends to other duties.

That evening, at home, Käthe explains what she found and the problem with Tutu.

Michel immediately reminds her, "But you said that they speculated that he had a twin!"

Throwing her hands up, she says, "That's it. I am stupid. That is the explanation ... it is a long shot, but do you realize that you and I are related to Fern and Runt!"

"Incredible, which explains everything. Amazing!"

"The only thing about all of this is that it is totally implausible. Who is going to believe that after, how many generations would that be, let's see 39,000 years times twenty generations per millennium that is roughly 800 generations."

"Wow, that is more than all the 'A begat B begat C' etc. in the bible. I agree, no one will believe that."

201

"Well, I will tell you something, the Homo sapiens genome has been remarkably stable through all that time. In fact, all the way back for the last 300,000 years. So it is possible."

Taking her in his arms, "My darling Käthe, no matter what people think, it will remain our romantic certainty. I feel it in my bones."

# The End.

# ABOUT THE AUTHOR

At university, the study of Business Economics, Information Systems, and Marketing Management prepared him for a career as a project manager. He developed extensive experience in proposing corporate computer systems and the installation and support of them.

In this fast-changing environment, it was always necessary to stay abreast of the latest trends and apply these in a pragmatic way that ensured a return on investments for the stakeholders.

For Maurice, with the demands of a career in the corporate world addressed, a standout subject at university was astronomy. There to test the practical application of computer science, quantitative methods, and statistics led to an interest in astronomy and, by extension, to the evolution of life under different environmental conditions. The emergence of life under exotic conditions intrigues and, closer to home, raises questions about our anthropologic past.

The incredible advances in astronomy and our understanding of the universe laid a tabloid for the mind to feast on. In parallel, this led to an interest in our past and how we secured a position of dominance on a planet with so many competitors.

This is Maurice's second excursion into fiction, where plausible science fiction remains the objective.

Email Address: maurice.schmidt@telus.net
Website: https://storylinebooks.com

*Other Books by the Author:*
*Mars Interrupted*
*ISBN: 978-1-7770574-0-4 (Paperback)*
*ISBN: 978-1-7770574-1-1 (eBook)*
*ISBN: 978-1-7770574-5-9 (Hardcover)*

# REVIEW

Please take time to review the book on your supplier's website and drop me a line in an email. It helps fledging authors establish a footing in this competitive field. Your support is appreciated.

Be assured that I will read your review.

Thank you.

Maurice Schmidt

www.ingramcontent.com/pod-product-compliance
Lightning Source LLC
Chambersburg PA
CBHW071107100726
47908CB00008B/2297